GLUED TO SEE YOU

A Die-Cut Cozy Mystery Series

JUDITH DICKENSON
ACKARET

JAT Trax Studios

Judith Dickenson Ackaret

Published by JAT Trax Studios
PO Box 230151, Tigard, OR 97281-0151

First printing, May 2020

Cover design by DLR Cover Designs
Etsy.com/shop/DLRCoverDesigns

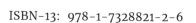

ISBN-13: 978-1-7328821-2-6

eISBN-13: 978-1-7328821-3-3

This book is dedicated to

Sue, Jacquie, Kathy, and Sheryl.

Acknowledgments

Writing a second book is much more difficult than the first. With that, I want to thank a number of people who kept encouraging me to keep going and not give up:

First of all, my husband, Jerry, who listened to my ideas with glazed looks on his face. I love you for setting your iPad aside for a moment of your time.

My mom, who at the age of 93, has retained her brilliant sense of humor, especially while listening to me talk about my book.

My sister, Deborah Menenberg (author of Uniquely Stella), who kept feeding me with proper writing techniques, and then when editing my book called me up to say, "Write in your own style. Forget what I said earlier."

To my dearest friend, Sue Stoller, who stayed up way past midnight to finish reading my book. You are a brave, honorable, sensitive person with a loving spirit. Go forth and heal.

Since I self-publish my books, I rely on a handful of people to read, edit, and make suggestions. My sister-in-law, Debbie Dodd, has been a great help with this book. As she remarked, "I left you twelve pages without red ink." This is out of over two hundred pages of book material! Thank you, Debbie.

A special thank you to Linda Parker (papercraftwithcrafty.co.uk) for teaching thousands of us the art of box making. I have made the most beautiful boxes due to her YouTube lessons.

Thank you to my family and friends whose names I have borrowed (mostly without their permission) to provide my book with colorful characters.

And lastly, thank you to all the people who have encouraged me to keep writing.

Author

Judith has been writing from the moment she learned how to put letters on paper. In grade school she wrote and directed plays, created comic books, and teamed up with her friend to write short stories. Her passion was to work behind the scenes in the police field and after some years in the accounting world, Judith was hired by a police department, spending the majority of her career in the Criminal Investigations Division as a Records Technician. In that position, she became a Composite Artist, transcriber, and a youth peer court advisor. Judith's love of paper-crafting has exploded from a small desk area to a full blown two-room studio. (Some of you can relate!) A line of vintage greeting cards and love of box designing is her current distraction from writing.

Along with their three adorable cats, Judith and Jerry (husband and Systems Reliability Engineer) spend a lot of time watching whales from their home on the Central Oregon Coast in the Pacific Northwest.

Books by Judith Dickenson Ackaret

Scored for Life
Glued to See You

Reviews of *Scored for Life*

"**Multi faceted**...A very good book with strong plots and subplots. This beginning book of the series goes into great detail establishing the characters and their relationships. There is plenty of action, new romances and quirky characters."...... *Good Reads Review*

"**You will not be able to put it down once started.** This book is amazing. Held my interest from the very beginning." ......*Amazon Review*

Judith Dickenson Ackaret

PROLOGUE

Two Weeks Earlier

Walter watched as his wife lay still on the bed. Placing a cover over her, he left the room to sleep on the couch. He would check on her in the morning. Walter took one last look and quietly closed the bedroom door, then walked down the hall to the expensively furnished living room. He hated the living room, but loved the last six months of lavish living with a wealthy woman. It took some work to convince Meredith to marry him, but it was all going to be worth it in the end. He would be taken care of for life.

Turning on the television, Walter flipped through channels with the remote control. He stopped on a news documentary of whale watching in a small coastal town in Oregon. He watched the last fifteen minutes of the program and then turned off the television. Picking up his laptop computer, he logged in and searched for the town of Bridgewater Harbor, Oregon. The community was large enough to offer senior independent living apartments, a senior community center, and social activities for seniors. Walter knew immediately that it was exactly what he needed.

Walter had been stashing money away and moving funds from Meredith's account to his personal accounts a little at a time. Six months of this had left Walter with a decent sum of spending money. He had been clever enough to get the password to her banking accounts soon after they were married. Meredith's current health indicated he would be a widower once again. He had tried to get her to change her Will to include him as sole heir, but she insisted leaving it as it was. At this time her daughter was the sole heir to her estate and he would get nothing. He made one last transfer of money into his private account. In the morning he would go to the bank, withdraw all of his cash, and close his accounts.

Putting his computer away, Walter fluffed the pillow on the sofa. He pulled the blanket over his reclined body. He was tired, but sleep evaded him. The large grandfather clock in the foyer seemed to be ticking more loudly than ever. Walter heard thumping noises, but excused them as normal house sounds. His eyelids finally became heavy.

♦ ♦ ♦

Morning sunlight danced on Walter's face. He lay still trying to remember where he was. He sat up and threw the blanket off as he got up quickly. He stretched and went to the bathroom, afterward to the kitchen to make a cup of coffee. He would eventually check on Meredith.

Slowly opening the bedroom door, he saw Meredith on the floor next to the bed. How in the world did she have the strength to get out of bed? He went to her side. She was cold. He felt for a pulse. There was none. She was dead...finally, he thought.

Next, he would call the paramedics. Later in the evening, he would make a call to Meredith's daughter who lived on the East Coast. He would then engage the previously made funeral arrangements, while acting as the grieving widower. She would be cremated immediately, before Meredith's daughter arrived. With Meredith's illness, there would be no question of why she died. But he needed the cremation before anyone could ask for an autopsy.

Walter sat calmly in the living room sipping his coffee. He thought about all the surfaces he touched. He wanted to make sure to clean the house of any fingerprints before he left. Walter picked up the phone to dial for the paramedics. Once the body was removed, he was free to leave.

His bags were packed.

CHAPTER 1

Saturday-Present Day

The captain's voice came over the intercom to announce the weather conditions in San Jose, California. Annie Weston sat in her first-class seat staring out the window, looking beyond the wing of the plane to a sea of white fluffy clouds. So many thoughts entered her mind as she pondered the events of the last two weeks. She wondered how so much had happened to her in such a short amount of time.

"Penny for your thoughts," Donald said after looking up from his laptop and noticing Annie in deep reflection. He was sitting next to her in the aisle seat. After being off work for two weeks due to the death of his aunt Helen Harper, Donald Harper was on his way back home in California to pack up and move to Bridgewater Harbor on the Central Oregon Coast. He had no idea the fortune he was to inherit when he first got on the plane heading to Oregon to handle his aunt's estate. Donald thought himself most fortunate though, when he first laid eyes on Annie Weston. It was love at first sight.

"Only a penny?" Annie laughed. "I can't even buy one-cent candy for a penny anymore."

Donald dropped his phone and groaned as he leaned forward, balancing his laptop on his lap, to retrieve the device. Annie turned her head to the window and stared into the fluffy white clouds. Her mind wandered back to Bridgewater Harbor to her paper craft shop, Ocean Loads of Paper, where she spent the majority of her time, at least until two weeks ago when she met Donald. Now, she realized, she wanted to be home at a decent hour and enjoy her time with family and friends, especially when they all gathered for dinner most evenings of the week.

Annie had fallen deeply in love with Donald from the moment she set eyes on him. She felt the instant attraction was mutual. When she first saw Donald, he looked tall, a bit muscular with brown wavy hair and brown eyes. Donald dressed rather nicely, considering he was a nerdy reliability engineer, Annie thought. She looked down at her clothes and wondered how long she owned the shirt she was currently wearing...ten years...maybe more like twenty. Oh, good grief! What kind of person keeps clothes for twenty years? Annie's thoughts were off on another tangent again. She often let her mind wander away with her thoughts.

Raising her left hand in front of her, she gazed at the large diamond engagement ring. She was getting married. MARRIED! She never dreamed she would ever fall in love and get married again. Her previous marriage lasted all of six months. When she found her first husband cheating on her, she vowed she was done with men. She buried her pain in long hours of work.

"Annie?" Donald was getting used to the times when Annie got lost in thought. "Is everything okay?" He had, after all, known her for almost two weeks!

Annie snapped out of her inner daydreams and said, "Yes, of course. I was just thinking of the last two weeks and all that has happened." In that time, her neighbor and mother's best friend passed away, she met Donald, she inherited a house, another business, and became guardian to a twenty-four-year-old Down Syndrome woman named Marie.

"It has been a bit of a roller coaster." Donald said. He closed his laptop and placed it inside his carry-on bag, then shoved the bag under the seat in front of him.

As Donald was putting away his laptop, a flight attendant walked up to him to ask if he wanted anything. He said he still had his coffee from Starbuck's, and lifted the paper coffee cup from the drink holder to show her. Annie noticed the flight attendant was cute. The young woman laughed and pushed a strand of hair behind her ear. She kept direct eye contact as Donald made some nerdy, 'must have been funny', talk about coffee. There was a pause in the conversation when a passenger pushed past the airline employee, causing her to plunge her chest into Donald's face.

Annie shook her head and rolled her eyes. She was about to ask for a drink, but the flight attendant disappeared. Really? The young woman did not bother to ask her if she wanted anything. Annie could hear the female attendant behind her asking the gentlemen on the other side of the plane if they needed anything. Donald, not aware that the flight attendant was flirting with him, turned his attention to Annie.

"We have a town car waiting for us at the airport." Donald said, "We should get Stella and Marie settled in the hotel, have dinner, and later we can take a taxi to my house and make plans to pack."

Annie nodded. Annie's mother, Stella, was sitting directly across from Donald and Annie, with Marie at her side. Stella had recently retired from the city as the librarian. Annie's father passed away from a heart attack years ago, and Annie had been living with her mother ever since. Annie's father, Richard Weston, had been a police captain at Bridgewater Harbor, the small town on the Oregon Coast where Annie currently lived. Ocean Loads of Paper was a dream of Annie's, and it only came true with the help of her mother over the years. Stella helped financially using Annie's father's insurance money. Annie was able to repay her mother over time. Stella never indicated she wanted Annie to move, so Annie remained in her family home until recently when she moved across the street due to inheriting the neighbor's house.

Annie leaned forward to see what her mother and Marie were doing. She noticed Marie munching on junk food Donald had purchased for her inside the airport. They were going to be eating a late dinner as it was, and now Marie would not be hungry. Annie tried to get her mother's attention, but her mother was fast asleep in her seat. Marie was holding her hand. Annie smiled thinking how sweet it all looked. Those two were going to have the best time in Disneyland, a gift from Donald for Marie mostly, but Stella seemed to be just as excited to join in the adventure. They would spend a couple of nights in Palo Alto helping pack Donald's house, then they would fly to Anaheim for the rest of the week.

Donald had taken a liking to Marie and they formed a big brother, little sister relationship. Marie was twenty-four and became under Annie's guardianship only two weeks ago when Annie's neighbor, who was caring for Marie, had passed under suspicious circumstances. Marie's mother died years earlier, leaving Marie with Helen Harper.

Annie was asking Donald questions about his house, his dog Laddie, and his parents. Time passed quickly and the announcement came over the intercom to stow their tray tables and return their seats to the upright position. Annie tightened her seat belt. She leaned over and noticed her mother was now awake and making sure Marie had everything put away and ready to exit the plane when they arrived at the gate. Annie's excitement was building. After making sure her mother and Marie were settled, she would soon be at Donald's house, meet his dog, and find out more about the man she agreed to marry.

◆ ◆ ◆

The taxi pulled up in front of Donald's house in Palo Alto. It was a cute, although small, house that Donald said was only a thousand square feet. The Craftsman exterior of the house gave it the appearance of being much larger. A walkway invited guests to the front door from the street, through a gate in the white picket fence, and up a few steps to a large covered front porch. Thick palm plants were displayed on both sides of the entrance in large gray ceramic pots. The house was a light grayish-blue with white trim. The white Craftsman-style front door had a window in its upper half.

Donald paid the taxi driver and carried the bags to the front porch. Annie could hear sniffing and whining from inside the house. Donald mentioned that his parents were taking care of Laddie while he was in Oregon. They must have dropped him off at home before Donald arrived.

As Donald opened the door, Laddie came bounding out to greet his missing person. The two danced around the porch for a few moments when Laddie stopped and looked at Annie. He tilted his head, and then looked at Donald. Donald introduced Annie to Laddie. Laddie took an instant liking to Annie and rolled over to have his belly scratched by both Donald and Annie.

"Come on, Laddie." Donald picked up the luggage and ushered Annie inside. "Let's show Annie around the house, boy." Laddie followed with glee.

As Donald turned on the lights, Annie was stunned by how beautiful and modern the interior of the house appeared. She never would have guessed it from the looks of the exterior Craftsman style.

She expected dark wood molding and dark floors. Instead, the walls were white with a hint of gray, and the woodwork was pure white. The furniture in the living room was medium to dark gray with dog blankets adorning each piece. Although the house was ultra clean in appearance, it still had a homey pet friendly feel. Must have been the toys scattered around the living room floor, Annie thought as she stepped over a terry-cloth toy shaped like a carrot.

Donald was on the floor wrestling around with Laddie. Annie could see how much they missed each other. Laddie was a black Lab, about three years old, and the size of a small horse. What is Callie, her cat, going to think when she meets her new 'brother'? Annie was not certain Callie would accept a dog in her house.

Donald got up off the floor and guided Annie through the house. She wasn't sure how Donald could leave such a beautiful home, sunny weather, and charming neighborhood. Donald hadn't experienced the gray, cloudy, foggy, gloom that was winter on the Oregon Coast. He would usually spend a week or two at his aunt's house in the summer as a kid, when it was sunny a fair amount of the time. Does he even know that it rains in Oregon? Annie was contemplating whether Donald would want to move back to California after the first winter. Her mind was wandering again.

Donald guided Annie to his bedroom. He stopped short at what appeared to be packed and labeled boxes lined up against one wall, halfway up to the ceiling. "I think my folks were here packing for me. Mom had mentioned something about helping out, but I thought she meant when we got here."

On top of one of the boxes was a handwritten note from Donald's mother explaining what was packed and that there were empty boxes left in his office for him to pack up his work materials. She said she had cleaned out the refrigerator and cupboards and packed up anything that was not perishable. Donald told Annie that his mother was very organized and probably had the place packed in a day with his father's help.

"Are you planning on keeping the house or selling it?" Annie asked, as she had not thought about it until now.

"The house actually belongs to my parents." Donald walked into the kitchen to look through the cupboards and open the refrigerator.

Annie followed and stood, watching Donald open and close cupboard doors.

"They wanted to give it to me, but I told them that it would be better if I just rented it from them. This house in Palo Alto is worth around three million dollars."

Annie staggered back into a dining table chair. She slowly sat down with her mouth open.

"I actually pay the taxes, insurance, and utilities for them in return for living here. I did pay to have the house painted and the kitchen remodeled, but that's about it. My father stops by weekly to mow the lawn. They only live a block away," Donald said, continuing to look around for anything that might have been missed during the packing of his belongings.

"Three million dollars?"

Donald stopped and looked at Annie. "Property is expensive here. It's high-tech country. Stanford University is near this neighborhood. I really did not think you would want to keep the house. If you do, I am sure my parents will give it to us as a wedding gift."

"No, I think one house is enough." A dazed Annie stood and followed Donald to his office down the hallway. Three million dollars for this tiny house, Annie thought as she looked over her shoulder at the living room while she walked slowly down the hallway.

Donald pulled out his cell phone and called his dad. Laddie followed close on Donald's heels. He was not going to let Donald out of his sight anytime soon. "Hi, Dad!" Donald said into his cell phone as he walked to the bedroom.

Annie began walking around the house. She wondered what it would be like to live in California where the sun shines most of the year. She was imagining living in the house she was walking through. Then it dawned on her that this particular house looked like a model home waiting to be sold. It was void of any personal touches. Probably, because Donald's mother packed up all of his personal belongings. Of course, Annie told herself, that is why the house looks so vacant of personal belongings.

Donald walked out of the bedroom and announced to Annie, "I am going to go take a shower." He went back into the bedroom and Annie followed. Donald had placed the suitcases on the bed and opened his to pull out his bathroom bag. He stripped down and walked to the bathroom.

Annie began to remove her clothes to join Donald in the shower. As she took off the last article of clothing, she heard a thump at the front door. She quickly grabbed a dress shirt from Donald's suitcase and put it on over her naked body. She poked her head around the bedroom door into the hallway and called out to Donald. There was no answer. The shower was running, so she figured Donald could not hear her. Annie decided to check the front door. Laddie was at the door when Annie approached through the living room. She looked out the peep hole, but saw no one. She listened at the door. No sounds. Laddie cocked his head sideways and looked as if he was listening at the front door too. He picked up a toy and tossed it in the air. He stopped and looked at Annie.

Annie put her hand on the doorknob and slowly opened the front door. She stepped on the threshold of the door, holding the front of the shirt closed with her right hand. The sleeves of Donald's shirt were long and the tail of the shirt went down pass her thighs. She kept close to the front door as to not let Laddie outside. She was leaning forward to look down the sides of the front porch when Laddie jumped up on the front door from inside, knocking her forward and closing the door. Annie struggled to turn around. Her shirt was caught in the closed door. She reached for the doorknob. Sudden fear struck as she realized the door was locked! Her shirttail was stuck in the door, and no matter how hard she tugged on it, the door was not letting the shirt go free. Annie could hear Laddie playing with a toy, which was making high-pitched squeaking noises.

It was now dark, and Annie looked around to see if anyone was walking down the street. Thank goodness, she thought, she was alone outside. Annie pounded on the door and called out for Donald. Laddie barked and jumped up on the door from the inside of the house. Annie assumed that Donald would not be able to hear her while the shower was on. She was wondering how long she could just stand in the doorway with nothing on but a shirt, which was stuck in the door.

As the minutes ticked by, Annie became more and more uncomfortable waiting on the front porch for Donald to finish his shower. She looked around for something to cover her naked body.

Once she left the shirt behind, she could venture around the side of the house to find the bathroom window. She decided she was going to try and knock on the bathroom window to get Donald's attention. Her only available option for body cover was right next to her in the large ceramic pots on each side of the front door. She stretched her arm out to break off a palm leaf. She tried it on for size by placing it in front of her. She decided she would only need three thick palms to cover her body. One palm would cover her in back and two palms to cover her upper and lower front areas. She was quite pleased with her problem-solving skills and began putting the plan in action.

Slipping out of the shirt, she quickly placed the palms in strategic locations on her body and edged her way cautiously to the side of the house, being careful where she stepped in her bare feet. She stopped short when she discovered that the bathroom window was located behind a fenced area. The window to the left of her was to Donald's bedroom. She slipped between the waist high bushes and began pounding on the window and calling Donald's name.

A patrol car pulled up to the curb. Two police officers exited the squad car. They walked up to the side of the house where they found Annie, with palms in her hand, pounding on the window.

"May we help you, Ma'am?" a female voice asked.

Horror suddenly enveloped Annie as she turned to face two police officers. Annie ducked behind the bushes to hide her body. "Um, I seem to be in an embarrassing predicament. I actually got locked out of the house."

"I can see that," said the female officer standing in front of Annie. A male officer was talking on his radio to dispatch several feet away. "Did you forget to put on your clothes before leaving the house?" the female officer asked sarcastically.

◆ ◆ ◆

Donald finished his shower and walked out of the bathroom with a towel wrapped around his waist. As he was walking down the hall to the bedroom, he noticed Laddie pulling on a piece of cloth which was stuck in the front door. The closer he got to it, the more the cloth appeared to be his nice dress shirt, at least part of it. Curious, Donald opened the door. The shirt dropped to the floor. He picked up the shirt and stuck his head outside. Not initially seeing anything unusual, Donald pulled his head inside and quickly grabbed Laddie before he could dash out the door. Donald turned to hear pounding on the bedroom window and Annie calling his name. He raced to the bedroom, raised the blind, and stopped suddenly to see the female officer standing a few feet behind a naked Annie. A male officer was standing nearby.

"You have got to be kidding," Donald muttered to himself as he hurriedly reached up to unlock and raise the bedroom window. As luck would have it, Donald's towel dropped and he provided a full-frontal view of his naked body to the female officer, who did not seem to mind a bit.

Donald grabbed his towel and wrapped it around himself. He tossed his shirt to Annie through the opened window. Annie was facing the window when the shirt came flying through the air landing on her face, causing her to stumble backward toward the male officer who caught her before she fell onto the shrub.

"Maybe the two of you could contain your sexual play inside the house with curtains drawn before we start getting calls from the neighbors," the male officer said lifting Annie into an upright position.

Mortified, Annie dashed behind a shrub to put on the shirt. Donald handed a blanket to Annie through the opened window. She wrapped the blanket around her as she walked to the front door. The officers followed.

"I got my shirt caught in the front door. The door was locked so I could not get back inside." Annie stepped up to the front door to show the officers that it was locked. She turned the knob and the door opened! Donald quickly walked from the bedroom wearing a robe and holding onto Laddie's collar. Laddie was excited to have company.

"I am really sorry about this officer," Donald said. "It was just an accident. It will not happen again." Probably true, Donald thought to himself. Annie will not repeat the same mishap, she will just create a new one.

The officers said good-night and left Donald and Annie standing on the front porch as they walked to the patrol car. Reaching the car, the female officer opened the driver's side door, and glared at Donald and

Annie, causing them to nearly jump and simultaneously back into the house and close the door.

"Is this a good time to ask...?" Donald began.

"No!" Annie cut him off short. She walked to the bedroom to get something to put on other than a blanket. Donald followed, feeling a bit amused.

Annie plopped down on the bed and said, "Donald, why in the world would you want to marry me?"

Donald walked up to Annie, pulled her up to him and wrapped his arms around her. He looked straight into her tear-filled eyes and said, "I cannot imagine living my life without you. I have met the most fascinating woman I will ever meet in my lifetime. How can I not marry her?"

"You are one brave man, Mr. Harper!" Annie kissed Donald and said, "Let's get married as soon as we get back to Oregon before you change your mind."

"I will marry you any time, but would you go take a shower? There appears to be leaves growing out of your head, and you smell earthy," Donald said as he walked to the hallway. "I'll look for something for us to snack on, and you can tell me all about your excursion outside."

Annie grimaced as she raised her hand to her head and pulled out small leaves entangled in her hair.

After a long hot shower, Annie was feeling much better. She dried her hair and pulled her nightgown over her head. She was definitely going to sleep well tonight. She walked into the hall where she found Donald carrying two bottles of cold water.

"The place has been cleaned out!" Donald handed a bottle of water to Annie. "This is all that is left. We should get up early tomorrow and go have breakfast with Stella and Marie before we bring them over here."

Donald took Laddie out to the backyard for a night time potty break. When he returned, he found Annie fast asleep in the middle of the bed. Laddie quickly jumped up on the bed and settled in at the foot.

"I don't think so, buddy," Donald said. Pointing to Laddie's dog bed, he said, "Go to your own bed." Laddie reluctantly hopped off the bed and walked to his dog bed. He sniffed it, turned to look at Donald, and groaned as he settled down. Donald stood looking at the bed and the woman he loved taking up all the room. Should he move her over, or just grab a blanket and sleep on the couch. He really did not want to disturb her. It was the couch then. He grabbed a blanket from the closet and a pillow from the bed.

CHAPTER 2

Sunday Morning

Annie awoke to the sound of Donald's voice in the distance. She opened her eyes and wondered who was sleeping next to her. She rolled over to find Laddie stretched out on the bed with his head on a pillow. She sat up and looked at the time on her phone. It was ten minutes after six in the morning. Annie noticed a text message from her mother. She pulled up her mother's phone number and after a few rings her mother answered.

"Good morning, Annie," Stella Weston said. "Did you sleep well?"

"Actually, I did." Annie did not want to relate the events of last night. "How did you and Marie sleep?"

"Wonderfully," Stella said, with Marie in the background talking about how comfortable the beds were. "Marie wants to go swimming and then get breakfast. Would you ask Donald to pick us up later this morning? You don't mind, do you?"

"No, of course not," Annie said with relief that she did not have to get up and get moving before she had a cup of coffee. "The packing is pretty much done." Annie explained that Donald's parents came in and packed most of his things for him over the last week.

"Come pick us up at ten and we can help you finish packing."

"Okay, Mom," Annie said. "Tell Marie she is going to love Laddie, Donald's dog."

As Annie disconnected her call, Donald walked into the bedroom with his cell phone to his ear. "Just a minute, Dad, I will ask." Donald told Annie that his parents were asking everyone to breakfast.

"Do they have coffee?" Annie asked, crawling out of bed.

"Yes, and they happen to have the brand you like so much."

As Annie accepted the invitation for herself, she told Donald that she had just spoken to her mother and was told that Marie wanted to go swimming and then they would have breakfast there. Donald was to pick them up at ten this morning.

Donald walked back out to the living room, letting his father know that they would be there within the half hour. He ended the call and walked back into the bedroom with a blanket and pillow, which he threw on the bed. With most of his clothes packed, Donald went through his suitcase to find suitable clothing to wear for the day. He took Laddie out for a morning walk. This gave Annie time to relax and get dressed.

The first thing to do, before anything else, was to get a cup of coffee. Annie put on Donald's robe and walked barefoot to the kitchen. There was not an appliance to be found resembling a coffee maker. Packed boxes were lined up against the far kitchen wall. Somewhere in those boxes Annie imagined a coffee maker was stored. Should she go through all the boxes to find out? She stared a bit longer. Her day was not starting off well. She thought she should probably get dressed and attempt to look presentable for meeting the in-laws-to-be.

Annie came out of the bathroom and was walking down the hall to the bedroom when the front door opened and a large black Lab came bounding through the doorway and raced up to greet her. She bent down to greet him with a hug.

"So, that is how it's going to be? The dog gets to sleep with you, and then he gets the first hug in the morning?" Donald walked up to Annie expecting a kiss. Instead Annie ruffled his hair.

"Good boy!"

Donald grabbed her hand. He picked Annie up and carried her to the bedroom and laid her on the bed. He was about to kiss her neck when she interrupted him, "Did you tell your parents that we would be at their house for breakfast a half an hour ago?"

Donald stood up and offered his hand to Annie. He pulled her close and they kissed. Laddie jumped up on Donald's back, knocking the two onto the bed.

"I think Laddie believes we should cancel breakfast and stay here."

"I think Laddie needs to be trained to stop jumping up on people and DOORS!" Annie said looking straight at Laddie. Laddie cowered and walked over to his bed.

◆ ◆ ◆

Fifteen minutes later, Donald, Annie, and Laddie entered Donald's parents' house. Donald's father greeted Donald with a hug and a pat on the back. Donald introduced Annie to his father, Randolph "Rand" Harper, who then gave Annie a hug and welcomed her to the family.

Annie thought Rand was so different from his brother, Robert Harper, who had been married to Donald's aunt, Helen Harper. They were both doctors, but the commonality ended there. Donald spent a week during the summers with Robert and Helen when he was growing up. He only found out yesterday that Helen was his biological mother. His parents did not know what he knew and at this point he was not willing to talk to them about it. Donald was not sure he would ever tell them that he knew.

Helen was found dead only two weeks ago, leaving Annie to inherit her house and properties, which included R&H Enterprises. Donald also inherited from Helen. She had left him her cash accounts, insurance policies, and various expensive collectibles from Robert's estate. Robert had died only a few months before Helen. Just two days ago, Annie and Marie were confronted by the man who caused Helen's, as well as Robert's, death. Annie was still attempting to catch her breath from all the excitement.

R&H Enterprises was a business which owned and leased two buildings located in the downtown area of Bridgewater Harbor on the central Oregon Coast. The buildings housed boutique-type stores and one bed & breakfast. Her own shop, Ocean Loads of Paper, was in the building overlooking the ocean. There, a boardwalk stood between the ocean wall and the shops. In the summer, tables and chairs were set out on the boardwalk to invite people to stay and visit, shop, and enjoy the view. Summer was a great time to whale watch from the area set above the rocky shore to the water below.

Patty Harper, Donald's mother walked up to Donald and gave him a hug. Donald gave her a kiss on the cheek, which Annie found endearing. Donald then turned to Annie and introduced her to his mother.

"Mom, this is Annie, your soon to be daughter-in-law." Donald put his arm around Annie.

"Oh, Annie." Patty reached for Annie and pulled her in for a long hug. "We have heard so much about you. Welcome to our family!"

"Breakfast is on the table," said Rand. "Let's eat!"

Donald's parents led the way through the house to a beautiful covered patio in the backyard. There sat a table with four place-settings, and a beautiful flower arrangement in the center. Next to the table was a built-in barbecue and outdoor kitchen. Large ceramic pots contained flowering plants which were thoughtfully scattered about the yard. Several trees shaded parts of the yard to add coolness on a summer day.

Donald walked up to the table and pulled out a chair for Annie. Although no one had ever pulled a chair out for her before, she seemed right at home with the gesture. Donald then waited until his mother sat down before taking a seat himself. These were manners not seen in today's society, but definitely welcomed, Annie thought. She smiled at Donald.

Annie was enjoying conversation with Donald's parents so much that she was eating slowly and savoring her second cup of coffee. It was at this time that Laddie began whining to go for a walk. Donald excused himself and grabbed Laddie's leash as they walked to the front door.

While Donald took Laddie for a walk, Annie began asking his parents questions about Donald's childhood, his schools, sports, and what he did during the summer months. She laughed as Rand and Patty reminisced with stories about Donald and their family vacations.

"I remember Donald visiting his Aunt Helen when he was just about six years old, Patty began. "He was to spend a week in Bridgewater Harbor, but then asked to stay an additional week. He met a boy about his age who lived across the street. The two of them were inseparable."

Patty took a sip from her coffee cup as she stared off into space. "I think his name was Davey or Danny."

"Danny?" Annie asked.

Patty set her cup down and looked straight at Annie. "Yes," Patty said excitedly. "Danny was the boy, and he had the most adorable little sister. I don't remember her name, but I remember seeing her standing on her porch with her hands on her hips pouting, because the boys would not let her play with them. It was so cute!"

"My brother...Danny?" Annie began to remember Dan playing with a boy who came to visit the woman across the street during the summer. It was Donald! Danny was Dan Surely. Annie confessed to Rand and Patty that she believed she was the young girl on the porch and Danny was Dan, the boy who came to live with her family when he was very young. Although Dan visited his biological mother on a regular basis, Annie's parents referred to Dan was their son.

The front door opened and Laddie came running into the house. Donald followed, removing the leash from Laddie's collar and placing it on the table by the front door. Donald walked to the patio to find his parents and Annie laughing over conversation.

"What did I miss?" Donald asked as he sat down next to Annie.

"We were talking about the young boy who lived across the street from Helen during the time you spent summers at your aunt's house," Annie said and then paused to let Donald think about what she said.

Donald stared at Annie for a moment and then sat up straight and looked over at his parents, and then again at Annie. "Dan? Dan was the kid I played with when I was at Aunt Helen's the summer before I went into first grade?"

"Do you remember his adorable little sister?" Annie asked coyly.

"No, I just remember an annoying little girl who put up a fuss, because we would not let her play with us." Donald said teasingly.

"And to think that annoying little girl grew up to be the woman you fell in love with and are going to marry", Rand said.

Donald smiled at Annie.

"Danny and I had great times in Bridgewater Harbor," Donald thought out loud. "We fished, crabbed, clammed, camped in the backyard, played baseball, and explored the beaches. We were never without anything to do all the time I was there."

"Your Aunt Helen would remark about not seeing much of you," Patty said.

"I wonder why I never realized it before?" Donald said looking at Annie. "There was Dan right in front of me, and it never dawned on me that he was Danny from my youth."

Annie squeezed Donald's hand. Frankly, she did not remember 'Donny' from childhood, but not much could survive the new memory of when she first met Donald two weeks ago coming down the staircase of his Aunt Helen's house with a towel wrapped around his waist. Why would she want to remember anything else? It was a surprise meeting, as she had no idea, when he arrived in town to settle his aunt's estate and was staying at Helen's house. She had only stopped by to deliver a photo album belonging to Helen Harper, which Marie had taken and needed to return.

"Wow! Look at the time" Donald said standing. "I need to go pick up Stella and Marie at the hotel at ten."

"You can all head back to your house," Rand said to Donald. "After I help your mother clean up here, we will meet you there to finish packing."

Donald called Laddie and attached the leash to his collar. They said a quick good-bye and were out the door.

◆ ◆ ◆

Donald and Annie walked back to the house with Laddie stopping at each tree to mark his territory. Annie decided she, too, needed to go to the bathroom and asked Donald to unlock the front door so she could go inside before they went to pick up her mother and Marie. As they approached the front door, Donald heard his neighbor, Ingrid, calling out to him. He unlocked the door and Annie quickly entered. Donald closed the door and walked down the porch steps to the side yard fence to greet his neighbor.

Annie was just exiting the bathroom when she heard the front door open. Patty entered with Laddie, who raced up to get attention from Annie. Annie petted Laddie and gave him a hug. The two walked into the living room.

"If I were you," Patty said, "I would go outside and introduce myself to the neighbor."

Annie wondered why Patty wanted her to meet the neighbor. She walked up to the window and saw Donald and Rand talking to a beautiful young blonde woman. Voluptuous, thin, and scantily dressed she seemed to be twirling strands of hair in her fingers as she talked and leaned in toward Donald. Annie turned to Patty and nodded in agreement. She exited the front door with Laddie in tow.

As Annie approached Donald and placed her arm around his waist, the young woman stepped back. The friendly smile shrank to a smirk as Donald introduced Annie, his fiancée, to his neighbor. "Annie, this is Ingrid, my neighbor."

"It is very nice to meet you, Ingrid." Annie held out a hand, but Ingrid nodded instead. "We would love to stay and chat, but we must rush off to pick up my mother and Marie."

"I understand you are moving," Ingrid said to Donald.

"Yes, today," Annie quickly answered. "We will be all packed up and leaving as soon as possible."

Donald gave a surprised look at Annie. "Uh, yes, we had better be going. Dad, Mom needs your help in the house."

Rand said his good-byes and entered the house with Laddie.

"Well, it has been so wonderful having you as a neighbor. I wonder who will be living here after you leave?" Ingrid said, attempting to continue the conversation. "At least let me say good-bye properly with a kiss."

"Oh, too bad there is a fence between you two," Annie said, pointing to the three foot fence and nudging Donald toward the truck. "I guess just a simple goodbye will have to do."

Donald waved to Ingrid as he opened the passenger side door for Annie. He turned to Annie and smiled playfully. Annie gave him a disgusted look as she climbed into the truck. Donald closed the door and walked around to the driver's side. He quickly got in and started the engine. As they drove out of the driveway, Annie turned to look at the house and noticed Donald's mother giving Annie the 'thumbs-up' gesture. Annie laughed.

Donald shook his head. "You have nothing to worry about."

"I know."

◆ ◆ ◆

A few minutes later Donald and Annie were pulling up to the entrance of the hotel, where they saw Stella and Marie waiting outside. Donald turned off the engine and got out to open the back-passenger door for Stella. Marie climbed in the truck from the other side. There was lots of excited chatter as the group headed back to Donald's house. Annie told her mother that Donald and she would be leaving very early the next morning to head back to Oregon. Stella and Marie would be taking an early flight to Anaheim to spend a few days at

Disneyland. Marie was over-the-top with excitement. She had never been to Disneyland before and was a huge fan of princesses. She made a list of all the princesses she wanted to meet. Annie was regretting not being able to go with them, but she knew there would be another time to go. Still, she longed to spend time with her mother and Marie at Disneyland.

Donald looked over at Annie as he listened to Marie talk about all the exciting things she had planned to do while at the parks. He had made reservations for them to stay at the Grand Californian Hotel & Spa, and even had a surprise waiting for both Stella and Marie when they got to their room. Donald realized that Annie might be wishing she was going with Stella and Marie.

"I was thinking it would be fun to go to Disneyland on our honeymoon," Donald said. "What do you think about that?"

"Well, yes. I mean, if you really wanted to go, I would not object." Annie was trying to hold back the excitement. "When did you want to get married?"

"We should probably wait until Marie and Stella get back on Saturday."

"I agree with Donald," Stella said. "You cannot get married until I'm there."

"Me either," Marie jumped in, "I'm going to be the flower girl."

"A flower girl?" Donald asked.

"Yes, she's going to be my flower girl, and Lizzy is going to be my best woman." Annie said.

"I thought Lizzy was the maid of honor?"

"Do not call her the maid of honor in her presence," Annie cautioned Donald. "She hates the word 'maid'. She decided she would be the best woman."

"I'm so happy!" Marie exclaimed. "I get to go to Disneyland and be a flower girl. I'm going to buy a princess dress to wear to the wedding."

Annie smiled at Donald. She rather liked the idea. It was going to be a small gathering in the backyard. The weather had been unseasonably warm and she hoped it would stay sunny until the weekend after next, when her mom and Marie had returned. Annie was thinking about a late afternoon wedding. Did she happen to tell

Donald she was planning a wedding in two weeks? Annie was shaken from her deep thoughts when she heard the truck doors open and everyone exiting.

As Annie and Donald walked to the house, Annie said, "Did I happen to mention that I am planning a wedding ceremony in the backyard in two weeks?"

"The sooner the better!" Donald said, taking Annie's hand in his. "We should probably let my folks know so they can make plans."

"They already know and they're driving to Oregon in their RV."

Donald stopped and turned to look at Annie. "How did you manage to make all these plans without me knowing?"

"Your mom and I made all the plans while you were talking with your Dad." Annie smiled and turned to walk up the stairs of the porch. "It's a simple ceremony in our backyard. Your folks, my mother, a few friends, and Princess Marie."

CHAPTER 3

Sunday Afternoon

Donald packed his office, with help from his father, while Annie, Stella, Marie and Patty sat in the backyard chatting about the wedding plans. When everything was boxed and ready to go, Rand helped Donald pack his truck. Boxes of kitchen appliances and other items were placed in the back of the truck, where a canopy would ensure everything stayed secure and dry on the trip to Oregon. Rand had walked back to his house earlier and brought over his own truck. Into it, he and Donald loaded the boxes Donald was storing at his parent's house. They unloaded them and returned to Donald's house. Everything was ready to go. With Donald's office equipment packed and sitting in the living room, ready to go in the morning, he backed his truck inside the garage in the backyard and locked it up. Donald and his father then joined the women on the patio.

"Is anyone ready for lunch?" asked Patty. "I have sandwiches and salad prepared and waiting at our house. I thought we could go there to eat."

"We've finished and I am ready to go anytime," Donald said, pulling out a patio chair. Just as he was about to sit down, everyone stood up from their chairs and began to enter the house through the kitchen door. Donald stood by the chair for a moment, sighed, and then followed the group inside the house. "I meant after I sat down for a moment," Donald mumbled to himself. He was exhausted from loading packed boxes into the truck.

◆ ◆ ◆

Rand, Patty, Stella, and Marie rode back to the Harper's house in Rand's truck, while Donald, Annie, and Laddie walked. While walking hand-in-hand, Donald stopped suddenly and turned to Annie, "What do you think about driving back to Oregon right after lunch?"

"You mean drive all night?"

"We could make it by midnight if we left around two this afternoon."

"I'm willing to give it a go. If we get tired, we can always stop and spend the night somewhere." Annie was getting excited. She wanted to get back to the shop, but she did not indicate such to Donald. She had so much work to catch up on, and being away for a few days caused her to spend more hours trying to catch up. Lizzy would be busy just handling customers. Yes, Annie thought. We can do this.

"It's decided then," Donald said, squeezing Annie's hand. They began their walk to his parent's house,.

♦ ♦ ♦

Annie pulled her cell phone from her pocket and looked at the message on the screen. It was from Lizzy. Lizzy was reporting that the cousin of Suzette, the owner of the bed & breakfast across the street from Ocean Loads of Paper, just arrived in town. Annie sent a text back saying she would call Lizzy in a few minutes.

"Suzette's cousin just arrived in town," Annie told Donald. "I don't remember Suzette saying that anyone would be staying at the bed & breakfast while she was in Europe." Annie was thinking she should probably text Suzette about it, since Annie was entrusted with the key to the B&B in case anything happened while Suzette was gone. Annie realized that it might be too late in the evening in Europe for Annie to be texting. Instead, she decided to email Suzette to let her know a cousin of hers had shown up at the bed & breakfast. If Suzette was not aware of this, she would text Annie as soon as she read the email.

Once Annie reached the Harper's home, she sat down on the cushioned front porch chair and pulled out her cell phone to call Lizzy. Donald continued into the house to join the group for lunch. Lizzy answered on the first ring and began explaining the situation to Annie.

"Her name is Janette Parker." Lizzy stopped to have a conversation with a customer. Annie could hear Daisy in the background answering a customer question. It sounded busy in the shop. All the more reason to get back home sooner, Annie thought. She waited for Lizzy to get back to the phone conversation, but could hear how busy it was in the shop.

"Lizzy, should I call you back later?"

"Call me in a couple of hours." Lizzy said.

"I feel bad not being there when the shop sounds so busy."

"It just got busy. It was quiet all morning long. Talk to you soon." Lizzy ended the call. Annie stared at her cell phone. How was Janette going to get into the B&B? She would not know that Lizzy had a key to the business, so Annie did not think that Janette would be asking her for a way in the building. Still, it seemed odd that a cousin would show up expectantly when Suzette was out of town. Annie trusted Lizzy would never let a stranger into Suzette's B&B.

Lizzy was the person Annie called upon to help her run R&H Enterprises after Annie inherited the business from Helen Harper. It was a dream job for Lizzy with her Master's Degree in Business Administration. She was going to manage R&H Enterprises for Annie, and would no longer need to find a part-time job during the winter months when the shop business slowed down. Shop hours were usually cut due to lack of tourist traffic. That meant both Annie and Lizzy made less money. As for Annie, she no longer needed to worry about money due to her inheritance from Helen's estate.

Lizzy, in the past, was single and barely making it paycheck to paycheck. Things now were certainly beginning to go Lizzy's way. She was in charge of R&H Enterprises, still working in the shop with Annie, and dating the hottest police detective in town, Dan Surely. Lizzy always had a crush from afar on Dan, and once he met the tall, beautiful woman with long, brown curly hair, he was smitten. Things were definitely going great for Lizzy! Annie was making sure of that. She was the one who introduced her brother, Dan, to Lizzy and they hit it off immediately.

♦ ♦ ♦

Annie went through the house, to the sunny patio where she found everyone seated and deep into conversations. Donald stood and pulled out a chair for Annie. Once she sat down, plates of sandwiches, salads, and other side dishes were passed over to her. Annie was hungry for some reason. She dug in while Donald caught her up on the conversations they had been having.

"I told Mom and Dad that we were leaving right after lunch," Donald said passing the potato chip bowl over to Annie. "They were okay with the idea."

"Annie," Rand broke in, "Patty and I are going to drive the motor home to Bridgewater Harbor. Donald said we could hook up to utilities next to the garage. I hope having a motor home in the backyard will not distract from your wedding plans."

"I am okay with it. I wasn't aware we even had a utility hook-up for motor homes in the backyard."

"I remember a large motor home being parked there when I was a teenager." Donald stated, "We would spend time traveling when I came to visit. Sometimes Uncle Robert and Aunt Helen would come to California and we would spend time traveling from here."

Rand explained that Patty and he would start out in the next couple of days and take their time driving to Oregon. He assured Annie that they would be in Bridgewater Harbor before the wedding. The plan was to bring along in the motor home any boxes and other items that were not able to fit into the truck, to save Donald another trip back to California.

◆ ◆ ◆

It was nearly 2:00 AM, when Donald and Annie pulled up to their house in Bridgewater Harbor, Oregon. Donald had driven the last two hours of the trip and although Annie had shared the driving and should have been exhausted, she was actually excited just to be home. She exited the truck and grabbed as much as she could carry to the house. Donald pulled out his laptop and a few bags. The rest he said would be fine until morning. Donald used his key fob to turn off the house alarm. Annie punched in the code for the kitchen door keypad and opened the door.

Callie stood at her food dish and meowed once she saw Annie. Annie placed her things on the floor and picked up Callie. Laddie was the next to enter and immediately began to explore the house. Callie tensed in Annie's arms, all the while keeping her eyes on Laddie. Callie hissed when Laddie came face-to-face with her. It might take a bit of time to get these two to like each other, Annie thought. Annie kept Callie in her arms. She was not sure when it would be okay to let her down. Donald called Laddie over to him. He introduced Laddie to Callie. Laddie sniffed once and then turned to continue exploring the house.

"They will be fine." Donald said carrying his laptop and bags upstairs.

"Just the same, I think I will keep Callie with me for a while." Annie carried her purse and Callie upstairs to the bedroom. "It seems a bit quiet in the house. I guess I never realized how large it was until now." Annie was thinking about how grateful she was to have Donald with her in the house. She was not sure she could have lived in the house alone. Her thoughts wandered to her mother and Marie. They would be off to Disneyland about six hours from now.

As Annie walked down the hall to the master bedroom, she noticed the door to the guest room was open. She walked up to the door half expecting Lizzy to be there, but instead found the room vacant and the bed made. She walked to her bedroom and stood in the doorway as she looked with disbelief at how beautiful the room was. It was cozy, yet spacious, with light turquoise walls. White blinds adorned the windows. Her favorite place was a seating area with an incredible view of the ocean. There was a partial wall separating the bedroom area from the seating area. A small love-seat backed up against the partial wall in the cozy nook. Comfortable chairs flanked the sofa. On one wall was a built-in cabinet with a coffee maker. Donald thought of everything when he designed the remodel of the house; a house that Annie inherited from Donald's aunt.

Donald walked out of the bathroom in nothing but his underwear. He went to the alarm pad on the wall and punched in the night code. He then crawled into bed. Laddie jumped up and settled in at the foot of the bed. Annie stared at Donald.

"Where is Callie going to sleep?" Callie was still in Annie's arms.

"It's a big bed. Just bring her up here with us." Annie walked over to the bed and set Callie down between her side and Donald's side. Callie took one look at Laddie, hissed, and hopped off the bed. She went over to her food dish and began eating.

"We need to figure out a better eating area for Callie. Eating cat food will make Laddie sick." Annie realized she was talking to herself. Donald and Laddie were fast asleep. Annie went to the bathroom to brush her teeth and get ready for bed. Exhaustion was setting in now and she was looking forward to sleep.

CHAPTER 4

Monday Morning

Annie woke at eight o'clock in the morning. Callie was snuggled next to her, between Donald and Annie's pillows. Both Donald and Laddie were nowhere to be found. Annie knew Donald wanted to get back to work on Monday. Annie, too, would be heading to the shop early to catch up on the missed days. She crawled out of bed and headed to the bathroom to shower and dress for the day.

Thirty minutes later, Annie was in the kitchen making a cup of coffee. She noticed that Donald had picked up Callie's food dish and placed a large dog food dish by the kitchen door. Next to the food dish was a water bowl. Water was splashed on the floor around the sides of the bowl. Annie wiped up the mess with paper towels and made a mental note to get a place mat for Laddie's bowls.

Annie took her coffee and wandered into the office to let Donald know that she would be going to Ocean Loads of Paper early today. She saw him at her desk with his computer monitors set up and spread across the desk. It was a good place for Donald to work undisturbed by the rest of the household.

"Good morning, sweetheart," Donald said, looking up from his work. He pressed a few buttons and then pushed his chair back to give Annie a kiss. He helped himself to a sip of coffee from Annie's cup.

"Would you like me to get you a cup of coffee before I go to the shop this morning?" Annie said, patting Laddie on the head. He was lying on a giant dog pillow on the floor next to Donald.

"I would really love that." Donald's computer began beeping and he walked around the desk to answer a call. He put on his head set and looked up at Annie. She smiled and turned to walk out of the office. In an afterthought, she walked back into the office and set her coffee down in front of Donald. She was leaving anyway, and would stop by Ione's Coffee Shop and Bakery to pick up her usual coffee and chocolate croissant.

Annie was walking back to the kitchen, when she saw Callie descending the stairs cautiously. "Come on down the stairs and I will get you some breakfast."

Callie meowed, remaining on the stairs, as Annie opened a can of cat food and placed a scoop full in Callie's dish. She cleaned the water bowl and filled it with fresh water. As she picked up the dishes from the counter, she turned and realized that she would need to feed Callie in the laundry room on the counter, where Laddie would not be able to reach her food. Annie called to Callie to follow her, and placed her food on the counter. Callie jumped up, surveyed the area, and began eating.

"I guess you approve for now," Annie mused out loud.

When Annie placed her hand on the front door knob, her cell phone chimed indicating a text message was awaiting her answer. She pulled her cell phone from her jacket pocket.

"Are you coming to the shop early today?" Annie read the message from Lizzy and smiled. Annie recalled Dan remarking how predictable she was. She did not want to admit it, but she was predictable. Annie typed in a text that she was heading out the door to walk to the shop. Ocean Loads of Paper was only a few blocks away from where Annie lived. She walked to work most days.

Lizzy was practically living with Dan while he was taking care of Stella's house. Stella and Marie would be back the following Saturday. Annie thought Lizzy might be enjoying the spaciousness of the house compared to her small studio apartment.

Dan had lived with Annie's family since he was six years old. His biological mother was not able to care for Dan after his father left them. Annie's mother and father stepped in and Dan lived with her family since that time. She had always considered him to be her brother in every sense. Like true siblings, Annie often respected Dan, but there were times when Dan overdid the protective big brother role. It was those times when Dan and Annie got into arguments. Oftentimes, Annie's mother would step in and bring them to their senses.

Annie opened the door and found Lizzy standing on the side walk waiting for Annie. They smiled at each other as they began the short walk to Ocean Loads of Paper. Lizzy was dressed to the nines, as usual. Her long, brown, curly hair was styled into a ponytail low on the back of her head. Annie often thought that Lizzy was the best dressed person in town. She wondered how Lizzy could afford such nice clothes when she was making not much over minimum wage in the shop. Lizzy never complained and never asked for more money. In the winter months, when tourism slowed, Lizzy would find a second job working part-time to make her rent payments. She lived in a small studio apartment above a shop several blocks south of Ocean Loads of Paper. It was beautifully decorated and always neat and tidy. Annie and Lizzy had been friends for years, from the first day Lizzy entered the shop and asked for a job.

During the walk to the downtown section of Bridgewater Harbor, Lizzy caught Annie up on the activities of the previous weekend.

"Suzette's cousin arrived late Saturday morning," Lizzy began. "She contacted me at the shop to say she would be staying in Suzette's apartment at the B&B. Her name is Janette. She looks almost exactly like Suzette."

"I'm looking forward to meeting Janette," Annie said. "Did she say how long she was staying?"

"Not really. She said it was to get away from stress at home." Lizzy continued, "Apparently, her grandmother passed away about two weeks ago. There was some issue with her mother's inheritance and missing money. She did not go into detail."

Annie and Lizzy changed the topic of conversation to upcoming events at the shop. Lizzy suggested an event to draw more people to the downtown area. They decided to brainstorm with the shop owners and come up with a plan. An event would be exciting, Annie thought. She loved planning events. It was the actual 'doing' that she needed Lizzy's help completing. Annie smiled to herself thinking about all the plans she had and how patient Lizzy was about listening to each one. Most of them never came about due to money, but that had all changed two weeks ago.

Lizzy and Annie walked directly past the paper store and entered Ione's Bakery and Coffee Shop. As they stood in line, Lizzy recognized Janette, ahead of them.

"Janette?" Lizzy asked the woman standing in front of her.

"Oh, hello, Lizzy", Janette said, as she looked up from digging in her purse to locate her wallet. "It's so nice to see you again."

"How are things going for you at Suzette's Bed & Breakfast?" Lizzy asked.

"It's quiet without Suzette around and the business being closed while she is in Europe," Janette commented. "I decided to walk around and visit the shops while I am staying here."

"You have my number, so please feel free to call anytime." Lizzy turned to Annie, "By the way, Janette, this is Annie."

Janette shook Annie's hand and said, "It's a pleasure to meet you. I love your paper shop."

Annie, Lizzy, and Janette chatted casually as they moved up in line to the order counter. After the three women ordered drinks, Annie offered to pay and the group sat at a table near the street side of the coffee shop. Annie's curiosity took over as she plied Janette with questions about her life, family, and how she came to Suzette's bed & breakfast. Annie sensed that Lizzy sometimes got annoyed with her for asking too many questions and appearing nosey. She attributed it to being a police officer's daughter. She had a natural tendency to ask questions.

Janette's eagerness to have someone be interested in her life was obvious in her attentive and open body language. She had a few friends in Connecticut, where she currently lived about a mile from her mother. Janette explained her friends were more interested in themselves, their husbands, and what local gossip they could obtain. She was nothing like that.

Forty-five minutes later, and many questions answered, Lizzy looked up and noticed Daisy standing in line to order coffee.

"Oh, boy!" Lizzy exclaimed, looking at her watch and standing up. "We need to open the shop."

"Would you mind starting without me?" Annie asked Lizzy. "I think I will introduce Janette to a few of the shop owners."

Lizzy eyed Annie suspiciously. Janette excused herself to use the restroom. Lizzy jumped at the opportunity to talk to Annie.

"What are you up to?" Lizzy said in a low whisper.

"I have a funny feeling about her," Annie whispered back. "I just want to talk to her a bit more. Did she mention having a key to the B&B?"

"No," Lizzy answered looking in the direction of the restroom door. "I think she has a code to the backdoor entrance."

"I will just walk to a few stores and casually introduce her to some of the shop owners."

"Be careful," Lizzy urged Annie. "I think she is sweet. I don't see her as a con-artist or burglar."

"Me either. But there is something off about her."

"Welcome back, Annie." Daisy said as she approached the two women.

"It is nice to be back, even though I was only gone for a couple of days." Annie thought about how it seemed like weeks since she left for California. Donald and she had not even had a chance to settle in as a couple, and yet they had a wedding nearly all planned to take place in two weeks. Will life ever slow down again? Will I be able to concentrate on my crafting anytime soon? Annie was lost in thought again as Janette approached and said she was ready to leave.

Annie was about to introduce Daisy to Janette when Daisy said, "Hello, Janette. How are things going so far? Are you getting to know the town?

"Somewhat," Janette answered back. "I really appreciate you having pizza with me last night. It was nice to have a friendly person to talk with."

Lizzy and Annie both looked at Daisy. Annie realized she would need to talk to Daisy later and find out more about Janette. She knew Lizzy was thinking the same thing.

Annie and Janette walked out of Ione's Bakery and Coffee Shop on the street-side of the shop and began walking down the street. As it was not quite ten o'clock, most of the shops were not opened yet. Annie and Janette talked as they continued to walk. Janette stopped and looked in the window of Spencer's Gallery. She gasped and stepped back. Inside the shop, a woman was in the process of hanging a beautiful painting, of a garden scene, on the wall inside the shop.

"Is something wrong?" Annie asked, noticing how startled Janette seemed.

"No," Janette said, a bit shaken by what she saw in the window. "Let's go inside and look around." Janette moved to open the door. It was locked. As she placed her hand on the glass door to peer inside, a nicely dressed woman of about sixty-five years old, with light brown chin-length straight hair approached and unlocked the door.

"Good morning. Please come in. My name is Jacquie Spencer. I'm the owner. If you have any questions, please do not hesitate to ask me."

Janette entered the shop and walked directly to the painting Jacquie had just hung.

"Thank you, Jacquie," Annie said as she introduced herself. While crossing the threshold and entering the gallery, she noticed which painting Janette was viewing. It was a beautiful painting and Annie could see why it must have caught Janette's eye.

"Oh, good morning, Annie," Jacquie cheerfully greeted Annie as she held the door open. "I understand from the other shop owners that you are the new owner and landlord of the building. It will be a pleasure to do business with you."

"Actually, Lizzy, my associate, is managing R&H Enterprises," Annie said as she walked further into the gallery and viewed the various art pieces. "I want to continue concentrating on my paper shop."

"I understand."

Annie was not sure why, but watching Janette closely viewing the painting nearby made the hair on the back of her neck stand up. She tried to suppress a shiver that made its way through her body.

By this time, Jacquie noticed how intrigued the young woman was with the painting she had just displayed. She walked up and stood behind Janette. Startled, Janette turned around and faced Jacquie.

"It is a beautiful painting," Jacquie stepped to the side of Janette.

"Yes," Janette said in a soft voice.

"Who is the artist?" Annie asked Jacquie.

"A person by the name of Sharon Parc." Jacquie answered. "I'm not that familiar with her work. I just found the piece in my backroom this morning and decided to display it, as I believe it will sell right away. My assistant must have recently acquired it through consignment while I was gone for a few days. Lawrence did not leave me a note about it. He is off today, but I will ask about it when he works again. I can try and find the paperwork on the painting if you are interested."

Annie thought she saw Janette's jaw muscle tense. Maybe it was her imagination, but there was certainly an air of tension around Janette. Maybe it was due to Jacquie standing so close to her that made Janette tense. Annie's mind was wandering again and she realized that Janette and Jacquie were carrying on a conversation and she had heard not one word of it. She really should try to pay better attention to those around her. Annie began to walk around the gallery. As she made her way back to the front of the shop, she noticed that Janette and Jacquie were still standing in front of the painting and in conversation.

"Janette, I really should be getting back to my shop." Annie said as she approached Janette. "Would you like to join my family and me for dinner tonight?"

"Yes, that would be lovely. Thank you."

"I will text you the address." Annie said looking at her cell phone. "It's an easy walk nearby."

"Thank you, Annie." Janette took one last look at the painting and turned to Jacquie. "Thank you for your time. I will contact you soon if I decide to purchase the painting."

"I really do not believe this painting will be here long," Jacquie told Janette.

"I understand," Janette pushed through the door to the sidewalk outside. Annie rushed to keep up with her as they walked briskly toward Ocean Loads of Paper.

"Well, here is my shop." Annie put her hand on the door and as she began to push it open, she said, "It was nice meeting you!" Janette continued walking and raised a hand to her eye. Was she crying? Annie continued to watch Janette as she crossed the street, barely turning her head to look for oncoming traffic. She was now in a jog to the end of the building across the street. She disappeared behind the building. Annie just watched for a moment, and then walked inside Ocean Loads of Paper.

♦ ♦ ♦

The shop was empty of customers when Annie walked in and approached the checkout counter. Both Daisy and Lizzy were standing there unpacking a boxed delivery.

"That was the strangest thing that happened to me." Annie took her jacket off and hung it up in the office. She set her purse in the lower drawer of her desk and walked back out into the shop.

"What happened?" Lizzy asked.

Annie began to tell both women of the events that just took place. Lizzy pulled out her laptop and began searching for the artist by the name of Sharon Parc. Although she found many photos of artwork on a website, there was no photo of Sharon Parc. Annie looked over Lizzy's shoulder, searching through the various works of art. The piece that Annie saw in the gallery was not shown on the website. What was the story behind that particular painting, Annie pondered?

In an impulsive move, Annie grabbed her coat and purse and walked out the shop door on the ocean side of the building. She left Lizzy and Daisy perplexed and knew she would have some explaining to do later. Annie could feel the cool morning breeze sweeping off the ocean as she practically ran to the gallery. She burst through the door and found Jacquie at a small counter area.

"I want to purchase that painting," Annie said pointing to the beautiful painting Janette could not keep her eyes away from. "How much is it?"

"Well, the young woman was actually interested, but since you are here to make a purchase, I will sell it to you."

Jacquie gave Annie a price. Annie handed her a credit card. After the transaction was made, Jacquie packaged the painting to protect it from the salty sea elements for Annie to carry it home.

Annie grabbed her package and headed for the door. She turned as she pushed open the door. Jacquie smiled and Annie walked out of the gallery. She had bought a painting for no good reason. Something was bothering her about this painting. What was its secret?

♦ ♦ ♦

Annie struggled to get herself and her newly purchased painting through the ocean-side door of her shop. The wind had picked up and a dark cloud bank was on the horizon. It was an ominous sign, Annie thought to herself. She closed the door and stopped to catch her breath.

"What in the world do you have there?" Lizzy questioned as she walked around the corner of the counter and approached Annie.

"I went out and impulsively purchased the painting."

"Why?" Lizzy asked with her hands on her hip.

"I feel like this painting has a secret," Annie carefully moved the painting to her office. She was trying to find a place to hide the work of art, but finally just set it up against her wall under the jackets. She loosened the wrappings to allow Lizzy a quick look at the work of art.

"A secret?" Lizzy said, taking a closer look at the canvas.

"Yes, a secret." Annie continued her story about the incident in the gallery and Janette's reaction to the painting. Then she related how Janette left the gallery quickly and practically ran across the street to the B&B.

"Do you think the painting is stolen and Janette knows something about the theft?" Lizzy asked, leaving the office and moving to her laptop on the counter. Lizzy began typing on the keyboard. "What is the name of the painting?"

"Meredith's Garden was written on the receipt. It was the name written in pencil on the back of the painting." Annie said pulling out the paperwork and handing it to Lizzy.

While Lizzy was busy searching the internet for information on the painting, Annie sent a text to Donald asking him to pick her up at the shop after work.

Donald responded with a return text, "Was last night too much for you?"

Annie smirked, "I have something large to bring home."

"I'm not sure how to respond to that! I will be there at five."

Annie suppressed a laugh and set her phone on her desk. She walked out of the office in time to help customers entering the store.

CHAPTER 5

Monday Evening

The last customer exited the store at 4:35 PM, which allowed Lizzy and Annie to begin closing procedures. Daisy was scheduled to work until six o'clock, but Annie told her to finish what she was doing and she would be paid for her entire shift. Daisy happily agreed and quickly finished. She grabbed her jacket and purse and was out the door within fifteen minutes. Lizzy smiled at Annie.

"She has a date tonight," Lizzy told Annie. "Daisy was worried she would not be ready and get to the movie theater in time. You saved her date."

Annie was about to ask Lizzy how things were going with Dan, when Donald entered the shop.

"You're early," Annie said with a smile. She was still in that giddy-feeling stage whenever she saw Donald. Could it be only two weeks ago when they met following the death of Donald's aunt, Helen Harper? Annie's mother, Stella, had been best of friends with Helen, who was the guardian to Marie, a young woman with Down Syndrome. Since Helen's death, Marie came to be under the guardianship of Annie and now lives in the house that Helen left to Annie.

"I finished work early and decided to help you with that 'large' object."

"It's in my office leaning against the wall," Annie said to Donald as she continued to count out the money in the cash register. "It has a story behind it. I think it might be of some value."

Donald walked into the office and walked back out with the wrapped painting. He set it behind the counter and asked if he could help with closing. Lizzy held out a broom and pointed toward the classroom area. Donald looked at the broom in Lizzy's hand for a minute, deciding whether she was joking or not, then took the broom and headed over to the assigned area.

Lizzy nudged Annie and said, "Wow! Is it always that easy to get him to help?"

"I hadn't really noticed," Annie said closing the cash register and taking the drawer to the safe in the office. She came out a moment later with her cell phone in her hand, looked around the corner to the classroom area where Donald was dutifully sweeping and said, "He really does help out a lot. I guess I have been so busy lately, I was not appreciating how much he had been doing."

Annie typed a message to Janette on her cell phone, giving her directions to the house, and suggested six-thirty as a time to arrive for dinner. Janette answered immediately and apologized for leaving so suddenly. She messaged to Annie that she would explain later. Annie was happy that Janette did not cancel dinner tonight.

"What time do you think Dan will be home for dinner?" Annie asked Lizzy.

"He told me this morning that he would be home by five-thirty this evening."

◆ ◆ ◆

At six-thirty that evening, Annie answered the door and invited Janette inside the house. Annie made every effort to make Janette feel comfortable, but she could sense that Janette was nervous about something. Janette handed Annie a bouquet of flowers as a hostess gift. The flowers had the familiar look of floral arrangements from Bonnie's Belle-Flower Shop a block away from Ocean Loads of Paper. Annie thanked Janette, and took the flowers, asking Janette to follow her to the kitchen to meet everyone. As usual when Annie was making dinner, people tended to congregate in the kitchen while she cooked.

"Janette, you already know Lizzy," Annie said as she was opening cupboard doors looking for a vase. Donald, noticing the bouquet of flowers, went into the laundry room and came back with a medium-sized vase. Annie took the vase and began to fill it with water while Lizzy introduced Dan to Janette.

"And, this is my soon-to-be husband, Donald," Annie said as she set the flowers inside the vase.

Donald shook Janette's hand, "Would you like a glass of wine?"

"Yes, thank you." Janette walked up to Annie and asked, "Can I help you with anything?"

"I have meat and taco shells warming in the oven, and all the fixings on the table in the dining room. I think we are just about ready to eat." Annie went to the oven and pulled out a bowl of ground beef, a smaller bowl of refried beans, a tray of warm taco shells, and some warmed chips. She handed them to Donald, who took the food to the dining room table. Annie pulled a large stack of burrito shells from the microwave and placed them in a warming tray.

Dan and Lizzy were talking in the living room. They looked very cozy with each other. Annie paused, smiled, but decided to interrupt them.

"Dinner is ready, you two love birds."

Lizzy walked to the dining room with Dan close behind her. As he reached Annie's location, he rolled his eyes at her. Annie laughed. Dan and Annie had a typical brother/sister relationship and neither one took any nonsense from the other.

The group gathered around the table and began passing dishes of steaming meat, beans, and rice around the table. To allow for everyone's tastes, Taco night usually included burrito wraps, crispy taco shells, and flat tortilla shells. There was much laughter and chatter as everyone tried to make Janette feel comfortable. It seemed to work, Annie thought, when Janette pulled Annie aside after dinner and said she wanted to explain her attitude earlier in the morning.

"There is a story behind the painting," Janette began.

Lizzy walked into the kitchen with the last of the dishes from the dining room table. She set the dishes down and Annie began to scrape the food scraps into the trash.

"Would you feel comfortable telling all of us the story behind the painting?" Annie asked, hoping Janette felt at ease with Dan being a police detective. During dinner, Janette had asked everyone what their occupation was, but as Annie thought about that conversation, she realized no one asked Janette directly what she did for a living. If Annie hinted at the subject, Janette seemed to redirect the conversation back to Annie. Clever. Annie wondered what Janette was hiding. She decided that Janette offering to tell the story of the painting was a way to work the conversation to what occupation Janette had.

Janette looked into the dining room at Donald and Dan chatting about crabbing. She turned to Annie and said, "Can I trust them to not mention what I say to anyone else?"

"If you ask them to not repeat it, they will honor your request." Lizzy said as she rinsed off the last dish and placed it in the dishwasher.

Annie added dishwasher soap, closed the door, and started the wash cycle. She wiped her hands on the dish towel while asking who wanted coffee. She made coffee and with Janette and Lizzy's help they were sitting in the living room within minutes. Annie was eagerly anticipating finding out the story of the painting and why it held such interest for Janette. She watched Janette thoughtfully sipping her coffee. Annie wanted to shout "Get on with it already!", as she gripped her coffee cup in her hands. The room was quiet. Janette looked at Annie as if to ask if it was a good time to begin. Annie nodded and smiled slightly hoping to reassure Janette.

"Fifteen years ago, while I was still in school, I gave my grandmother a painting for her birthday," Janette began in barely a whisper. "My grandmother loved the painting." Tears welled in Janette's eyes. "Until recently, that painting hung in her foyer."

"What happened to the painting?" Dan asked in his usual interview tone of voice.

"My grandmother had become quite ill over the last year," Janette continued. "She had a heart condition. She was doing fine until six months ago, when she married a man five years younger. She knew nothing about him. I believe she was lonely and longed for the love that my late grandfather gave to her. When my grandmother and this man married, we were not invited to the wedding ceremony. In fact, she did not mention the marriage until a week after she was married." Annie and Donald looked at each other. Annie asked herself, were they rushing into marriage? Donald seemed to sense what Annie was thinking. He squeezed her hand.

Janette took a sip from her coffee cup and continued to tell the attentive group that her grandmother had passed away two weeks ago. The man she was married to for six months called Janette's mother and to report the death. Janette's mother was the only surviving child and sole heir to Janette's grandmother's estate.

Annie and the others learned that the man's name was Walter Smith. Smith, Annie thought to herself, is certainly a common name, not too traceable. The marriage seemed suspicious to Annie. Why would Janette's grandmother have kept such a happy and joyous union from her only daughter? Was Walter a con-artist? Annie was deep in thought again when she felt a nudge from Donald. He was used to Annie drifting off in thought. Annie sat up straight and directed her attention to Janette, hoping she had not missed anything important.

Janette continued to explain that her grandmother's body was quickly cremated before her mother and she could fly out to California from Connecticut. Walter had waited until late in the evening to make the call that her grandmother had passed earlier that morning. He rushed a cremation. By the time they had arrived, Walter had packed up and moved out of the house. He left a note saying he was deeply troubled by his wife's death and could not stay. That was the last they heard from him.

A week later, Janette reported, her mother discovered Walter had been siphoning a large amount of money from his wife's bank accounts. She contacted the police, who in turn stated that there was nothing they could do. Since the couple were married, she may have approved the transfer of funds. As her mother and Janette went through her grandmother's belongings, they discovered jewelry and artwork were missing. One of the art pieces was the painting Janette saw in the gallery in Bridgewater Harbor. The very work of art Janette gave to her grandmother.

"What do you know about Walter Smith?" Dan asked Janette.

"Nothing, really," Janette said, looking as if she was trying to pull any shred of information about this man from her memory. "My mother was not even aware Grandma was dating him, and all of a sudden she is married."

"Did she have a marriage certificate?" Dan asked, trying his best not to turn this into an interview involving an investigation.

"Yes. My mother did find a signed marriage certificate." Janette wiped her eyes and continued, "It listed the address of the groom as my grandmother's address and the name of Walter Smith. That is all we know about him."

"Did you or your mother ever see a photo of this person or meet him at some point in their six-month marriage?" Dan asked.

"My grandmother was in California and we live in Connecticut," Janette began to sob. "I was just too busy to go to California. Now I wish I had, but it's too late."

When Annie looked over at Lizzy, she saw tears welling in her eyes. Annie realized she did not know much about Lizzy's past life. Somehow the conversation they were having with Janette triggered something emotional in Lizzy. Dan must have noticed the same thing, as he quietly placed his hand on Lizzy's hand. Annie knew deep down inside Dan was a sympathetic guy, it was just a rare moment when she actually saw it.

Dan continued to ask Janette questions about Walter Smith. It was apparent that she did not know him at all. Dan asked Janette if she could contact her mother and ask her to locate any photos or information regarding her grandmother's husband.

"Does this mean you will be able to investigate my grandmother's missing painting?" asked Janette to Dan.

"With your permission, I would like to ask around and see if I can find out anything on this Walter Smith and his background." Dan said as he stood up and walked to the kitchen to get another cup of coffee.

Lizzy gave Annie a stern look, indicating that it might be time to tell Janette about the painting. Annie stood, excused herself, and walked to the office. She returned shortly with the covered painting and placed it on the floor in front of Janette. She carefully removed the paper protecting the piece of art. As she did, Janette gasped in shock as she realized Annie had her grandmother's painting.

"Annie," Janette whispered, "This is my grandmother's painting that was in the gallery. Did you buy it?"

"Yes. I noticed that it meant something important to you." Annie continued, "I was afraid someone else would buy it and you would not see it again."

"My mother is sending me money to purchase the painting," Janette advised Annie. "Please, may I buy it from you?"

"It is my gift to you, Janette," Annie said. "You have been through so much, and I thought it might be a bit comforting knowing that you have the painting back."

Janette jumped up and hugged Annie.

Dan walked back into the living room, handing a glass of water to Lizzy. He stopped and stared for a moment at the painting. He gave Annie a suspicious look and then sat down.

"Is that the painting you were talking about?" Dan said as he set his coffee cup down on a side table.

"Yes," Janette said excitedly. "I had no idea Annie purchased it for me. She is so sweet and kind."

Annie turned to see Dan glaring at her. It was his 'What are you up to?' look. It seemed that Annie once again, somehow, aggravated Dan. She knew she should not be enjoying this moment, but could not help herself.

Donald asked Janette, "How do you know Suzette?"

"Suzette is my cousin on my mother's side," Janette said. "Our mothers are sisters. Suzette's mother passed away years ago." Janette went on to explain that Suzette lived in California near her family until she married and moved to Washington. She had only been married a short time when she divorced and moved to the Oregon Coast for an opportunity to own and operate a bed and breakfast. It was her dream. Janette explained that she and Suzette were the same age and looked very much alike. "As kids, we used to love the 'Patty Duke Show' reruns, because it was so much like us," Janette reminisced. "Our mothers are of French descent, so we even had the European equivalent of Patty's cousin, Cathy."

"I loved that show when I was younger," Annie commented. "We had a TV station that played old shows."

"I understand Suzette has been traveling in Europe for the last few weeks," Dan asked. "What brought you to Bridgewater Harbor? Did you know that Suzette was out of town?"

"Oh, yes," Janette answered. "I contacted Suzette and she told me to stay in her apartment while I was here. She said she was cutting her vacation short and returning back to Bridgewater Harbor."

"But what brought you here while your mother was in California after your grandmother's death?" Dan persisted after Janette did not answer the initial question.

Janette paused, looking down at the floor. Annie sensed that Janette was keeping something from the group. Lizzy stood up and walked over to the painting that was resting against a table. She lowered her body to read the name of the artist in the lower right-hand corner.

"Sharon Parc," Lizzy read the name out loud. "Isn't P-A-R-C French for park? Your last name is Parker."

Janette looked up at Lizzy and said, "Yes. My name is Sharon Janette Parker. I am the artist of this painting. I paint under the name of Sharon Parc. It was my mother's suggestion that I paint under a French name."

Dan looked at Lizzy with surprised admiration. Lizzy realized she might have revealed a bit about herself that she did not want anyone to know. She knew Dan was not aware that Lizzy spoke fluent French due to her frequent trips to France while growing up. She meekly smiled back at Dan.

"So, tell us why you are here in Bridgewater Harbor, Janette," Dan stated, turning his attention back to Janette. "Did you know the painting was here?"

"No," Janette said, tears stinging her eyes. "When I arrived at my grandmother's home after her death, I noticed a pillow and blanket on the sofa in the living room. I am assuming Walter had slept there the night of my grandmother's death. On the coffee table was a blank pad of paper and a pencil. I was suspicious of Walter leaving before we got there, so I was looking around for some reason as to why."

Janette explained that she used the pencil to gently rub across the top paper in the pad to reveal the name of Bridgewater Harbor, Oregon. She was surprised in seeing that name. It was the town her cousin lived in. She knew that Suzette was out of the country. Why would Walter be interested in this particular town? Was he interested in contacting Suzette? Janette ended up with so many unanswered questions, that she thought it might be to her advantage to travel to Bridgewater Harbor. She contacted Suzette, who in turn gave her the door code to enter the bed & breakfast and her separate apartment.

Janette had no idea she would find the painting here in a gallery, but knew she was on to something important when she did. But now, Janette explained to the group, she did not know what to do next.

"Let me make some phone calls and find out more about this Walter Smith," Dan told Janette. "I am wrapping up a homicide case right now, but I will try and make some calls tomorrow."

"Annie and I can hold onto the painting for you while you are in town," Donald said. "We can lock it up in a safe until you are ready to go home."

Janette agreed and said she felt much better knowing that she had the painting back. Meredith's Garden was a very special painting. Janette said that her grandmother used to joke that it held a secret. Janette laughed and said that she was sure there was no secret, since she was the one who painted the piece of artwork.

Lizzy stood and announced that it was getting late. She picked up her water glass and Dan's coffee mug and walked to the kitchen. Dan stood and asked Janette if he and Lizzy could drive her back to the Inn.

"Thank you, but I drove my rental car here," Janette said. "I did not want to walk home in the dark. I appreciate the offer."

Dan and Lizzy said their goodbyes as Annie walked them to the front door. Dan held the door open for Lizzy, but before walking out he turned to Annie and whispered, "Don't get any ideas about investigating this case. Leave it to the professional."

Annie smirked at Dan and said nothing. After he walked out the front door, she closed it and turned her attention to Janette. Laddie followed Janette and sat next to her. Janette placed her hand on his head and scratched his ears.

"Thank you so much for a wonderful meal and conversation," Janette said. "I feel much better telling someone about this whole situation. Do you think Dan might be able to find Walter?"

"He will try his best, Janette," Annie said, thinking she too, would do some checking and see what she could find. An idea of how to get this information was forming in her head. She said goodnight and waved as she watched Janette get into her car and drive down the street into town.

Donald walked from the office where he had taken the painting to the vault room downstairs. "Do you think Dan was suspicious that we had a safe large enough to house a painting that size?"

Annie thought for a moment and said, "We may want to tell Dan and Mom about the vault room at some point. For now, I would like to spend more time down there and find out what it contains. Why did Helen leave all of this to me?"

CHAPTER 6

Tuesday Morning

Annie was up, showered, dressed, and heading downstairs with Laddie close at her heels in a race to reach the bottom step. It was five-thirty in the morning and light was just making an appearance in the sky. After filling Laddie's food dish with dry food, she filled his bowl with fresh clean water. She walked into the laundry room to check on Callie's food and water dishes. She filled Callie's water bowl from the sink faucet in the laundry room.

After making a cup of coffee, Annie opened the living room curtains and sat in the dark room looking out over the yard and into her mother's front yard across the street and the neighboring yard of Millie. Millie, who once lived alone, now lived with LaVerne, Lorraine, and Elsie. They referred to themselves as the Silver Sleuths. Although in their late seventies and early eighties, they managed to get around with ease, and knew absolutely everything that was going on in Bridgewater Harbor. Annie sat sipping her coffee, formulating a plan. She smiled to herself and wondered what Dan was going to say to her if, or when, he found out what she planned.

By six-thirty, Donald was making his way down the stairs and into the kitchen for a cup of coffee before going to work in the office. He stopped short when he saw Annie sitting in the living room in the now dim light of morning.

"Why are you sitting in the dark?" Donald asked of Annie.

"Oh, good morning," Annie said, shaken from her thoughts. "I was just thinking."

"About me and how sexy I am?" Donald said, leaning against the wall with his arms folded in a manly pose.

"Nice thought, but no. I was thinking about the painting and why it turned up in Bridgewater Harbor."

"Do not let Dan know you are thinking about that painting." Donald said standing upright and walking to the kitchen to start the coffee brewing. "I have plans to go crabbing with him this weekend. I would prefer he was pleasant, not crabby."

"I was just thinking that's all." Annie stood up and walked to the kitchen. She wrapped her arms around Donald and gave him a good morning kiss. He smelled wonderful and she wanted to stay in his arms all day. Unfortunately, he had work to get to and she had...plans to engage.

"I need to work on some crafting ideas for classes, so I am thinking of contacting Lizzy and letting her know that I may stay home today. Tuesdays are not the busiest day of the week. There is no need for three of us to be at the shop."

Donald took a sip from his coffee cup and stopped to look at Annie. "Are you feeling okay?" He knew that Annie's life was in that paper shop. For her to want to stay home on purpose was out of character.

"Of course," Annie said. "I just have craft projects to prepare for classes. It takes time to get everything together. I have a few things to do in the house and then I think I will take my laptop out on the front porch and work."

Donald gave Annie a kiss on the cheek and said, "I will be in the office if you need me."

It was almost seven in the morning. Annie figured she had at least a couple of hours before she began her plan. She decided to check the washing machine and maybe start a load of clothes. As she walked through the kitchen to the laundry room, she looked out into the backyard. She stopped and looked at the little yellow cottage in the far corner of the yard. Donald had the cottage cleaned and painted. It had been covered in vines and barely noticeable only a couple of weeks ago. It would make a perfect office for R&H Enterprises, the business she inherited from Helen Harper.

Annie walked out the back door and over to the cottage. She stood in front of the cottage and continued to think about setting up her business in this spot. She walked to the front door and tried the doorknob. It was locked. She knew it would be, but she had to try anyway. She walked over to the front window and peered inside. It was a large room with a small bathroom, a kitchenette, and a small fireplace. On the left side of the front door was a wall of built-in bookcases. As Annie stared at the built-ins, she thought they looked out of sync with each other. Was it her imagination? Probably just poor workmanship, she told herself.

Annie diverted her attention to the floorplan. It was large enough to house a desk and file cabinets for Lizzy, a small loveseat, chair, and end table, and most importantly, over by the built-in bookcases was room for Annie to set up a table for crafting. It was perfect. Now all she had to do was convince Donald that he should remain in the office and not move his work out to the cottage as he had planned.

As Annie continued to think about R&H Enterprises, she thought about the few boxes she gave to Lizzy which had R&H Enterprise's records. She did not recall coming across the tax records. Who did the taxes for R&H Enterprises? Annie decided it was probably late enough in the morning to contact Lizzy. She pulled out her cell phone and sent a text to Lizzy.

While waiting for Lizzy to answer her text, Annie walked over to the garage door. It, too, was locked. Annie returned to the house and gather up the keys she needed to get into the backyard buildings. As she walked to the kitchen door of the house, she heard the chime of her cell phone. It was Lizzy stating that she would be over in a few minutes.

The front door bell chimed and Annie opened the door to Lizzy. She was dressed in a light turquoise and white cotton summer dress, which wrapped around the waist, and sandals. It was Lizzy's casual look, but she appeared to have walked out of a fashion magazine. Lizzy wore a diamond necklace with matching diamond stud earrings. Her makeup was impeccable. When they stood together, Annie seemed to disappear in the glow that surrounded Lizzy. Men would make fools of themselves to get her attention, but she only had eyes for Dan. She never noticed other men.

Annie let Lizzy inside and began to explain her thoughts about the little cottage being used as an office, and her concerns over the files, tax records, and other papers. Lizzy had previously been through the four boxes of files that Annie had turned over to her. There were no tax records or mention of who prepared the taxes. The records had to be in the garage where all of the boxes had been moved to when the cottage was cleared out.

"I was thinking of staying home today and trying to make sense of this business I inherited," Annie said to Lizzy as they stood in the kitchen talking.

"Since I am going to be managing the company," Lizzy began, "What if I walked to the shop, opened it up for Daisy, and then came back here to help you organize all the records?"

"That sounds perfect." Annie said, as she walked to the kitchen door and looked at the cottage through the window. "Let Daisy know that we are willing to come down if it gets busy."

"It's never that busy on Tuesday," Lizzy remarked, "But I will tell her to call if she has any issues."

Lizzy was out the door and on her way to the shop. She wanted to get to the shop early and get things set up for Daisy, the young college student who was working as many hours as she could to help pay for tuition. Daisy had a keen mind for crafting and wanted to learn all she could about owning and operating a shop.

Annie thought it would be a good time to talk to Donald about staying in the office and letting her use the cottage for R&H Enterprises. Donald had planned on moving to the cottage this weekend. It was a place where he could work in private and not be interrupted. She grabbed a cup of coffee and a small dish of snacks to take to Donald. Her gesture was not a bribe at all, she told herself, she was just being nice.

Donald was disconnecting from a meeting when Annie knocked softly on the door. "Come in," Donald answered.

"Am I interrupting anything?"

"No. I just finished a meeting and so far, the rest of my day is clear."

"Good. I wanted to talk to you about the cottage."

"Not even married yet and you are moving me out to the cottage." Donald stood up and took the snack dish and coffee from Annie.

"Don't be silly. Laddie can have the cottage. I'll have a dog house built for you!"

Donald set the dish and coffee down on his desk and pulled Annie close to him. He wrapped his arms around her and placed his lips on hers. Annie was feeling tingly all over her body. She was trying to remember why she came into the office.

"When did you want me to move my office out there?" Donald continued to hold Annie close.

"That is what I wanted to talk to you about," Annie said. "I was wondering if we could rearrange this office so I could have a desk for household bill paying and computer work, and you could have a desk for your work."

Donald stood back and surveyed the large office area. Opposite the door was a wall of windows that looked out into the backyard. Floor to ceiling curtains covered the windows. A loveseat was backed up to the windows and upholstered chairs flanked the loveseat. A coffee table stood in front of the small sofa. Tall bookcases stood against the outer wall of the office area on one side of a window, which faced the side yard driveway leading to the back-yard garage.

"If I put a desk here in front of the bookcases," Donald said pointing to the corner of the room, "I can place the upholstered chairs in front of my desk." Donald moved one of the upholstered chairs in front of an imaginary desk by the bookcases. He stood back and visually surveyed the placement. "I can order a desk and office chair this afternoon."

Annie looked around the room and said, "That makes sense."

Donald and Annie discussed the furniture needed to make both the office and the cottage workable environments. Donald made a list and assured Annie that he would take care of ordering and setting up both rooms.

"Would I be bothering you if I came in this afternoon to spend time in the vault room?" Annie asked Donald. "I thought I would try and make some sense of it all down there."

The vault room was accidentally discovered by Annie over a week ago. There was a hidden staircase behind the bookcases, to the right of the door in the office leading to a finished sitting room at the bottom of the stairs. Behind a floor to ceiling painting was a vault door. Opening that door revealed a very large room where Robert and Helen Harper kept all their secrets. It was the first place Donald had kissed Annie.

"If you wait until after four o'clock, I will be happy to go with you." Donald offered. "I must admit, I am curious as well. If you don't want the company, I will understand."

"Don't be silly," Annie said flirtatiously. "Lizzy and I will be finished by four o'clock. We can have the whole house to ourselves."

"Let's be on the safe side and lock the office door." The phone rang and Donald reached for his headset while saying, "I do not want a repeat of what happened last time in the safe room." He answered his phone and Annie turned to leave the office.

◆ ◆ ◆

Making a fresh cup of coffee and retrieving her laptop from the kitchen table, Annie walked out to the covered front porch and sat down in a wicker chair. She set her coffee cup on a side table and viewed the neighborhood in front of her. Then she rose, moved a few pieces of furniture, and again sat down in the chair. She wanted to make sure she was noticeable where she sat. She decided to get up and water the hanging petunias. She turned on the water and began walking the length of the porch stopping at each hanging basket to give the flowers a drink of cool liquid. She had just enough time to finish, turn off the water, and sit back down when her plan began to work.

The sun was shining and a light cool breeze drifted through the June air as LaVerne, Lorraine, Millie, and Elsie walked from Millie's house and crossed the street. Nothing got past these ladies, Annie thought. She opened her laptop and pretended not to see the ladies as they approached.

"Well, good morning, Annie," Millie said as the four ladies walked up the stairs of the porch. "This is certainly a beautiful day to be sitting out on the porch."

"Good morning, ladies," Annie said looking up with a warm smile on her face. "Would you please join me?"

"Don't mind if we do," Lorraine said sitting down on the wicker loveseat and straightening her dress.

As Elsie sat down next to Lorraine, she said, "We thought you would be at work by now. Are you not feeling well?"

"You're not pregnant already, are you?" LaVerne asked as she sat in one of the previously and carefully placed chairs on the porch.

"Heavens, no!" Annie said, thinking about the times she and Donald had been romantically inclined...or was it reclined. Annie smiled to herself. "No. No. No. There is no pregnancy. I was taking some time off to get caught up on everything that has happened to me in the last two weeks. It is a bit overwhelming."

"Oh you poor dear!" Elsie said to Annie. "But you are young. You can handle anything. We are here to help, if you need us."

And the door was open, Annie thought to herself. They offered and she was going to accept their offer. Now, how should she approach the subject and let them do their magic of finding out information? She had to be careful. These ladies were not easily fooled. They were smart and feisty.

"We want to hear all about California," Lorraine asked. "Did anything exciting happen?"

Annie stared at Lorraine for a moment, hoping the ladies did not hear about her mishap of being caught naked by the police outside of Donald's house. No, she thought. There is no way they could have found out about that. Calm yourself Annie. Do not panic.

Annie began by telling the ladies about meeting her soon-to-be in-laws and Laddie the dog. She told them of the wedding plans and how she would be waiting until her mother and Marie returned from Disneyland to make final plans.

"I hope we are still invited," LaVerne said.

"How could I get married without my favorite crafting ladies present?"

"We can help decorate, or make invitations, or wedding favors," Millie said. "Oh, Annie, you have just got to let us help."

"I will let Mom know," Annie said. "I am sure she will be happy to have the extra help. We were planning on getting married in the backyard a week from Saturday."

"Oh, that does not give us much time to plan," Lorraine said as the ladies shook their heads in agreement.

"On another topic," Annie said, changing the subject. "It is well known that you ladies have a knack for knowing what is going on around Bridgewater Harbor. I was wondering if you had the time to help me out with a problem."

"A case?" said LaVerne.

"Oh, yes," added Lorraine. "The Silver Sleuths are at your disposal."

"What information are you looking for, Annie?" asked Millie.

Annie began to tell the senior ladies about a man, Walter Smith, who married a young woman's grandmother under suspicious circumstances. Walter Smith was the person she wanted to find out more about. Who was he and why was he suddenly in Bridgewater Harbor?

"Well," LaVerne started, "The only men in town that we know of who have recently moved here are living at the senior apartments. They all moved in about two weeks ago."

"What does he look like?" asked Millie. "I have been introduced to all three of them. I would say two of them are charmers."

"Bart Jones has the hots for you, Millie," LaVerne said.

"Handsome, yes, but he is too pushy for my taste," Millie responded. "I rather liked Calvin Atwater. He is a bit shy."

"I think they all have eyes on Millie," LaVerne said. "She owns her own house and has money. These old guys are just looking for someone to take care of them."

"You know what they say," LaVerne added. "Old guys are looking for one of two things: A nurse or a purse!"

"I think Henry Kenner is hot," Lorraine spoke up. "He used to dance in movies. He is tall and has long dancer's legs. His hair is light brown with a bit of graying at the temples."

"Oh, Lorraine, he dyes his hair," LaVerne stated, giving Lorraine a tap on her arm to wake her from a dreamy state of mind.

"Well, I would certainly dance with him, if he asked," Lorraine said, returning to her thoughts of Henry.

Annie inquired if the ladies knew any more information about Bart Jones, Calvin Atwater, and Henry Kenner. She realized she should not focus solely on those three men, but since they arrived in town only two weeks ago, they would be her first choice.

"You want us to get information on these guys?" LaVerne asked. "We can get the men in our Silver Sleuths group to do some asking around."

"I will ask Morty," Millie said. "He likes me. He will do anything I ask."

"Morty likes anything in a skirt, Millie," LaVerne said as she stood to leave.

Annie knew Morty. He was spry, cantankerous, old as dirt, and walked with the assistance of a four-wheel walker with a seat. Morty flirted with all the women. He was often seen sitting on his walker watching traffic during the day. Sometimes he would sit on benches with other older men and watch the world go by. Annie imagined that he was gathering information. What information, she was not sure. He just seemed like a crafty old man.

Annie thanked the ladies for their visit and willingness to ask around about Walter Smith.

"Annie," LaVerne leaned in toward Annie, "we will just keep this to ourselves for now. We do not want that detective getting on our case again."

"We should have a code word," Millie said. "You know, like they do in the spy movies"

Annie said she would think about that and get back to them. Lorraine told Annie not to worry, that they would come up with the code word and let her know later.

CHAPTER 7

Tuesday Afternoon

Annie spent the next hour working on ideas for her upcoming classes. She made notes of supplies she needed and sketches of her designs. She was looking forward to getting back to crafting again. Her ideas were of summer projects, but her mind began drifting to wedding decorations. She was actually getting excited to marry Donald in a simple, quiet, ceremony in the backyard. They really had not made too many plans, as her mother and Donald's mother seemed to have everything under control. For Annie, the formalities were not important. It was all about being married to the love of her life.

Just as Annie was thinking about asking Lizzy to help her find a simple white dress for the wedding, she saw Lizzy walking up the street toward the house. In her hand was a bag with the familiar logo from Ione's Bakery and Coffee Shop. Annie realized she had the best friend ever.

Lizzy walked up the stairs as Annie was closing her laptop and standing up. She took a coffee cup from Lizzy, and they both went inside the house. Lizzy placed the bag of food on the counter. As Lizzy was removing plates from the cupboard, and Annie was getting bottles of water from the refrigerator, Donald walked into the kitchen.

"Hello Lizzy," Donald said as he took a bottle of water from Annie and kissed her on the cheek.

"Hi, Donald," Lizzy said placing sandwiches on a platter. "I thought we might want to have lunch before setting up an office in the cottage this afternoon," Lizzy said to Annie as she handed her a napkin. "I hope you are hungry, Donald, because Ione makes the best sandwiches on the Oregon Coast."

"I love Ione's sandwiches," Donald said to Lizzy. "Thank you for including me."

"You think of everything, Lizzy," Annie said.

Lizzy continued to pull items out of the bag. When she finished, there were potato chips, macaroni salad, and what Annie thought was the best, chocolate brownies for dessert. Laddie's nose was stretching up to the table hoping for anything he could sink his teeth into. Donald reached into a cookie jar and pulled out a couple of dog biscuits for Laddie. Laddie immediately knew what Donald was holding and turned his attention to the dog biscuits. He danced around Donald as they headed for the kitchen door.

"Come on, boy," Donald said to Laddie, picking up his plated food and walking outside to the patio table. Lizzy and Annie followed with their food and water.

◆ ◆ ◆

By three-thirty in the afternoon, Lizzy and Annie had moved all the boxes from the garage to the cottage office. They managed to move in a small table, which was also stored in the garage. This gave Lizzy a work surface where she could immediately begin setting up a working business environment. Annie noticed Lizzy reaching into a tote bag she had brought over and retrieving a calendar, pens, mechanical pencils, highlighters, marking pens, sticky note pads, large yellow pads, a stapler, tape dispenser, and various other desk items. Lizzy appeared to really enjoy her new environment.

Lizzy and Annie had accomplished a great deal by four-thirty and decided to walk to the shop to help Daisy close up for the day. After sending Donald a text that she was heading to the shop, Annie grabbed her purse and tote bag and followed Lizzy out the front door.

The sun was shining and a light breeze made the summer day perfect for walking into town. As Lizzy and Annie walked, they talked about setting up a meeting of all the shop owners and plans they wanted to make for the future of R&H Enterprises. Annie left the details to Lizzy. It was a short walk, and they soon entered Ocean Loads of Paper to find Daisy at the counter with a customer. No other customers were in the store, but Daisy was being very helpful instructing the woman on various types of glues.

After the customer made purchases and left the shop, Annie put up the closed sign and locked the doors while Lizzy conducted closing duties. Daisy began straightening up what she had not completed earlier. When they all finished their tasks, Annie suggested they go next door to Ione's Bakery and Coffee Shop to get coffee and talk. She unlocked the door and followed Daisy and Lizzy as they walked out. After locking the door, Annie took a moment to look out over the ocean where she happened to see a gray whale spouting in the distance. She loved watching the whales and the ocean.

Once inside, the women ordered coffees and sat down at a table on the street side of the shop. Annie asked Daisy how she liked the job so far. Daisy spoke excitedly about the shop and the people she met. She reached for her purse and pulled out folded papers with sketches and ideas for projects. Annie was impressed and asked if Daisy was interested in teaching some classes. Daisy was thrilled to do so and thanked Annie for giving her the chance to help with classes. Annie told Daisy that she could use the table in the shop to work on her projects and create samples. Annie would begin scheduling more project-type classes, as she had been getting requests for them.

As Daisy and Lizzy talked about project ideas, Annie's attention was drawn to a gentleman entering the coffee shop through the street-side doorway. Annie was looking at an incredibly handsome man of about fifty-five years old. He had slightly greying hair at the temples and was clean-cut in appearance. He was very well dressed for a tourist on the coast. He almost seemed out of place. Annie wondered who he was and why he was here of all places.

Lizzy noticed Annie's attention on the man standing in line at the coffee counter. She and Daisy stopped talking and watched as the employee at the counter pointed to the table where Annie, Lizzy, and Daisy were sitting. The gentleman thanked the employee and walked directly over to their table.

"Good afternoon, ladies," the tall gentleman began. "My name is Lawrence Smyth. I am the manager of Spencer's Gallery. I was told I might find Annie Weston sitting at this table."

"I'm Annie Weston, Mr. Smyth," Annie spoke up. "How may I help you?"

"If I may…" Mr. Smyth asked, gesturing for permission to join the ladies at the table.

"Please do."

"I will get directly to the point." Mr. Smyth pulled the chair out and sat down. "I understand you purchased a painting at Spencer's Gallery. I was hoping to convince you to let me purchase the painting from you, at a generous profit, of course."

Lizzy and Daisy looked curiously at each other, not knowing whether to stay or make an excuse to leave. They decided to stay.

"Why would you want that particular painting?" Annie leaned in as she asked the question. Annie was concerned why there was sudden interest in the painting that was missing from Janette's grandmother's home and how it suddenly turned up in Bridgewater Harbor.

"Actually, I was considering purchasing the painting myself as a gift for my mother when the painting arrived at the shop. She loved gardens and the colors in the painting reflect her personality so beautifully." Mr. Smyth fidgeted in his chair. "I made the mistake of not telling Mrs. Spencer that I wanted to purchase the painting and therefore left it with other inventory in the back room. It was a terrible mistake on my part."

"How did the painting end up in Spencer's Gallery, Mr. Smyth?" Lizzy asked.

Annie smiled inwardly at Lizzy's question. Dan's police background was definitely becoming an influence on Lizzy. It was a question that Annie was about to ask.

"It came in with other paintings for sale from a source we sometimes use."

Annie made a mental note to ask Jacquie Spencer who the 'source' was the next time she saw her in the shop.

"I am very sorry, Mr. Smyth," Annie said as apologetically as she could. "The painting was purchased as a gift. I no longer own the painting."

"May I inquire as to who the recipient is then?"

"I am afraid not," Annie said as she stood, indicating the meeting was over. "The particular person who received the gift has no desire to part with the painting."

Mr. Smyth stood, realizing the meeting was over, and said, "I appreciate your time, Miss Weston." He nodded to the two women seated and left the coffee shop. As he walked out the door, he turned and eyed Annie, who was watching him closely.

A curious chill ran through Annie's body. It was the look. Other than that, he seemed like a perfectly charming man. But for a moment, his look seemed sinister, in a way. Annie chided herself for thinking such thoughts. Good grief, she told herself, he was just trying to buy a beautiful painting for his mother. He took a chance on buying it back. That was all there was to it. Just because the painting had a story behind it, there was no reason to be suspicious of this man.

Annie turned to Daisy and Lizzy, who were also watching the man walk away. There was a long pause before Daisy said, "Wow! He was hot for an old man." Annie and Lizzy looked at each other and laughed.

Ione was standing at the next table and turned to pick up empty coffee cups and clear the table where Annie, Lizzy, and Daisy sat. "What did Lawrence want with you ladies?" Ione was not afraid of asking personal questions. She was known for having the latest gossip in town. Annie would never admit it to anyone, but she loved to listen to what new information Ione had to offer about anything happening in Bridgewater Harbor.

"I purchased a painting yesterday, and he wanted to buy it from me."

Ione pulled out a chair and sat down at the table saying, "Meredith's Garden."

"How did you know?" Lizzy asked.

"Janette was in here this morning," Ione said, happy with the fact that she was still on top of the news in town.

The doorbell chimed and attention was turned to Donald walking into the coffee shop. He spotted the group and walked over to the table. Ione got up and wiped the table surface as she greeted Donald and walked to another table to clear.

"Funny finding you in a coffee shop," Donald said to Annie.

"You were looking for me?" Annie said.

"Always looking forward to you," Donald smiled suggestively. "Actually, I was going to pick up Chinese food across the street, but noticed you in here. I guess now is a good time to ask if you had plans are for dinner."

"Dan and I have our own plans tonight," Lizzy jumped in. "I am spending the night at my apartment and Dan is working late. I guess you two are on your own."

Annie turned to Lizzy, "Is everything okay with you two?"

"Of course," Lizzy said quietly, not looking directly at Annie.

Daisy stood and made her excuses, thanking Annie for the coffee. She said she would see them both in the morning. She left through the boardwalk side of the coffee shop and walked out of sight.

"I will be over at the Chinese restaurant picking up takeout," Donald said. He bent down and kissed Annie on the cheek.

Annie watched Donald exit the shop and immediately turned to Lizzy. "What is going on?"

"Nothing!"

"Lizzy, we have been friends too long. Has my brother done something stupid?"

"No," Lizzy said in a loud whisper, looking around to see if anyone was listening. "It's me, not him."

"I'm listening."

Lizzy kept looking around the room. Annie could tell something was upsetting her and that she really did want to talk about it, but the coffee shop might not be the best place to discuss anything personal.

"Let's go outside to the boardwalk," Annie said. "There doesn't seem to be a lot of people out there right now."

Annie sent a quick text to Donald as to where he could find her, then she and Lizzy walked out to the ocean wall of the boardwalk. Lizzy leaned up against the rock wall, which stood thirty inches high and was about eighteen inches deep. It was enough to sit on, but with the late afternoon sun beating down on the rock, it seemed a bit warm. Annie faced the wall and turned to Lizzy, waiting for her to speak.

"Dan wants me to move into the house after Stella moves out and turns the house over to him." Lizzy paused.

"That's great, right?" Annie sensed there was more.

"Yes, except..." Lizzy was finding it difficult to express her feelings. "It's not exactly an offer of commitment, is it?"

"I see your point," Annie looked out over the ocean and watched the waves splashing up against the rocks that jutted out into the water.

"Well, any words of wisdom? You know him better than I do."

"My advice would be to go with your gut feeling," Annie said to Lizzy. "You have to ask yourself why you are doing this and if you will be happy."

"I have never felt this way about another man," Lizzy said, brushing off a twig that was resting on the rock wall. "He stimulates me intellectually. He makes me laugh. I find myself thinking about him all the time." Lizzy looked up at Annie. Her eyes were filled with tears, "Annie, I think I am in love with your brother."

Annie hugged Lizzy, and then said, "I am truly happy for you. You do know he can be a pain in the 'you know what' at times, right?"

"I call that charming."

Annie and Lizzy were laughing as they talked about the brother/sister relationship that Dan and Annie had while growing up. Annie related stories that had Lizzy bent over clutching her stomach laughing. It was then that Annie remembered Donald had been there as well. Thinking back on some of the things that she did to Dan and Donald when she was young, she wondered if Donald would remember them. She made a mental note to ask him.

Donald walked through the coffee shop and out the ocean side door, carrying a large bag of Chinese food.

"Are you sure you want to pass up dinner with us?" Donald asked Lizzy.

"I appreciate the offer, but I have laundry to do tonight and I need to get home." Lizzy hugged Annie, "Thanks for listening. I feel so much better. I know what to do now."

♦ ♦ ♦

Donald and Annie sat in front of the television, watching the news and eating their takeout. It was eight o'clock in the evening when Donald announced he was going to bed early, as he had an early meeting at six o'clock in the morning. Annie was happy to go to bed early. She cleaned up the kitchen, fed Callie crunchies in the laundry room, and made sure the doors were locked. Donald turned off the lights downstairs and the two headed to the bedroom.

As Annie was brushing her teeth, she thought about the conversation with Lizzy about her childhood. She thought about Dan and Donald as close friends back then. She was remembering how sad Dan would be when Donald went back to California after spending a week or two with his aunt and uncle in Bridgewater Harbor. She was not sure if they ever kept in contact during the year.

"Donald, did you and Dan ever keep in contact after your visits here."

"Not really," Donald said finishing brushing his teeth. "We just seemed to pick up where we left off each year."

"Do you two talk about the times you spent here as a kid?"

"I have not really given it much thought."

Annie followed Donald out of the bathroom and stopped to turn off the light. She stood in the doorway for a moment watching Donald pull the covers back on the bed and slide in under the covers. Laddie was already in his giant dog bed and fast asleep. Callie was in her kitty tower watching the scene below her. Annie walked to her side of the king-sized bed and crawled in, pulling the covers up over her body. She lay thinking about her childhood.

An hour had passed and Annie was not able to fall asleep. She began breathing deeply and trying to clear her mind in an attempt to drift off to sleep.

Donald sprang upright in bed and said, "Annie! Wake up."

"I'm awake."

"I remember Dan and I playing in the backyard of this house and finding a doorway to what Uncle Robert told us was a root cellar."

"A root cellar?" Annie said questioned.

"Yes, in the very place that a cottage now sits." Donald threw the covers off and sat at the edge of the bed. "Come on. Get dressed. We should go check out the cottage. I would bet there is a secret room below it."

"Donald, you have an early morning meeting and its dark outside." Annie said. "It will be there tomorrow. We can check it out after work."

Donald reluctantly got back into bed. As Annie lay in bed thinking about the possibility of another secret room, she decided it would not be impossible to believe. What was in the secret room was not something she was sure she wanted to find out. In a few minutes she heard soft snoring from Donald. It certainly did not take much time for him to nod off. It was going to be a long day tomorrow. She will need plenty of coffee in the morning, she thought. Annie was awake for an hour, thinking about the many secrets this house was revealing before she finally drifted off to sleep.

CHAPTER 8

Wednesday Evening

Annie's afternoon was moving along quickly as the shop was busy and she had a class with a regular once-a-month crafting group. She also had to prepare for the senior crafting group on Thursday afternoon. Fortunately, Daisy was helping out with this afternoon's class and had pretty much organized everything. Annie was so grateful to have Daisy working for her.

At three o'clock, Annie noticed Lizzy working at the counter. There was one customer waiting for the class to begin, and Annie knew the other class members would be arriving soon. It was a good time to take a break.

"How was your evening last night?" Annie asked Lizzy.

"Lonely," Lizzy said as she closed the catalog she was ordering from. She placed the catalog under the counter and walked to the printer to pick up the list of items ordered for the shop.

"You should talk to him," Annie said. She pulled up a stool and sat down. "Sometimes Dan gets busy and does not see the world revolving around him."

"It's okay. We'll be fine."

As if Annie had willed it to happen, Dan walked into the shop from the street-side door. He walked up to the counter and greeted the two women.

"Lizzy, would you like to go out to dinner with me tonight?" Dan asked.

"I would love to, Dan."

"Great. What time should I pick you up?" Dan asked as he pulled out his cell phone and looked at a text message.

"The shop will be closing at six o'clock today," Lizzy said, noticing Dan's attention was diverted. She was hoping he was not getting called out on a case tonight. She wanted to spend some time with him.

"The Deputy District Attorney wants to meet with me tomorrow on a case," Dan told Lizzy. "I need to make a call to him right away."

Lizzy nodded and Dan left the shop. Lizzy turned to Annie with a hopeless look in her eyes. Annie knew things would be okay between them. They just needed time together to get it all figured out.

"Oh, I just realized, I told Donald I would be home at four o'clock today," Annie said as she jumped off the stool. "Lizzy, I'm sorry, but would it be a problem if I left early?"

"Good grief, no," Lizzy said. She looked around the shop. "The only thing going on right now is the class, and Daisy has that handled. Are you ready for the senior crafting class tomorrow?"

"No, but I can get it set up tomorrow."

Lizzy laughed and shook her head. Sometimes Annie was known to procrastinate, but she always came through in the end.

♦ ♦ ♦

At four forty-five in the afternoon, Annie walked through the front door. She started to walk upstairs to drop off her purse and tote bag when Donald exited the office.

"Ready to tackle the root cellar?" Donald said as he closed the door to the office.

"Looks like I got here just in time," Annie said coming back down the stairs and placing her purse and bag on the kitchen table.

"I saw you walking up through the cameras. I have a monitor on my desk with all the cameras displayed."

"Of course, you do," Annie said, feeling glad Donald was so security conscious. She was still a bit uneasy about answering the front door after what happened with the intruder in her house and a murderer forcing his way into her home at gunpoint. It had been less than a week ago, and the drama of it all was still near the surface of her feelings. Yet, she made it a point to let her life go on as normally as possible.

"Annie?" Donald said, trying to snap Annie out of her deep thoughts.

"Yes, that will be fine," Annie said, not knowing if Donald had been asking her a question or not.

Donald looked at Annie for a long moment. She realized he was staring at her. Great, she thought, he asked her a question she did not hear, because she was off in thought-land.

"Was I not paying attention again?"

"Yes," Donald said with a sly smile, "But, you said, 'yes, that will be fine'. So, I am going to hold you to that." With that, Donald walked to the backyard.

Annie stood for a moment playing the conversation in her head. What did she agree to or was Donald messing with her mind again? She reluctantly followed him out the kitchen door.

Donald and Annie stood outside the cottage front door. Annie was not sure what Donald was looking for, but kept quiet, taking in the scene before her. There stood the small yellow bungalow with white trim and a white door. Roses were planted in flower beds around the building. The aroma was intoxicating in the warm summer heat. Annie was watching a butterfly fliting across the flower bed when Donald suddenly moved to unlock the front door. Annie followed inside.

Donald walked around the room, which had been organized by Lizzy and housed the R&H Enterprise business. Donald pulled a measuring tape from his pocket and began measuring the length and width of the room. Annie grabbed a notepad from her crafting desk near the bookcase and began writing down the numbers Donald was calling out to her.

Donald and Annie walked outside and measured the length and width of the outside of the building. Donald stood back and began looking around the yard. He walked to the main house back door and began taking measured steps to the middle of the yard. Donald stopped, thought for a moment, turned and walked up to the cottage.

"Danny and I found a...I want to say trap door in the ground around here," Donald said pointing to the area where the cottage now sat. "We stepped it off after Uncle Robert told us it was just an old root cellar. He warned us to not get too curious, as it was a dangerous hole and we could get hurt. We went on to other activities and I never gave it another thought. I think he gave us money to go into town and buy ice cream."

"Do you think there is another secret room that is accessible from under the cottage?"

"I am beginning to think Uncle Robert liked secret rooms," Donald said with a smile.

"He certainly had the funds to build them."

"Let's search inside for a doorway," Donald said as he walked back into the cottage.

"If you think about it, your uncle seemed to like moving bookcases. That seems like a good starting point." Annie walked up to the bookcases and began looking for the area that had looked out of place when she was peering through the windows earlier before she and Lizzy moved the files and furniture inside the small building. She walked out the front door, closed it, and began looking in through the window. She found it. The area of the bookcase that looked like it was not lined up with the other structure.

Annie quickly opened the front door and walked inside. "Donald, right here," she said pointing to the misaligned shelf area. "This area looks like it might be off from the rest of the bookcase."

Donald walked over and began pushing and pulling on the bookcase, but it did not budge. He opened the lower cabinet doors and began feeling for a switch or button that would open the doorway.

"Is there a flashlight somewhere in here?" Donald asked Annie.

"There is a First Aid kit hanging in the bathroom," Annie said, and she walked quickly to the small room adjacent to where they were inspecting the bookcases. There on the wall stood a white metal box with a large red cross blazoned across the front. She opened the lid of the box and noticed a flashlight. As she pulled the flashlight from its resting spot, she noticed a toggle switch inside. She flipped the switch. The next thing she heard was a loud thud. She peeked out of the bathroom to find Donald lying on the floor. Apparently, when she flipped the switch, the bookcase popped open and surprised Donald, causing him to fall backward.

"Are you alright?" Annie asked as she helped him to his feet.

"I take it you found a way to open the bookcase doorway?" Donald said.

"Sorry, Donald," Annie said. "I probably should have said something before flipping the switch inside the emergency box. Now we know where it is."

Donald and Annie looked at the opening in the bookcase. Donald moved to open the doorway further and felt for a light switch. Finding one on the right-hand side of the opening, he flipped it to illuminate narrow stairway leading down. Annie was close at Donald's back, nearly touching him, as they descended the stairs. Odd, Annie thought, the whole stairway is nicely finished. She would have thought it to be dark and creepy, but instead the walls were a light yellow and the stairs were finished wood.

The two kept going and turned a corner, where they came across a small room with wooden boxes.

"Are those coffins?" Annie exclaimed shakily.

"No," Donald said. He looked at her and shook his head.

"Well, they look like coffins at first glance."

"First of all, they are too small for coffins," Donald said moving to one of the wooden crates. "Second, they are shipping crates." He opened the lid to a crate and looked inside. The wooden box was empty. He walked around the stacked crates and opened the lid of another one. Again, empty. Annie was looking in the boxes after him.

"These crates are empty," Annie said. She was noticing the wood of the shipping crates and wondering what she could create from all that wood. Her mind was in the creative mode. She was imagining birdhouses, feeders, flower boxes, and such. She thought the wooden boxes would give her and Lizzy a great reason to use the workshop inside the garage. Her father had taught her how to use power tools and she was always looking for projects to create. This was wonderful, she thought.

"Annie, over here," Donald said. He was examining the wall on the far side of the tiny room. "I think there is a doorway here."

"Another one?" Annie asked.

"See if you can use your switch-sniffing skills to find out how to open it," Donald teased. Annie gave Donald a look and proceeded to search the room. When they both came up with nothing, Annie suggested it was not a door. Donald relented and they decided to go back upstairs. It was just a secret room with empty wooden boxes.

As they reached the upstairs cottage room and closed the bookcase doorway, Annie told Donald that they should eat some dinner and try to figure out why there was a room down there. Annie was getting a bit hungry and thought that taking a break would help them think this situation through more clearly.

While Donald threw a couple of hamburgers on the grill and toasted the buns, Annie made a salad and prepared lettuce, tomato, mayonnaise, and mustard on a plate. She put slices of ham, Tillamook cheddar cheese, and onions on a separate plate that she took outside to Donald to add to the cooked burgers on the grill. She set up table outside and went back into the kitchen. As she was walking back out with iced tea for both Donald and herself, Donald was setting the plated burgers on the table.

"You know what bothers me about that room?" Donald asked Annie as he picked up the salad dressing bottle. "Regardless of what was in those shipping crates, it would have taken two people to carry them down that narrow stair case. Who helped Uncle Robert carry them downstairs?"

"Do you ever recall a time when your uncle received wooden crate shipments here when you were a kid?" Annie asked as she added mustard to her hamburger bun.

"Not that I remember," Donald said, pulling his phone from his pocket. "I bet Dan would remember."

"No!" Annie shouted to Donald. "Do not call him tonight. He is on a date with Lizzy."

"He is always on a date with Lizzy," Donald said, pausing with the phone in his hand.

"Yes, but tonight they need to be left alone. Dan is taking Lizzy out to dinner."

"Do you know something you are not telling me?" Donald put his phone down.

"Lizzy spent last night in her apartment alone," Annie began. "She said that Dan had asked her to move in once Mom turns the house over to him."

"Well, that is good, right?" Donald took a bite from his hamburger and looked for Annie to respond.

"Let's just say Lizzy did not take it as a gesture for a long-term commitment."

"Marriage?"

"She wants some kind of commitment."

Donald was quiet for a moment. He picked up his fork and began eating his salad.

Annie eyed Donald suspiciously, "Did Dan say anything to you?"

"Dan and I like to talk about crabbing and fishing," Donald said.

That did not answer her question, Annie thought. She decided not to ask further questions, and instead returned her focus to the secret room.

"Donald, do you think it might be a good idea to take a look into the journals Helen left in the vault room?"

"Couldn't hurt," Donald said finishing the last bite of his hamburger. "That was a great hamburger. I'll help you clean up and then let's head on down to the vault room."

♦ ♦ ♦

Annie and Donald had stacked Helen's journals in decade order. Each book represented a year in her life. Not every day was filled in, but it was enough to get an idea of Helen's life and the events that happened to her.

Annie read excerpts from the journals to Donald. There were many entries of Donald as a child and the time he spent visiting in this house. Annie wondered if Donald ever thought about how things might have been different if he grew up as Robert and Helen's son. Would he have been an engineer?

Donald looked up and noticed Annie looking thoughtfully at him.

"Did you find something interesting?"

"Donald," Annie began, "Have you ever thought about what it would have been like to be Robert and Helen's son?"

"Sure," Donald replied. "I also think that I am lucky to have the parents I have. They gave me the life I am enjoying now. I don't want to look back. Helen gave me up for a reason. It is her reason and has nothing to do with me. I have loving parents. I am grateful I had the time I did with Aunt Helen and Uncle Robert though. They were, to me, just my aunt and uncle."

Annie pulled herself up from a sitting position and walked on her knees the two steps over to Donald to give him a hug. As she did, she made a feeble attempt to maneuver across stacks of books on the floor, which caused her to slip and tumble into Donald's arms. As she landed on Donald, Annie's legs kicked out from under her. Her foot stretched out and pushed through the back of a painting resting against a chair.

"Oh, Donald!" Annie exclaimed, rolling over to see the damage that she had caused. "What have I done?"

Donald slowly sat up and crawled to the painting near them. He lifted the painting to inspect the hole. It was a small rip in the canvas.

Annie was horrified to discover that it was Meredith's Garden, Janette's painting that Donald and Annie were keeping safe in the vault room. She looked at the rip in the back of the painting, and then moved to see the front of the painting. Again, she inspected the back, where she saw a three-inch rip in the canvas. She looked again at the front. There was no damage.

Donald looked at the back of the art piece and then the front. "Annie, I think we have discovered the secret of this painting." Donald pulled his cell phone out and turned it on flashlight mode. He focused the light into the ripped area and noticed three large envelopes attached to the back canvas. There were two canvases in one frame. It was cleverly disguised as one painting.

"I don't think you damaged the painting," Donald said, still looking inside the ripped area to see if he could find anything else. "We should contact Janette and have her take a look at this."

Annie looked at her watch. It was ten o'clock at night. Too late to call Janette, Annie thought. She would text tomorrow morning. Annie pointed out that it was getting late. Donald stood and began stretching.

"We can leave this," Annie said, standing. "We are the only people who know what is here." Annie shuffled through some of the journals, searching for the year of Donald's birth. She wanted to find out the story behind Helen and Robert giving Donald up at birth. She found the right book and walked out of the vault room with Donald. They closed the vault door and secured all doors to the office.

Laddie was jumping up and down, wanting to go out for a walk. Donald picked up his leash and the two headed out the door. Annie went to the laundry room to feed Callie and clean her water bowl. Annie made sure the house was locked up, and then headed upstairs to get ready for bed. She was tired, but wanted to read a portion of Helen's journal.

Annie heard Donald and Laddie enter the house. Laddie was excited to go to bed. He jumped onto his bed and turned around to find the right spot to settle. Donald brushed his teeth and joined her in bed. He was quickly asleep. Annie could only read for a half an hour before she, too, was asleep.

CHAPTER 9

Thursday Morning

I t was five forty-five in the morning when Annie walked into the sitting nook of the master suit, bringing with her the journal she had been reading the night before. Grabbing the remote control, she opened the curtains to reveal the vast ocean in front of her. She stared into the dark colored water. The sun would be shining soon, causing a turquoise transparency in the waves that always amazed her.

Opening the journal to where she left off last night, Annie began to read. She read about Helen traveling with Robert to Africa to help with medical needs for the people there. Helen also wrote a steamy passage of a passionate encounter with Robert in a small hut. Annie decided to skip a few pages ahead for other details of her trip to Africa.

After an hour of reading journal entries, Annie finally came across the day Helen discovered she was pregnant. She was so overjoyed. The emotion in Helen's statements brought tears to Annie's eyes. It was obvious that Helen really wanted to have a baby. So, why did she give Donald away to Rand and Patty, Annie asked herself.

It was seven o'clock when Annie set the journal down on the end table and stood up to stretch. Callie was in her cat tree fast asleep. Annie walked into the bedroom area and noticed that Donald and Laddie were already up. The bed was made and the bathroom door was open. Donald usually started work at seven in the morning. Already being dressed for work, Annie made her way to the office downstairs to let Donald know she was leaving for work.

♦ ♦ ♦

The sun was shining bright as Annie walked down the boardwalk between the sea wall and the shops. She pushed open the door to Ione's Bakery and Coffee Shop. The shop was fairly busy with people ordering coffee to go, and picking up bags of donuts to go back to their rented rooms. Ione was busy helping customers when she spotted Annie.

"The usual today?"

Annie practically cringed at the word 'usual'. Dan's mention of Annie being predictable was really beginning to irritate her.

"Yes, of course." Annie moved up in line to the cash register. She paid for her chocolate croissant and coffee to go.

"Is Suzette back from Europe?" Ione asked as she handed Annie her coffee.

"No. Not that I have heard." Annie said.

"I thought I saw her in the window of the B&B." Ione said, turning her attention to a customer ordering a coffee cake.

Ione turned back to Annie, who replied, "Janette, her cousin, is still staying there. She looks a lot like Suzette."

"Hmm...that might be who I saw," Ione said as she rang up the coffee cake order.

Annie waved goodbye and walked to her shop. She unlocked the door and let herself inside, locked the door and walked to her office. After setting her coffee down, Annie turned on a few lights to illuminate the crafting desk that she liked to use to design crafts for class. She had her senior citizen group coming in today, which included the Silver Sleuths, and she was looking forward to finding out if they had any information for her.

Annie began organizing materials for the crafting session. She had planned to make decorative notebooks for sticky pads. As a bonus, she would have them add a small fan embellishment to the front cover. Daisy had punched out the shapes to make the fans and organized them in groups for each class member. Annie was now cutting papers to make kits for the elders to put together the notebooks. She went to the storeroom to find the sticky pads she had ordered months ago.

Annie walked from the storeroom to the classroom area with a stack of sticky notes in various colors. Suddenly, a flash of something caught her eye. She looked out the shop window to the windows of Suzette's B&B across the street. The B&B was closed. Maybe it was Janette moving around in one of the rooms, Annie told herself. She looked for a moment longer and then went back to setting up her class.

As Annie walked back to her office, she remembered she needed to contact Janette about the damaged painting. She looked at her watch and thought it might still be a bit early to bother Janette, so she made a mental note to contact Janette in an hour or so. Annie told herself she was not procrastinating about telling Janette of the damage she had caused to the painting. Annie would take full responsibility for repairing the damage. What was interesting though, were the envelopes behind the main painting. Donald had not pulled the envelopes out, as it was Meredith's painting and she may have placed them there for her daughter or granddaughters.

At nine o'clock, Lizzy unlocked the shop door on street side and entered. She locked the door and walked over to the office.

"Good morning, Annie," Lizzy said, smiling.

"I take it you and Dan had a nice evening?" Annie said looking up from her cutting paper task.

"We had a wonderful time together at dinner." Lizzy hung her purse on the peg behind the office door and walked out with the money tray from the safe. She punched a few buttons on the cash register, placed the tray inside, and closed the drawer. She stopped and look at Annie with a smile.

"You have got that goofy love look," Annie said.

"I know," Lizzy said walking around the counter and pulling out a stool at Annie's crafting table. She sat down. "Annie, do you think Dan would ever want to get married?"

"It is not something Dan and I talk about," Annie said taking a sip from her coffee cup. Realizing the coffee had gotten cold, she set it down. "You should ask my mother. She and Dan talk all the time."

"I would definitely move in with him," Lizzy said twirling a strand of hair while staring at the ceiling in a dreamy state of mind, "if I only knew that he was willing to get married at some point. Married to me, that is."

Annie laughed and told Lizzy she did not think Dan would marry anybody else. The two women continued to talk until Daisy knocked on the door. Annie was surprised that time had passed so quickly. She stood and walked over to the door.

"Good morning," Daisy said. "I'm thinking it's going to be a busy day at the shop. The weather is incredibly warm and people are already lining up at the coffee shop."

Annie frowned. She was hoping to get to the coffee shop and buy another donut before she opened the shop. Lizzy noticed Annie's expression and said, "I will go stand in line at the coffee shop. I have not had a cup of coffee yet this morning." Lizzy went to the office to get her wallet and then exited the shop.

"Is this the sample for the class today?" Daisy asked picking up a sticky pad notebook. Daisy was impressed with how the shapes she punched out yesterday developed into a cute little fan that adorned the cover.

"Yes," Annie said, handing Daisy a different notebook.

"They turned out cute," Daisy said as she took the notebook from Annie. "I think the ladies are going to love them."

◆ ◆ ◆

The morning did prove to be busy with customer traffic. The tables and chairs that were set out on the boardwalk, for people to sit and eat or just drink their coffee and view the ocean, were filled most of the morning. By eleven-thirty, Annie walked into her office and realized she had not contacted Janette. She pulled her cell phone out of her purse, tucked inside her bottom desk drawer.

"Hello, Janette. I need to talk to you about the painting. Do you have time to come over to the shop?" Annie sent a text to Janette. She waited for a few moments, but did not receive a reply. Not everyone is attached to their phones, Annie reminded herself. She certainly did not carry her phone around with her all the time. She decided to go back to what she was doing and wait for a response from Janette. Annie placed the phone in her pants pocket and walked out of the office.

About fifteen minutes later, Annie heard her phone chime. She pulled the phone out of her pocket and read the text from Janette.

"I have gone to Portland to visit some friends for a few days. Is the painting you are referring to Meredith's Garden?" the text read.

"Yes," Annie replied. Annie thought it odd that Janette would ask such a question about the painting. She knew Donald had put it in the safe. Janette thought it was a good idea for Donald and Annie to keep the painting safe.

"I have sold the painting to Lawrence Smyth at the gallery. You can give it to him," the text went on.

"I would like to talk to you about the painting first. It would be better if you gave the painting to Lawrence Smyth personally." The hairs on the back of Annie's neck were up and red flags were raising in Annie's mind. There were no further text messages from Janette. Annie was now wondering if she should feel concerned. It was highly likely that Janette went to Portland, but she had been so emotional about getting the painting back. Why would she suddenly sell it? It made no sense.

Annie walked to her classroom and looked up at the windows of Suzette's B&B. Was Janette there this morning? Annie chided herself for not sending the text message earlier. She had no idea when Janette would have left for Portland. With Janette out of town though, Annie was then responsible for making sure the B&B was secure. Maybe she should talk to Dan. She dialed Dan's cell.

"What?" Dan answered the phone, knowing from caller ID that it was Annie calling.

"Hello, Surely," Annie teased Dan.

"Why can't you call me Dan like everyone else?" Dan asked impatiently.

"Because I am your little sister and I like to annoy you," Annie chuckled.

"What do you want?"

"Would you have time to help me walk through Suzette's B&B to make sure everything is okay?" Annie asked.

"I thought Janette was staying there until Suzette came back," Dan responded.

"She sent me a text that she was in Portland," Annie told Dan. "Then she told me to give her painting to Lawrence Smyth at the gallery. Dan, she loved that painting. Why would she suddenly want to sell it?"

"I don't know," Dan said. "I am in Newport at the District Attorney's Office right now. I can help you later tonight, when I get off work. I'll call you."

"Thanks, Dan."

Dan disconnected and Annie put her phone away in the office. She wondered if she should go over there on her own, but decided it would be best if Dan accompanied her.

Annie decided to walk over to the gallery and talk to Jacquie Spencer about Lawrence Smyth. She let Lizzy and Daisy know that she would be back shortly and exited the shop with her purse and phone. Annie walked down the boardwalk to Spencer's Gallery. As she pushed on the door to enter, she found it to be locked. She peered through the window and noticed all the lights were on, but no one seemed to be inside. She knocked loudly on the door and waited a few minutes. No one appeared. It is lunchtime, Annie thought. Of course, Jacquie would lock up if she needed to get a bite to eat, but usually there was a sign on the door letting potential customers know she would be back shortly.

Instead of walking to the many restaurants and eating places to find Jacquie, Annie went back to Ocean Loads of Paper. She was glad she did, as shoppers were filling the store. The street-side door chimed and Annie noticed the Senior Center bus unloading the ladies for her class.

As the seniors came through the opened door, Annie noticed several men arriving also. One in particular was Morty. His spindly legs were barely keeping up with his walker as he found his way to the classroom.

"I hope you don't mind a few extra people in the class today, Annie," Lorraine said as she scooted pass Morty. Morty reached out to pinch Lorraine on the back-side, but Lorraine was too quick for him. He snapped his boney fingers in an 'aw-shucks' motion. Then he turned and smiled a toothy grin at Annie. Morty was harmless, as he really could not move fast enough to cause anyone harm.

Annie asked Daisy to run over to Ione's Bakery and Coffee shop to pick up the coffee and donuts for the group. Annie had ordered them earlier. While Daisy was running the errand, Annie made sure the older ladies were seated and comfortable.

"Any word on what we had talked about Tuesday morning?" Annie whispered to Lorraine.

"That is why we brought the entire Silver Sleuths group," Lorraine told Annie in a loud voice. "We wanted to tell you what we found out."

LaVerne pulled out a chair next to Lorraine, located at the center of the table. Annie began to sit down and realized that the people at the table across the room stopped talking and they all turned their attention to Annie. The Silver Sleuths suddenly seemed much larger than Annie originally realized. Annie sat down and moved her chair closer to the table.

"So, what did you find out?" Annie asked quietly.

"What did she say?" Morty asked loudly.

"She wants to know what we found out about Bart Smith, Calvin Atwater, and Henry Kenner," Millie said into Morty's ear.

"Turn up your hearing aids, Morty," LaVerne shouted at Morty.

Everyone watched as Morty adjusted his hearing aids. He stopped and looked at the group. "Well, don't just sit there. Someone say something so I know if I can hear you or not."

"Why did we bring him?" LaVerne asked.

"I heard that!" Morty responded.

"Good. Now just sit there and listen." LaVerne told Morty.

"Bossy woman," Morty responded.

"There is not much to tell yet, but we are having a dance at the Senior Center tonight after dinner and we will be able to do some sleuthing then," Lorraine spoke up. She looked around the tables for the project they were going to be working on today.

"Why are we just sitting here?" An older lady across the room asked loudly. "Let's get to work."

Annie stood and walked to the counter where she had project packets prepared for the group. She handed them out and the ladies all began chatting. Daisy arrived with the donuts and coffee. She set the food on the counter and the ladies instantly moved to the donuts.

LaVerne asked Elsie to get a donut for her and Lorraine while they talked with Annie. Annie's interest was piqued at what they wanted to say. She sat down next to Lorraine. LaVerne motioned for Annie and Lorraine to lean in so their conversation would not be heard by anyone else.

"If anyone is suspect, in my opinion, it would be Bart Jones," LaVerne said seriously.

"Bart?" Lorraine asked surprised.

"Yes," LaVerne argued. "I attempted to get to know him better and he avoided my advances. If that does not prove he is suspicious, I do not know what does."

"Oh, LaVerne," Lorraine said disappointedly. "He only goes after wealthy women. Everyone knows we live on our pensions."

"So," Annie turned to LaVerne, "he could have asked around about all the women and found who had money and who did not. That's why he didn't return your interest." Annie was trying to make LaVerne feel better. She was an interesting woman, but men might feel intimidated by her.

"You're right, Annie," Lorraine said. "We should focus on who the wealthier women are and find out if Bart is flirting with them."

"You know who is wealthy? LaVerne said, looking around the room and then moving in closer to the women.

"Agnes?" Lorraine asked.

"Yes, but not her. Millie. Millie is stinking rich. She doesn't need us living with her to save money. She is just lonely." LaVerne sat back and had a look of smug satisfaction on her face.

Lorraine sat back, thinking about what LaVerne had said.

Annie thought LaVerne might be on to something. Elsie came to the table with donuts. Annie stood and began to discuss the craft project at hand. Everyone stopped chatting to listen and then began to put together their notebooks. The room was filled with happy chitchat.

At three-thirty, the bus pulled up in front of the shop to waiting seniors. Annie and Daisy finished clearing the classroom and joined Lizzy at the counter.

"Did either of you know that Janette was going to Portland for a few days?" Annie asked Lizzy and Daisy.

"When?" Daisy asked. "She and I were going to a movie tonight. She didn't say anything to me about going to Portland." Daisy walked to the office and returned with her cell phone. She was looking through text messages.

"I haven't heard from Janette," Lizzy spoke up.

"There is nothing from Janette saying she was not going to the movie with me tonight," Daisy said, disappointed that Janette would not at least send her a message.

Annie was wondering if she should be concerned, but was soon distracted by customers entering the shop. It was busy until closing time at six o'clock. Lizzy locked the door on the ocean side and Daisy locked the door on the street side. Annie counted down the till and pulled the tray to place in the safe.

"Would you and Dan like to have dinner with us tonight? I can make spaghetti," Annie asked Lizzy. "Daisy, you are welcomed to join us."

"Let me call Dan," Lizzy said pulling out her cell phone and walking a short distance away to call Dan.

"Thanks, but I think I will go home and do laundry tonight," Daisy said. "Janette may still be planning to be back for a movie later."

After Lizzy called Dan to meet her at Annie's for dinner, Lizzy and Annie grabbed their purses and followed Daisy out the door. Lizzy and Annie said good-night to Daisy and began the short walk home.

CHAPTER 10

Thursday Night

A s Lizzy and Annie approached Annie's house, they were met by Laddie bouncing his way down the street. He greeted Annie, gave a quick sniff to Lizzy, and turned his attention back to Annie. Donald approached and leaned in to kiss Annie. Laddie jumped up between them and licked Annie on the face.

"I think he likes you better than me," Donald said pretending to be jealous.

Annie was wiping her face and laughing. They walked up to the house with Laddie dancing behind them. After entering the house, Annie put her purse on the kitchen table next to Lizzy's. Donald walked over to Laddie's water dish and filled it with fresh water.

"How was the class today?" Donald asked.

"I think the Senior Sleuths are holding back on me," Annie said, thinking about their conversation. "But they may not know as much as they used to, now that they are living at Millie's."

"They might be busy with other cases," Donald said, with a twinkle in his eyes.

After pouring three glasses of iced tea, Annie, Donald, and Lizzy walked out to the backyard to wait for Dan to arrive. Annie decided that she could quickly make dinner once he arrived. She did not need to prep much for spaghetti.

"Donald, I received the strangest text from Janette today," Annie began the conversation sitting down next to Donald on an outdoor sofa. "She told me she was in Portland for a few days, and then told me that she had sold "Meredith's Garden" to Lawrence Smyth."

"That doesn't sound possible," Donald said after taking a sip of his iced tea and setting it down on a side table. "She was visibly upset when she thought the painting was sold in the gallery."

"I went to talk to Jacquie about it, but she wasn't in the shop," Annie said. "The shop doors were locked, but all the lights were on. I knocked on the door loudly, but no one answered."

"Do you have her cell phone number?" asked Lizzy. "Maybe you should call her and find out if everything is okay."

Annie wondered if she might be over reacting at the moment. Just because the lights are left on at a business, does not necessarily mean anything is wrong. Most of the shops did have lights on at night. Jacquie might have walked out for a few minutes to go to the bank. Things were casual in a small town on the coast.

Annie, Donald, and Lizzy sat on the patio for another thirty minutes talking about the gallery, Lawrence, and the painting. What connection did Lawrence have to the painting? Was he aware that Meredith's Garden held a secret? Did he know what the secret was?

Lizzy picked up her cell phone when it chirped to look at a text from Dan, stating he was on his way from the office. Lizzy passed on the information. The group stood and walked to the kitchen with their glasses.

Annie was about to start dinner when she received a text on her cell phone. She pulled it out of her purse and read a message from Dan. He was downtown and reported to Annie that the 'Senior Snoops' were setting up chairs in front of her shop. He asked if she had some event going on downtown. Annie was about to text back, when she heard Dan walk through the front door.

"I just got your text, Dan," Annie said holding up her cell phone. "I have no idea what the seniors are doing in front of my shop."

"They were setting up chairs," Dan said as he walked up to Lizzy and gave her a kiss on the cheek and said hello and nodded to Donald. He turned his attention back to Annie and said, "There must be at least ten of them. They brought chairs, and all seemed to be nicely dressed."

"Maybe I need to go downtown and check this out," Annie said. "They were going to a dance at the senior center tonight."

"And what's the deal with the gallery?" Dan asked. "Lights are blazing on inside. Patrol checked the business, but no one answered their knocks at the door. The guys asked if you had a key. They would be happy to check out the business."

"Something strange is happening," Lizzy said moving next to Dan.

"I agree," Annie told the group. "Would you mind if we postpone dinner and go downtown to check on the seniors and the gallery?"

"Tell you what," Donald added. "I will buy dinner at the Chinese restaurant after we check on things."

"Sounds good to me," Dan said, and walked to the front door, holding it open for Lizzy on his way out.

"I think he is hungry," Donald said to Annie with a smile, referring to Dan's quick exit. Donald locked the back door and made sure Laddie had a full food dish. He followed Annie to the front door, set the alarm, and locked up.

The four walked into town to a scene of now twenty seniors sitting and standing on the sidewalk in front of Annie's shop. The downtown shops were mostly closed, except for the Chinese restaurant, which was closing at eight o'clock.

Annie approached LaVerne, Lorraine, Elsie, and Millie who were seated in folding chairs at the curb. They were all looking up at Bridgewater Bed & Breakfast windows. Some of the seniors seated in the front rows had binoculars, and some had cameras. There was much chatter as the crowd was awaiting some spectacular event.

"LaVerne, what is going on?" Annie bent down near where LaVerne was sitting to talk to her. "Why are all these people here?"

"We are all glued to those windows until we see the ghost!" LaVerne said not taking her eyes off the windows.

"I saw a ghost once," a small, hunched-over, elderly lady spoke up. She was standing behind Millie, who was sitting on the other side of LaVerne. "I think it was my grandmother. I could smell her lavender perfume."

Elsie tapped Annie on the arm and leaned in to say in a whisper, "There is no such thing as ghosts. I think they saw a curtain moving. It might have been a draft near the window. Maybe it was not closed properly. Anyway, there is no such thing as a ghost."

Annie took a step back and told Dan, Lizzy and Donald what LaVerne had said.

"Of all the idiotic nonsense," Dan blasted. "These ladies have gone crazier than usual."

As Dan was talking to the crowd of people continuing to form, telling them that they needed to disperse, Annie looked up at the windows in curiosity. She remembered something catching her eye earlier today. Was someone in the bed and breakfast? She decided to ask Dan and Donald to go check it out with her. Dan was a police officer after all. He could walk in first, Annie thought to herself, in case there was any trouble. If there is a ghost inside, Dan can handle it. Annie smiled to herself. Flashbacks of childhood appeared in her mind. As a kid, she would make Dan go first in a scary situation.

Annie unlocked the door to her shop and grabbed the keys to the B&B from her office. She quickly looked around her shop as she made her way to the street-side exit. She locked her shop door and found Dan and Donald attempting to convince the seniors to go home. Annie asked them to inspect the building with her. Lizzy insisted on going with them.

"Annie, just give me the keys," Dan said. "I will call a couple of patrol guys to help me out."

"Dan," Annie began, "Do you really want patrol to show up to help you find a ghost?"

"No," Dan relented, looking at the 'Senior Snoops'. "We can check it out and if there is a problem, I will call dispatch."

Annie walked over to LaVerne and asked, "Who told you there was a ghost in the B&B?"

"Jeanne," LaVerne took her eyes off the windows to look at Annie. "She's one of the ladies in the senior apartments. She was at the dance tonight. Her daughter was driving through town when the granddaughter shouted out that there was a ghost in the window. Well, then Jeanne's daughter told Jeanne, and Jeanne mentioned it to us."

"She knows we are top-notch sleuths and we would get to the bottom of the situation," Lorraine added leaning close to Annie.

Annie thought the top-notch sleuths were a bit obvious on the street, but who was she to tell them how to run their sleuthing activity? They usually knew everything that was happening in town.

"If you ladies would make sure people stay off the street, Donald, Dan, Lizzy, and I will check out the inside of the B&B," Annie requested of LaVerne and the ladies sitting close to her. "We will let you be the first to know if there is a ghost or not."

"Will do, Annie," Lorraine said excitedly.

◆ ◆ ◆

Dan and Lizzy followed Donald and Annie down the sidewalk to a place where they could get past the crowd and cross the street. As they walked, Annie noticed a man knocking on the door of the gallery. She tugged on Donald's arm to signal him to look. The group stopped and watched for a moment. They could hear the man calling out for Jacquie.

Annie approached the man who introduced himself as John Spencer, Jacquie's husband. John was a clean-shaven man in his mid-sixties, with a sprinkle of gray in his thick black hair which was stylishly short. It was evident that John kept in shape. His broad shoulders caused the material on his knit shirt to stretch. His clothes were nicely tailored to fit his muscular body.

"I have not heard from Jacquie all day," John explained to the four standing near him. "She was planning on staying at the bed and breakfast, but it was closed, so she is staying at a motel at the south end of town. I checked the room, she is not there."

John and Jacquie lived in Portland and had just recently purchased the gallery. Georgeann Wells sold the prospering gallery to the Spencer's a few weeks ago in hopes of retiring in a more rural setting. Jacquie came to town to change out the signage and sign a new lease with R&H Enterprises. She hired Lawrence Smyth to manage the shop two weeks ago when she drove to town for the day. She had only met him once during the interview, gave him the keys to the gallery, and drove back home to Portland. His references were impeccable and the listed contacts gave her glowing reports of his capabilities.

As John explained to the group, Jacquie was now missing. She had not made contact with him since last night when they talked by phone. He was so worried, that he drove from Portland to find her. John explained that the two had kept in frequent contact while she was in Bridgewater Harbor.

"Does Jacquie have GPS tracking on her cell phone?" Dan asked.

"Yes, but her phone appears to be turned off," John said visibly shaken.

Dan pulled his phone out and called dispatch. He told John to stay where he was and that a patrol officer was coming to take a report. He said that he would personally look into Jacquie's disappearance.

Annie and Lizzy followed behind Dan and Donald as they moved around to the back of the building. There were several cars parked in the lot behind the building. Annie recognized them as belonging to employees at the Chinese restaurant. She then noticed a dark gray sedan parked close to the rear entrance of the bed and breakfast. Dan called dispatch and asked them to check the license plate. It came back as a rental out of Portland.

"Janette was driving this car the other night," Lizzy said. "She must still be here."

Dan instructed Annie to unlock the door. He opened it cautiously and proceeded inside. All of the lights were off. It seemed to Annie that the business was empty. They listened for a moment for any sounds of someone being inside. It was eerily silent.

Dan and Donald checked out the downstairs floor while Annie and Lizzy waited in the lobby. Seniors were now gathering on the sidewalk next to the lobby door of the bed & breakfast. Several were peering in through the window. The guys came back and shrugged, indicating there was nothing out of place. They proceeded up the stairs. Annie and Lizzy followed.

As the guys quietly walked through the upstairs main dining and kitchen areas, Annie and Lizzy were quietly testing the door knobs of the rooms down the hallway. They were locked. Lizzy tested the knob on the room at the far northside of the building, and it turned with her effort. Still holding onto the knob, Lizzy signaled Annie to follow her inside, then pushed opened the door.

A scream echoed throughout the building. Dan recognized Lizzy's voice. He and Donald ran down the hall, seeing that neither Lizzy nor Annie were in the hall. When they came across an open doorway, Dan cautiously entered and noticed Lizzy, with Annie directly behind her, standing stiff inside the room.

"It's a ghost!" Lizzy shouted.

"That is not a ghost," Annie said as she peered around Lizzy's shoulders. "That's a woman."

"Is...is she...dead?" Lizzy asked Annie in a loud whisper. Lizzy was shaking and grabbed Annie's hand.

Dan ran to the side of the woman lying on the floor. She was bound in duct tape around her ankles and her arms were bound behind her. She was entangled in a sheer curtain, which had been hanging in the window at one point.

"The lights...someone switch on the lights," commanded Dan. "Annie call 9-1-1. Get paramedics and an ambulance over here immediately."

Donald felt along the wall for a light switch. When the room was illuminated, the four heard a cheer from the street below. Dan rolled his eyes. Dan then noticed that the woman he was kneeling next to was Janette. She was unresponsive. Dan pulled a knife from his pocket to cut the duct tape ties.

"Uh...Dan," Donald said hesitantly. "There is a woman on the bed bound up the same way as the one on the floor."

Dan rose and walked over to the bed. Annie looked up from her phone call to dispatch. She gave the address and information and then disconnected.

"Jacquie!" Annie shouted. She ran to Jacquie's side. Jacquie was pale, but the look in her eyes when she saw Annie was one of utter relief. Her mouth was covered in duct tape, as were her hands and feet.

Donald took out his pocket knife and began cutting the tape on Jacquie's arms and legs. Lizzy ran to the sink to get a warm wet wash cloth to help remove the tape across the woman's mouth. As she removed the tape, Jacquie began telling Annie about the man who kidnapped them and left them here to die. She was so angry that she had to stop and take in a breath to continue speaking. Annie tried to get her to calm down. Dan went back to Janette and continued to cut the tape from her legs. She barely moved as he worked fast to get the bindings removed.

Donald finished cutting away the tape on Jacquie's arms and legs. While scraping off the tape from his knife, he heard sirens from the emergency vehicles approaching the inn.

"I'll go downstairs and let the paramedics in through the front door," Donald said. "Should we ask the seniors to go home?"

"I'll go with you," Annie responded, as she finished helping Jacquie sit up and swing her legs over the edge of the bed. "Lizzy, would you mind staying with Jacquie in case she needs help?"

Donald and Annie headed down the stairs to the front door. The paramedics arrived in a large fire truck and were gathering supplies to carry inside the building. Annie saw LaVerne, Lorraine, Millie, and Elsie standing on the side near the front door of the bed and breakfast.

"Ladies, I need your help," Annie addressed the four women. "Would you please ask everyone to go home? I will meet you back here as soon as I can." Donald alerted Annie after seeing John Spencer watching from across the street. John began walking through the crowd to join Annie and Donald. He seemed in a daze as he absentmindedly bumped into people. He walked directly up to Donald.

"Have you found my wife?" John asked Donald with a strained seriousness in his voice. "Is she...?"

"I think she will be fine," Donald reassured John. "Come with me. She will want you with her while the paramedics check her over."

Annie was more worried about Janette. She was pale and limp on the floor. She really hoped Janette would be okay when she returned upstairs. As the firemen filed in, Donald closed and locked the front door. He guided the paramedics and John to the north-side room upstairs. Annie watched the activity outside for a short moment and then followed the emergency people up the stairs.

The Senior Sleuths were asking people in the crowd to go home. The elderly women assured the crowd that they would update everyone soon. LaVerne and Lorraine took control of the street crowd in an orderly fashion. Soon everyone was on the sidewalk across the street and out of the way of emergency workers. After a short time, only the four women remained on the sidewalk in front of the B&B to make sure no one disobeyed them.

CHAPTER 11

Late Thursday Night

"Jacquie!" John called out. Jacquie was sitting up on the bed. She seemed to have regained color in her face. John raced to her side and hugged her tightly. Annie's eyes teared up as she looked to Donald. Annie sat on the end of the bed. Donald sat down next to Annie as they quietly watched paramedics work on Janette. After a few moments, the medical people started moving aside to where Annie could get a good look at Janette. Dan earlier cut away the shear curtain that entangled the still body.

"Suzette!" Annie cried out. She stood and pushed her way to Suzette, who was lying on the floor. It was not Janette at all, but her lookalike cousin who owned the bed and breakfast. Annie had no idea the owner of the bed & breakfast was back in town. Suzette's eyes began to flutter and she slowly opened them.

"Annie," Suzette said in a soft voice. "He has my cousin, Janette. The bookcase..." That was all Suzette could say before she lost consciousness. Paramedics gathered in to continue treatment. A gurney was waiting in the hallway to take the victims to a local hospital.

"Who?" Annie asked. "Suzette, wake up. Who has Janette?" A fireman pulled Annie out of the way. Suzette was loaded onto the gurney and taken away. Annie watched as a blanket was placed on top of Suzette and straps were secured across her still body for safety in transporting her to the hospital. She was still breathing, but her face looked pale.

A fireman stopped in front of Annie and Donald. "She will be taken to Newport Hospital. Do you know how to contact her next-of-kin?"

Annie nodded. She would check the emergency contact that Suzette had on her lease agreement.

A second gurney was brought up for Jacquie, as she was weak from dehydration, but angry and telling Dan that the next time she saw Lawrence, she was going to take a baseball bat to his head. Dan advised against such actions. John tried to calm his wife as he followed the medical people downstairs. He was not going to let Jacquie out of his sight. Soon the room was cleared of all the emergency workers.

"Where is Janette?" Annie asked Dan. "Suzette said 'he has my cousin'. Then she said something about a bookcase."

Annie, Donald, Dan, and Lizzy all looked at the bookcase in the room, against the north wall. Several items on the shelves of the bookcase were turned over. Dan signaled Lizzy, Annie, and Donald to leave the room. He sent a text to the officers who were downstairs. The officers quietly walked past the three in the hallway. Annie suggested they move further down the hallway in case there was trouble. If Dan was thinking what Annie was thinking, then the suspect was holding Janette inside a space behind the bookcase. Could it possibly be an old storage closet that Suzette covered up with a moveable bookcase?

There was a lot of noise, shouting, and scuffling by Dan and the police officers. Annie heard Janette scream. She raced to the room in time to see Janette being thrust into the men standing in a doorway. The bookcase itself was opened like a door into the guest room. Dan was hanging to the side of the bookcase attempting to upright himself. Annie saw Lawrence running down a set of stairs. Annie thought the stairs would lead to the empty shop on the north end of the building. She mentioned this to the officers.

One of the officers radioed that the suspect was escaping out the north end shop. Dan was hot on his trail. It was dark, and Dan was stepping on paint brushes, old paint cans, and other clutter on the stairs. Annie heard a door slam. Lawrence was off into the night. Dan was running after him.

Annie searched for a light in the stairwell behind the bookcase. She found one and turned it on, illuminating the entire staircase and hallway. There was a lobby area below. It looked like this might have been the main entrance to the hotel of long ago. In the center of the room was a large reception counter which must have been the check-in for the hotel.

Annie turned around and noticed Donald, Lizzy, and Janette looking at the same thing.

"Janette," Annie said, walking up to her and giving her a hug. "Are you okay?"

"Yes," Janette answered with tears in her eyes. "What happened to Suzette and Jacquie?"

"They are heading to Newport Hospital," Annie said. "Suzette and Jacquie are dehydrated, but they will be okay."

"Lawrence was trying to force me to go with him to your house to get the painting," Janette told Annie. "He warned me that if I did not cooperate, he was going to hurt Suzette and Jacquie."

"When did Suzette get back from Europe?" Annie questioned Janette.

"Late last night," Janette said. "Lawrence pushed his way inside when Suzette had unlocked the back door. He had Jacquie with him. I was inside. He held us all at gunpoint. He taped us up and made us lay on the bed in the north room. I was able to stand up at one point in the morning and try to get someone's attention from the window. He came in and knocked me to the floor. He left me there all day."

Janette told Annie that Lawrence came back and untied her to go to Annie's house. When he heard people outside the building, Lawrence grabbed Janette and hid behind the bookcase. He was going to try and sneak out the north end of the building through the unoccupied shop, but there were people gathering on the street, so he could not leave the building unseen.

Janette thought Suzette might have been trying to get someone's attention at the window. From behind the bookcase she could hear Suzette moving around. Lawrence threatened Janette to not make a sound. Janette panicked when she heard a scream and thought at first it was Suzette.

Janette was crying. Lizzy ran to the kitchen to get a bottle of water from the refrigerator. She returned and opened the bottle and handed it to Janette. Janette took a couple of sips and sat down on the bed. As Annie and Lizzy tried to comfort Janette, Donald went downstairs and let LaVerne, Lorraine, Millie, and Elsie inside the building. Most everyone else had left and taken the chairs with them.

"We were under the window of the room with the light on when Lawrence Smyth came crashing out of the empty shop and took off." Annie could hear LaVerne's loud voice as she told Donald their observations.

"He nearly knocked me over," cried Elsie. "Then Detective Surely came dashing out after him."

"He can certainly run fast," Millie added, walking into the lobby and looking around.

"We have seen Mr. Smyth around the senior center a few times," offered Millie. "He is a strange man. I do not know what he was doing around there."

"You ladies take a seat in the lobby," Donald offered. "It's warmer inside and you will be comfortable here." The ladies graciously agreed and Donald went back upstairs to the room where Annie, Lizzy, and Janette were seated. Annie was not sure what to do at the moment. She was waiting to hear from Dan.

After a half hour had passed, Annie received a call from Dan. The suspect had gotten away. Officers were searching with K-9s from other agencies, but it seemed that Lawrence had gotten into a car and driven off. The description of the vehicle appeared to be that of Suzette's car. He must have stolen it after Suzette arrived home.

Annie told Dan about Janette's statement that Lawrence wanted Janette to try and get the painting. Dan asked that Donald help lock up the building and take Janette to their house. He would meet them there.

Annie relayed the information from Dan. Janette packed an overnight bag. The group secured the building and left with the senior ladies. Donald told the ladies that it was late and he would talk to them in the morning. He also asked them to drive directly home. He knew that they really wanted information, but it was getting too late for that. Tomorrow would be another day.

Dan called Lizzy around ten o'clock in the evening and asked her to stay the night at Annie's house. The house was alarmed, had cameras, and a large black protective dog. Even though the house was a target for Lawrence to try and get the painting, he would be a fool to attempt a break-in at that house.

Lizzy handed her phone to Annie; Dan wanted to talk to her. Annie asked about Suzette and Jacquie. Dan told her that the last time he checked they were resting comfortably and spending the night at the hospital. John Spencer was staying by his wife's side. Her room was next to Suzette, who had a security guard outside her door for protection in case Lawrence Smyth showed up at the hospital. He asked about Janette. Annie told him that she seemed fine at the moment.

Dan asked Annie if the painting was in a secure place. Annie assured him that it was. She did not want to reveal the location of the vault room, so she told him it was in a safe. Dan did not ask further. He asked Annie to tell Lizzy not to wait up. He would see her in the morning. He disconnected and Annie handed the cell phone back to Lizzy and relayed the message.

Annie showed Janette to the guest room. She made sure that Janette was comfortable and reassured her that it was a secure place to stay. Annie told Janette that Suzette and Jacquie were going to be fine. They needed to be monitored overnight and would most likely be released the next morning. Annie made sure Janette had a bottle of water on her nightstand. She asked Janette if she was hungry, but Janette declined anything to eat and said she only wanted to rest.

Annie realized that they had not eaten dinner. She walked to the bedroom to ask Donald if he wanted something to eat. She found Donald fully clothed on the bed asleep. Boy, she thought, can he fall asleep fast. Annie decided to check on Lizzy. She would offer Marie's bedroom so Lizzy could get a good night's sleep.

Annie found Lizzy at the kitchen table holding her cell phone. Apparently, she had been texting Dan.

"Dan said he would contact you in the morning," Annie reminded Lizzy as she walked into the kitchen.

"I know," Lizzy said. Lizzy looked very tired.

"I am going to make a snack to eat," Annie said opening the refrigerator door. "Would you like something?"

"No," Lizzy said holding her phone up to see if Dan had sent a text.

Annie made a small snack tray of sliced summer sausage, cheese, and fruit. She set the food on the table. Next, she pulled out a couple bottles of water from the refrigerator, and set one in front of Lizzy.

"You know," Annie told Lizzy, "if you want to be a police officer's wife, you must get used to call-outs and not being in constant contact."

"I know, Annie," Lizzy said. "You must think I am being silly."

"Not at all," Annie said while placing a slice of cheese on a slice of sausage and placing it into her mouth.

Lizzy picked up a grape and held it for a minute before placing it in her mouth. She looked again at her cell phone. Then setting the phone down, she opened her bottle of water, took a drink, and eyed the food on the table. She picked up a small piece of cheese and ate it.

"Dan thinks highly of you, Annie," Lizzy spoke after a long silence.

"He is not too bad for a brother figure." Annie thought about it for a moment before saying, "I could have been a nicer sister."

"He told me that you were a stinker as a little kid."

"I was," Annie laughed. "The first time he would not let me join his friends, I began calling him 'Shirley', because his last name is Surely."

"I remember when I first saw him walk into the shop to talk to you," Lizzy reminisced. "I thought my heart stopped, he was so gorgeous and well-dressed."

"Really?" Annie chuckled. "He usually visited my shop any time he came to see Mom. Sometimes he only drove down for the day. Other times he would stay in his old room or at his biological mother's house."

"He never noticed me then," Lizzy said.

"I would not say that," Annie said as she sat up. "He would ask about the girl working in my shop. Unfortunately, he was dating a girl back then. He was trying to find a way to break it off, but the girl kept convincing him to stay together. He was miserable about the whole relationship."

"Really?" Lizzy perked up. "You never told me that."

"Well, Miss Lizzy, you have never told me much about your family," Annie said. "Let's talk about that."

A sly smile formed on Lizzy's lips, "I guess I have been a bit quiet about my family." She took a drink of water from the bottle she was holding and set it down.

Lizzy began by telling Annie that she was an only child. She came from a very wealthy family. She was well educated. Her father insisted she get a college degree in something worthwhile, such as business or accounting. He had her entire life planned out, including who she was to marry. She had a brief engagement to the son of her father's business associate.

Lizzy told Annie that after a few months of being engaged, Lizzy discovered that the man she was to marry had a girlfriend on the side. Apparently, the man thought of their marriage as only a business arrangement and nothing more. Lizzy broke off the engagement and had a terrible argument with her father. Her father cut off her allowance, took her sports car away from her, and she moved out. She told her father that she would make it on her own without his money.

"That's when I ended up here," Lizzy said. "You gave me a job and now look at me!"

"You have two jobs, a boyfriend, and a successful career," Annie added. "The only thing that bothers me is that you said your father took away your allowance. How in the world can you afford the designer clothes you wear?"

"Is it that noticeable?" Lizzy laughed. "My mother sends me the clothes and other things. She used to send money, but I would return it. The clothes were gifts. I had to prove that I was able to make it on my own."

"You did prove that," Annie remarked.

Annie and Lizzy's attention were drawn to the thumping of paws on the stairs as Laddie descended. Donald was right behind him.

"Laddie is upset with you, Annie," Donald said spying the snack platter on the table. "He could smell sausage from the bedroom and begged me to let him out."

Laddie's nose was sniffing along the table. He stopped next to Annie and sat down. Donald reached over and grabbed a slice of sausage and gave it to Laddie. Donald then walked to the refrigerator and pulled out a bottle of water. He sat down at the kitchen table and began to eat.

"So, what is the topic of conversation going on down here?" Donald asked, picking up a napkin and wiping his hands.

"Just girl talk," Annie smiled at Donald.

"Is that my cue to go back upstairs?"

"No," Lizzy said. "We can talk about anything."

"Oh," Janette said as she walked down the stairs, "I thought I heard voices. I did not know everyone was still awake."

"Come join us," Annie said. "We have a snack tray and conversation."

"Thank you," Janette said as she sat down next to Lizzy. "I heard from my cousin, Suzette. She is perfectly fine and wants to leave the hospital and go home as soon as possible. The doctor wants her to stay overnight."

Everyone chimed in about the good news. Janette seemed more like herself now, just a bit tired looking. As the group ate all the food on the snack plate, Annie prepared additional food and placed it on the platter.

Returning to the circumstances of her kidnapping, Janette told everyone that Lawrence had ripped the tape from her wrists and legs, he pulled her off the bed and threatened to kill them all if she did not cooperate.

"I could tell that Suzette was angry and probably scared for me," Janette said as she took a sip of water from the bottle that Annie had placed in front of her. "That is why she got up and tried to get someone's attention from the window."

Janette continued that Lawrence somehow knew about the secret bookcase panel that opened and led downstairs to the old hotel entrance. It would have cost a great deal of money to remodel, so Suzette decided to close up the downstairs and create an additional room for guests from the sitting area upstairs. She added a bookcase door to the room, thinking no one would ever discover it being there.

"Up until now, she pretty much forgot about the doorway," Janette said.

"I would bet with a little bit of investment capital, the entrance could be restored to its glory days," Donald said.

Annie looked at Donald and realized she was unexpectedly wealthy and would be able to help Suzette make the restoration of the entrance to the old hotel. She made a mental note to talk to Donald more about the prospect of helping Suzette. What point is having money if it is not doing a good deed? She did own the building after all.

"I was wondering if I could take a look at my painting?" Janette asked Annie, changing the subject.

Annie looked at Donald. Donald said he would go get the painting. He excused himself and Laddie followed him to the office.

"Janette, there is something I need to confess about the painting," Annie began. "I accidentally tore a hole in the back of the canvas."

Janette was quiet for a moment. Annie quickly pointed out that it did not damage the front of the painting. She explained what happened.

"I am sure it was an accident," Janette said. "I do not understand how the tear in the back does not show up on the surface of the painting.

"That's what is curious," Annie continued. "There are two canvases inserted into the large frame. The back canvas is much thinner and attached to the back of your painting."

"I don't know what happened," Janette said. "I framed the painting that I gave my grandmother. It only had one canvas."

Annie continued to explain the discovery. Donald appeared a few minutes later with the painting. Janette inspected the front and seemed relieved that it was intact. She then turned the frame around and noticed the rip in the back of the canvas. She again looked at the front, and then turned the frame to view the back. There indeed was an extra canvas inserted cleverly in the back of the painting. One would never have known it was there, except for the rip.

Donald grabbed a flashlight from the laundry room and handed it to Janette. He pointed out that the second canvas on the back contained envelopes. Janette handed the flashlight to Donald. She began to make the opening of the rip large enough to remove the envelopes. There were three in all. Each envelope was addressed to the granddaughters of Meredith.

Janette read each name aloud, "Sheryl Suzette, Samantha Collette, and Sharon Janette." She stared at the envelopes for a long time. The room was silent. Janette spoke again, "These are the names of my cousins and myself. Meredith is our grandmother. My aunt and uncle passed away years ago. Only my mother survived. That is why grandmother left her estate only to my mother."

"She must have left the envelopes in the painting knowing you would eventually receive the painting back," Annie surmised.

"I should wait to open my envelope when my cousins open theirs," Janette said.

Annie really wanted Janette to open her envelope now, but it was Janette's, after all. It was probably a sweet letter from her grandmother, Annie thought, attempting to console herself. Annie was trying not ask Janette to open at least one envelope. She felt Donald's hand in hers, squeezing as if he knew what she was thinking.

"I am tired," Janette said. She stood and picked up the painting. "Thank you for everything." Janette walked upstairs with the painting and envelopes.

"I think we should all go to bed," Donald said standing up. "Come on, Laddie. Let's hit the hay."

Lizzy said she was going to clean up first, and then curl up on the sofa. Annie gathered blankets and a pillow from the laundry room. She told Lizzy that she was certainly welcome to sleep in Marie's room. Lizzy said she would be fine on the sofa. Lizzy picked up her cell phone and looked for a text message from Dan. There was none.

Annie was happy to finally crawl into bed. Donald was fast asleep. She wished she could fall asleep so quickly. Once her head hit the pillow though, she was fast asleep.

CHAPTER 12

Friday

Annie was awake at five o'clock the next morning. Laddie was scratching at the bedroom door to go out into the hallway. Annie got up, quickly dressed, and walked to the door. She listened for a minute, then opened the door. Laddie raced downstairs. Annie was wondering if she should wake Donald, but realized he would be getting up in an hour for work. She let him sleep.

Annie descended the staircase quietly only to find Lizzy in the kitchen drinking a cup of coffee. She had her cell phone in her hand. It was plugged into a charger. Laddie ran up to her and sniffed. Lizzy must have been okay to him, as he went to his food bowl and ate a few bites of dry food.

"How long have you been up?" Annie asked as she walked to the cupboard to get a coffee mug. She pulled a coffee pod from a jar on the counter and plopped it into the coffee maker.

"Most of the night." Lizzy answered. She got up and rinsed her cup.

"Is Dan still working on the case?" Annie asked.

"Yes. He was able to interview Suzette and Jacquie at the hospital."

Annie asked Lizzy if Dan had any additional news about the kidnapping. It was pretty much what Annie had gathered from Jacquie and Janette. Suzette was doing much better. Both Jacquie and Suzette would be released today from the hospital. Annie was thinking she would go to Newport with Janette and help take Suzette home. She figured that Lizzy would want to sleep all day, so she decided to contact Daisy and let her know that she would not need to work today. Annie was not going to open the shop.

After texting Daisy, Annie looked over and noticed that Lizzy was fast asleep with her head on the kitchen table. Dan sent a text to Annie asking if she was awake. Annie told Dan to come over. She walked over to the alarm and disengaged the system. Dan knocked softly on the front door. Laddie gave a bark and ran to the door. Annie quickly opened the front door to Dan. She pulled Laddie inside and walked out.

Dan and Annie sat on the front porch in the cool summer morning air. He told her he believed Lawrence Smyth was hiding out locally. He and other police officers had served a search warrant on his apartment, but it looked like he had cleared it out. He had wiped down surfaces and left no fingerprints. Dan was going to get some sleep and then get back on the case later today. He said he would take Lizzy home with him. She needed sleep as well.

"On a personal note, Annie, can I ask you a question without you talking to anyone else?"

Annie perked up. She was curious, but keeping something from Lizzy or Donald, that was going to be difficult.

"Okay," Annie reluctantly agreed. "I will keep it to myself."

"Do you think Lizzy wants to get married?"

"Yes."

"To me?"

"Yes."

"So, if I asked her to marry me, she would say 'yes'?" Dan asked.

"Ask and you will find the answer," Annie said smiling.

Dan rolled his eyes and shook his head. He got up and walked into the house. He stopped when he noticed Lizzy with her head on the table. He gently woke her up and guided her out of the house to his house across the street.

Annie glanced around in the dimly lit living room. The blankets on the sofa had not been used by Lizzy, so she sat on the sofa, pulled the blankets over herself and laid down. Laddie jumped up on a chair, turned around once and curled up to sleep. It did not take long before Annie was asleep, too.

At six forty-five, Donald came downstairs. Laddie got up, stretched and went to Donald's side. Donald walked to the laundry room and let Laddie out a back door into an enclosed run. Laddie did his business while Donald made a cup of coffee and grabbed a banana from the fruit bowl. After a brief period outside, Laddie signaled he wanted inside. Laddie rushed inside, went directly to his food bowl, ate a few crunchies, and ran to Donald's side as Donald left the kitchen area.

Donald was walking through the living room to the office when he noticed Annie sound asleep on the sofa. He set his coffee cup down and pulled the blanket over the woman he loved. Picking up his coffee, he and Laddie went to work. Donald walked to his desk, set his coffee cup down and Laddie went directly to his bed on the floor next to Donald's desk.

♦ ♦ ♦

It was eight o'clock in the morning when Donald emerged from his office to make another cup of coffee. Annie awoke when she heard the office door open. She sat up and yawned.

"I cannot believe I fell asleep," Annie said as she pulled the blanket off. She stood and stretched.

"You needed the sleep," Donald said walking to the kitchen. Annie followed.

Donald pulled a coffee cup from the cupboard and set it on the coffee maker. He placed a coffee pod in the machine and pressed a button. Moments later the whirling noise stopped and the machine poured freshly brewed coffee into the awaiting cup. Donald handed the cup of coffee to Annie.

Annie lifted the cup to her face and inhaled the wonderful aroma before taking her first sip. She loved coffee. Coffee and chocolate. Annie looked up and noticed Donald smiling at her.

"What?" Annie said to Donald, curious as to why he had a silly smile on his face.

"I just cannot believe how much I love you."

"Well, you are stuck with me now," Annie said as she set her coffee cup down on the counter and grabbed Donald by his shirt to pull him to her. He wrapped his arms around her and they hugged.

"Good morning," Janette said as she descended the staircase and walked into the kitchen. "I hope I am not disturbing you."

"Not at all," Donald said, moving over to the coffee machine. "I was just getting some coffee and going back to work. Donald made a cup of coffee for himself and then said, "I will leave you ladies to talk." Donald and Laddie left the kitchen.

Annie made Janette a cup of coffee, which she gladly accepted. Annie offered to drive Janette to Newport to pick up Suzette, and possibly Jacquie and John if they did not have a ride back to Bridgeport Harbor. Janette was overwhelmed with the offer and quickly accepted.

"Janette, I know I really should not ask," Annie began. "But, have you thought about what might be in the envelope addressed to you from your grandmother?"

"Oh, Annie," Janette leaned forward. "Do you think it would be terrible to open the letter addressed to me before I meet with my cousins? I am curious as to what might be inside that would make Lawrence Smyth think it is valuable enough to want to kidnap or kill someone."

"Exactly what I have been thinking," Annie said excitedly. "It would be okay if you did open it and discovered something that would help Dan in his investigation."

"True," Janette said deep in thought. "Do you think my cousins would be mad if I knew what was in the envelopes?"

"You know them best," Annie said. "I may be a bad influence on you, because I am so curious right now. I assure you I can wait, and again, it is really none of my business."

"Nonsense," Janette replied. "If it wasn't for you, I would not have this painting back. It is a special bond between my grandmother and myself. It means so much to me. I want to read the letter with you."

With that said, Janette jumped up and ran upstairs to retrieve the letter. Annie was feeling a bit guilty for bringing it up. It was her curiosity that always got her in trouble. She decided to let Janette read it to herself first. She could always tell Annie that it was personal and Annie would be fine with that.

Janette came down with the letter in hand. She sat down, looked at Annie, took a deep breath and began to open the letter. Annie reached over and placed her hand on Janette's to stop her.

"Wait a minute," Annie said to stop Janette. "Maybe you should wait and read this with your cousins. Do not let me influence you to open the letter."

"Annie," Janette said, looking at Annie and smiling. "My mother is not here right now, but I know she would want me to open it and call her later to tell her all about it. I am so happy you are here to support me in whatever I find inside this envelope."

"Well, what are you waiting for? Open it!" Annie said with anticipation.

Janette carefully opened the envelope marked with her name. Annie could see the woman's hand shake as she looked inside. A look of confusion appeared on Janette's face as she pulled out a small stack of papers. To Annie, they appeared to be certificates of some type. Janette stared for a moment and then looked through the stack of papers. She looked up at Annie.

"My grandmother left me 'bearer stock certificates'," Janette said. "What does that mean?"

"It means the person in possession of these certificates is the owner of the said stock," Donald said as he stood behind the two women.

Annie was surprised to see Donald standing there. She was so engrossed in what Janette was doing, that she did not hear him walk up to the table.

"Do you think they are worth anything?" Janette asked Donald.

"I know of someone you can call and find out," Donald said taking his coffee cup to the sink and washing it out. As he dried the cup and placed it back in the cupboard he said, "The question is, does Lawrence Smyth know about the certificates and more importantly, how does Lawrence know?"

"Janette," Annie began, "You may want to contact your mother and find out if she knows about these bearer stock certificates. If Lawrence knows about the certificates there may be a connection between Lawrence Smyth and Walter Smith, which may be how the painting arrived in Bridgewater Harbor in the first place."

Janette ran upstairs to get her cell phone and call her mother. Donald picked up one of the bearer certificates and held it up to check for a watermark. The certificate appeared genuine at first glance. They would need to be examined by a professional to be sure. He set the paper down on the stack of other papers.

"You should let Dan know what has been found," Donald said to Annie.

"I was planning to do so, but he did not want to be disturbed until after noon today," Annie told Donald. "In the meantime, we can find out a bit more about the stocks."

"We?"

"Yes."

"By 'we' you mean you want me to call my friend and find out about the bearer certificates and what they are currently worth?"

"I bet the Silver Sleuths would make us honorary members if we solve this case," Annie mused.

"Can you imagine what Dan would say?" Donald laughed.

"Let's not go there right now." Annie said as her attention was turned to Janette coming down the stairs with her phone at her ear.

"Thanks, Mom," Janette said. "I will call you later. Love you!" Janette hung up the phone as she stood in front of Donald and Annie.

"Mom said she was able to get into the safe deposit box Grandma had. Apparently, Walter Smith did not know about the box. Mom had a key and was on the account to get into the box. Grandma left a letter there for Mom."

Janette told Annie and Donald that the letter mentioned giving the bearer stock certificates to her granddaughters. The stock certificates were given to her by her father in the 1960's. At this point, they could be worth a fortune.

Annie was elated. It was good news from a sad situation. At least now they knew why the painting was so important to Lawrence. The unanswered question was how did he know about the stock certificates? Annie believed there was definitely a connection between Lawrence Smyth and Walter Smith. Were they the same person? Would Janette's grandmother have married a much younger man? No one had a photo of Walter Smith and not much was known about him.

"Janette, would your mother send you a copy of the marriage certificate of your grandmother and Walter Smith?" Annie asked. She had the idea to contact the county where the marriage license was obtained. Maybe she would get more information about Walter Smith, like an age.

"Sure," Janette said as she began typing a text message to her mother. Moments later her mother said that she would send a photo of the certificate when she returned to her mother's home. She was out running errands.

"Annie," Janette began. "This is so exciting. I could not have done it without your help."

It was just the beginning, Annie thought. At least she had a clue to follow by tracking down the marriage certificate. She would tell Dan later. He really needed his sleep right now. Good thing Lizzy was not here, Annie thought. She would tell Dan and it would be out of Annie's hands. What fun would that be?

"We should be heading out to Newport to pick up Suzette," Annie said standing up from the kitchen table. "I bet Suzette is chomping at the bit to get out of the hospital right now."

◆ ◆ ◆

As Annie and Janette made their way to Newport in Annie's car, Janette received a text message from her mother stating that she sent a photo of the marriage certificate in an email to Janette. Janette then opened the email and pulled up the photo of the marriage certificate. Nothing looked suspicious to Janette. She forwarded a copy of the photo to Annie. Annie would look at it later.

Janette advised Suzette that they were on their way to pick her up. As Annie expected, Suzette was in her hospital room dressed and ready to go home. Jacquie and John were in the room, too, and waiting to ask if they could ride back to Bridgewater Harbor with the group. John had ridden in the ambulance with Jacquie and did not have a way to get them back. Annie could tell how very much in love the two were, as John was now holding Jacquie's hand after spending a sleepless night in the hospital room with her. She was happy to accommodate them. She thought Donald would do the same for her if she was the one in the hospital overnight. Annie wanted to talk with Jacquie a bit more about what happened and how she ended up in this predicament.

On the way back to Bridgewater Harbor, Annie was able to find out what happened to Jacquie. Jacquie told the group that she was in her gallery Tuesday when Lawrence came back to work after his day off. He noticed the painting missing from the back room and questioned her. She told him that she sold it to Annie Weston, the owner of the papercraft shop a few stores down. Lawrence seemed upset about the sale. He demanded that she go to Annie Weston and get the painting back. Jacquie tried to ask why he wanted the painting when he stormed out of the shop and did not return until later the next evening.

Jacquie was physically shaking and upset as she continued to tell her story. Lawrence returned on Wednesday evening, as Jacquie was getting ready to close the shop, and the two argued once again about the painting. It was then that Lawrence pulled a gun on Jacquie and forced her out of the gallery and to the back of the building housing the Bridgewater Bed & Breakfast. As they approached the back door to the B&B, they were met by Suzette, who had just returned home from Europe. Lawrence forced both Suzette and Jacquie into the building and tied them up in the room where Annie had found them. Janette was already in the room tied up on the bed.

Jacquie said that Lawrence was nervous and paced the floor trying to figure out how to get the painting from Annie. He came up with a plan to text Annie from Janette's cell phone to have Annie turn the painting over to him.

That was the strange text that she received from Janette, Annie thought. She continued to listen to Jacquie's story.

Lawrence left the room and they did not know where he went until the next morning. Janette managed to get up off the bed and went to the window to try and get someone's attention. It was then that Lawrence returned and knocked her down. He left her there until later in the day, when he was going to force her to go to Annie's house to get the painting. They heard noise outside and Lawrence noticed older people gathering on the street. When he heard people inside the building, he grabbed Janette and hid behind the bookcase. They were warned not to say anything or they would be killed. Suzette pushed herself off the bed and made it to the window to signal for help. She was startled by Lizzy entering the room.

"I thought it was Lawrence coming back to kill us," Suzette added.

Jacquie continued, "Lizzy entered the room and screamed, and Suzette fainted." You know what happened after that.

Annie was in deep thought about all of the information she had at this point. She really needed to talk to the senior ladies and find out what they knew. Walter Smith was either Lawrence Smyth or he was one of the three men who moved to Bridgewater Harbor recently. Could more than one person be involved? Her first step was to research the marriage certificate.

CHAPTER 13

Friday Night

I t was noon when Annie pulled into the parking lot behind the Bridgewater Bed & Breakfast. As she stopped the SUV near the rear entrance of Suzette's home and business, everyone sat quiet for a moment. No one made a move to get out of the vehicle.

Annie's cell phone chimed, which caused Annie to jump. It was Dan. He wanted to know how Suzette and Jacquie were doing this morning. Annie dialed Dan's cell phone number and lifted the phone to her ear. She told Dan that they were at the Bridgewater Bed & Breakfast in the parking lot. Dan asked that they all stay in the car and he would be there in a few minutes to check out the building before they went inside. Dan disconnected. Annie stared at her phone for a minute, then told the group what Dan had said.

"I am a bit hungry," Jacquie said. "Maybe we could go to the coffee shop and get something to eat."

Others quickly agreed with Jacquie. Annie sent a text to Dan saying she was taking the group to Ione's for a bite to eat. She asked him to join them when he finished securing the building. Suzette gave him permission the night before to enter the building during his investigation, and Annie had given Dan the building code to unlock the door earlier, so neither of them needed to be there.

Annie pulled the car out of the parking lot and drove to a parking spot in front of Ione's Bakery and Coffee Shop. As she did, she noticed the lights were on in Ocean Loads of Paper. She excused herself from the group and walked over to her shop. Once inside, she found a very tired looking Lizzy on the computer at the counter. Daisy walked out of the back room with an arm load of craft products.

"Hi, Annie," Daisy said, grabbing a pen set before it fell out of her arms. "I thought you were taking the day off today."

"I am, but I was not aware that Lizzy was working today," Annie said walking up to Lizzy.

Lizzy looked up from her computer and said, "Dan was up at 11:00 this morning, so I decided to get up and open the shop for Daisy."

"You look exhausted," Annie said to Lizzy.

"I need coffee," Lizzy said, closing her laptop and moving it to the office.

"Good," Annie said walking to the door on the ocean side of the store. "Come with me to Ione's. The gang's all there. Daisy, do you mind holding down the fort for a while?"

"Certainly not," Daisy said.

Annie and Lizzy exited the shop and headed over to Ione's for lunch. When they entered the shop, Annie noticed how busy it looked. She spotted Suzette, Janette, Jacquie, and John sitting at a corner table by the ocean side window. Ione was standing at the table taking their orders.

"Annie, Lizzy, your usual?" Ione asked.

"Sure." They both responded at the same time.

Annie looked around the room and then asked Ione, "It seems to be getting busier for you lately?"

"Yes, indeed," Ione responded. "I need to hire a part-time person to help with clearing tables and extra duties we are having a difficult time getting done right now. Do you know of anyone interested in part-time work?"

"How about William, Daisy's brother?" Annie asked Ione. "He was looking for a part-time job and Daisy said he is a hard worker."

"Send him in for an interview." Ione said. She heard an employee call her name and quickly walked off.

Annie sent a text to Daisy asking if her brother, William, was still interested in working part-time. If so, she should have him contact Ione for an interview. She thought Marie might like the idea of William working next door. They could take their breaks together. Annie knew Marie had a crush on William, but was not sure William felt the same way. Marie was much more outgoing and William seemed to be shy most of the time. At least they could have a friendship and talk about their work.

Annie put her cell phone in her pocket and turned her attention to the group. Suzette was looking at the building across the street. Annie noticed a patrol vehicle parked in front of the entrance to Bridgewater Bed & Breakfast. She saw Dan inside the building opening the front door for the patrol officer. He locked the door after the officer entered and the two moved away from the doorway.

"Looks like Dan will have the building checked out in no time," Annie said looking at the building and then at Suzette.

"I love my bed and breakfast, but now it just seems scary being in there with just Janette and myself," Suzette said with a shiver. "I guess things will get back to normal once customers begin to arrive again."

"When are you opening back up again?" John asked Suzette.

"I do not have bookings until a week from Thursday," Suzette responded. "I was not planning on returning from Europe until next weekend. That gave me four days to stock supplies and freshen all the rooms."

"Are you and Jacquie staying in town or going back to Portland today?" Janette asked of John.

"I really need to get my shop in order," Jacquie leaned forward as she answered Janette's question. "We will stay in town for a few days at least."

"Why don't you stay at my place?" Suzette asked. "There is a small unused studio apartment next to mine. Janette is not using it, so it is available. You can stay there anytime you are in Bridgewater Harbor."

"Oh, that would be wonderful," Jacquie exclaimed. "It will give me plenty of time to find a manager for my gallery."

"Then it is all set. You can move in immediately."

The food arrived at the table and everyone began to eat. Lizzy got up to get a second cup of coffee. Annie was secretly thinking about dessert. Those chocolate brownies in the display case looked exceptionally delicious today. Ione added extra dark chocolate chips to the batter.

Lizzy walked back to the table and set her coffee down. She noticed Annie staring at the chocolate chip brownies.

"I asked Ione to bring a plate of brownies over for dessert."

"Lizzy, you are so thoughtful," Annie teased.

"No problem," Lizzy said, taking a sip of coffee. "You're paying."

♦ ♦ ♦

By the time the group was finished eating lunch and dessert, Dan walked through the door of Ione's Bakery and Coffee Shop. He ordered a cup of coffee and a sandwich and joined the group at the table.

"The place is all clear and locked up," Dan said as he sat down.

"What about the old entrance on the north-side of the building?" Suzette asked.

"I wanted to talk to you about that. I spoke with Fred at the hardware store, and he said he would change all the locks for you, check out the security system, and board up the doorway behind the bookcase. Just give him a call and he will be right over."

"Thank you so much for everything," Suzette said. "In the years I have been here, there has never been a problem. I just hope this does not scare customers away."

"Nonsense," said Ione, walking up to clear plates from the table. "If people hear there was a ghost in the building, it will become a very popular destination spot."

The group thought about what Ione had said. A sandwich was set down in front of Dan and he began to eat.

"What is for dinner tonight, Annie?" Dan asked as he took another bite from his turkey and cranberry sandwich.

Annie thought for a moment, "Since it is sunny outside, how about a barbecue? Everyone here is invited."

Suzette was the first to accept Annie's invitation for dinner. She made the comment that she would not get to shop for food until the next day. She did not know how long it would take for Fred to change all the locks on the doors in the bed and breakfast.

"John and I will be there," Jacquie said. "What can we bring?"

"Just yourselves," Annie replied. "Let's plan on six-thirty."

Everyone agreed and began to stand up to leave. Dan was still eating his lunch, so Lizzy stayed behind to keep him company. Annie walked up to the counter to pay the lunch bill. When she got the bill, she noticed that Dan had put his sandwich and coffee on her tab. She smiled and looked over at Dan as she handed Ione cash from her wallet.

♦ ♦ ♦

After spending the afternoon in the shop with Lizzy and Daisy, Annie arrived home around five-thirty. She called Donald earlier to tell him that she invited everyone for a barbecue at six-thirty. Donald said he would make sure everything was ready to grill once he got off work. When Annie walked through the front door, she noticed Donald in the kitchen preparing hamburgers.

First giving Donald a kiss, Annie ran upstairs to put her purse and bag away and to check on Callie. Callie was sound asleep on her cat tree in the seating alcove of the master suite. Annie gave Callie a gentle pet and walked back downstairs to help Donald with the preparations for dinner.

At six-o'clock, Lizzy walked through the front door carrying dessert from Ione's Bakery and Coffee Shop. It was a chocolate pound cake covered in chocolate ganache and shaved chocolate on top. To most people, that would be chocolate overload, but to Annie it was perfect.

Guests began arriving at six-fifteen in the evening. By a quarter to seven, everyone was settled on the patio and eating hamburgers, potato salad, chips, and drinking iced tea. Donald handed Dan a beer and took one for himself. He motioned to John with a beer in his hand. John nodded and Dan passed a beer to him. Dan and Donald were the last to be seated around the dining table outside. The warm summer weather was inviting and conversation was lively.

"Did you get the problems solved at the bed and breakfast?" Donald asked Suzette.

"Fred from the hardware store came over this afternoon and changed all the locks and helped me reset my electronic code on the back door. He brought over plywood to seal up the entrance behind the bookcase in the guest room. No one will be able to come or go through that entrance anymore."

"That must make you feel a bit more at ease now," Lizzy said.

"Keep in mind that Lawrence Smyth is still at large and Walter Smith is suspected of being in this area," Dan said picking up his beer and taking a sip.

"That reminds me," Janette said. "Annie, I was wondering if you would lock these papers in your safe for Suzette, Collette, and me."

"Sure. What are they?"

"The letters given to us by our grandmother that contain the bearer certificates. I think they are valuable and that is what Lawrence was after."

"How would Lawrence know about the bearer certificates in the painting?" asked Lizzy.

Janette suspected that Walter must have known the bearer certificates were in the back of the painting. The painting disappeared from her grandmother's house and ended up in Bridgewater Harbor. It seems that Walter may have brought the painting to Lawrence at Spencer's Gallery.

"And I unknowingly found the painting in the storage room and set it out on display for sale," Jacquie added. "It is all my fault. I did not do a thorough background check on Lawrence when I hired him to manage my gallery. His glowing references were probably fake and he may have paid people to represent businesses when I called for a reference. It was foolish of me."

"If you think about it," Annie said while picking up the bowl of potato chips and placing a handful on her plate, "You may have saved the bearer certificates from getting into the wrong hands. If Lawrence had gotten his hands on those letters and certificates, Janette, Suzette, and Collette would never have received the personal letters from their grandmother."

Everyone was silent for a moment, deep in thought about what Annie had said. Annie was glad that Janette asked her to keep the documents safe for her. She had the painting in the vault room. At least the house had lots of security and a large goofy dog to protect her and Donald from Lawrence.

At the end of the evening, Dan offered to follow John, Jacquie, Janette, and Suzette back to the bed and breakfast. He offered to check the place out, but the group agreed that they felt much safer with the new locks and the secret doorway being sealed behind the bookcase. Janette did say she would text Annie after they arrived safely home.

As Dan and Lizzy were getting ready to go home, Annie pulled Dan aside. She asked him if he thought Lawrence would stop trying to get to the painting if he somehow knew the documents were found and placed in a secure vault.

"In a small town like this, conversation overheard at Ione's would get around quickly, but you did not hear that from me." Dan motioned to Lizzy and they walked out the front door. Lizzy said goodnight. Annie closed the front door and locked it.

Donald and Laddie entered the kitchen through the back door. Laddie had finished his business for the night and went to his water and food dish for one last sampling before going to bed. Donald began turning off lights as Annie activated the house alarm. The two of them walked up the stairs to their bedroom, with Laddie close at Donald's heels.

Annie looked at her cell phone when it buzzed. It was a message from Janette stating all was well at the bed and breakfast. She thanked Annie for dinner and friendship.

"Donald, did you put Janette's papers in the safe?"

"Yes, while you were cleaning up after dinner. I put them in the safe in the office."

As Annie brushed her teeth, she was in deep thought about Lawrence Smyth and Walter Smith. Were they related? Were they the same person? Did they both arrive in town on the same day? Where were they now? Annie set her toothbrush in its charger and rinse her mouth. She stood staring at the mirror in thought. She suddenly realized that Donald was talking. Was he talking to her?

"...which means we should do that first thing in the morning," Donald said as he walked out of the bathroom.

Annie stared at the bathroom door, wondering what Donald had said. As she chided herself for not paying attention to Donald when he talked, Donald poked his head into the bathroom.

"You did not hear a word I said, did you?"

"I heard 'first thing in the morning'," Annie grimaced. "Does it have anything to do with sex?"

"Well, now it does!"

Annie laughed and put her hand to Donald's forehead and playfully pushed him out of the bathroom. As she walked into the master bedroom, she saw Laddie already asleep in his large dog bed next to Donald's side of the bed. Callie was eating at her elevated food station. Annie picked up her water dish and walked back to the bathroom to rinse it out and refill with fresh water. Upon returning Callie's water dish to the feeding area, Annie noticed that Donald had already turned the light off on his side of the bed and was snuggled under the comforter.

Annie crawled into bed and pulled the covers over her. She was contemplating whether or not she wanted to read before going to sleep. Donald made up her mind as he pulled her close and began kissing her. She reached up and turned off the light.

CHAPTER 14

Saturday

Annie opened her eyes to early morning light filtering through the window in the seating area of the master bedroom. Her thoughts immediately went to the projected late afternoon arrival of her mother and Marie. They were finally returning from their vacation in Disneyland. Annie was excited to see them again. Marie must be full of stories, she mused.

Annie got out of bed and moved to the seating alcove to not disturb Donald. She made a cup of coffee from the coffee station that Donald had built in to the room when he did the remodel of the master suite. He thought of everything. Taking the coffee to the small sofa, Annie sat down and gazed at the ocean. The sun would be shining brightly on the water soon.

Turning her attention to a notebook, in which she made notes for crafting projects, Annie began paging through possible ideas for her next class. She turned a page and came across wedding notes she had made for herself. There in front of her was a page of ideas of what type of dress she wanted, what flowers she thought would be simple yet elegant, and the chocolate cake with white icing and chocolate roses. As she continued to look at the notes, she suddenly realized that the wedding was going to take place next Saturday...a week from today! Annie's stomach began to tighten.

Calm down, Annie told herself, it was never going to be a big wedding, just family and a few friends...a simple ceremony in the backyard. Her mother had it practically all planned out. Annie knew Ione was going to be making a cake, and Myra from the florist would be working on the flowers. Lizzy was her best woman and Marie was her flower girl. Annie's mother had also made arrangements with a pastor from the local church to perform the ceremony. The only thing missing now was a dress for her and Lizzy. Marie was going to wear a Disney princess dress. That was just fine with Annie.

Annie closed the notebook and set it on the side table when she heard Donald approaching. He sat down next to her. Reaching for her coffee cup, he took a sip, and handed it back.

"Am I interrupting anything?" Donald asked. He got up and made himself a cup of coffee and sat back down.

"No," Annie laughed softly. "I realized that we are getting married in a week. I have a few things to do to get ready."

"I just need to put a suit on and meet you on the steps of the cottage in the backyard, right?"

"You are in charge of Dan, your best man."

"Now, I am overwhelmed! How will I ever cope?"

Laddie jumped up from where he had been lying on the floor. He ran to the bedroom door and began to quietly woof. Donald and Annie walked up next to Laddie. They listened for a moment. The alarm made a noise as if being disengaged. Donald ran to the bathroom to put on clothes. Annie followed and did the same. Donald then grabbed his cell phone to check cameras around the house outside. He noticed a dark figure lurking at the front door, and then entering the house.

Laddie began to scratch at the bedroom door. Donald told Annie to call the police while he opened the door to release Laddie on the intruder. Laddie bounded down the stairs barking loudly. Donald caught a glimpse of the dark-clothed figure sprinting across the front yard and down the street. Grabbing Laddie, Donald ran outside to the street. Laddie was tugging on Donald's grip. He wanted to chase the bad guy, but Donald would not let him. The dark figure ran down the street and turned a corner. He decided not to give chase, as he did not know if the person had any weapons on him.

Donald turned to see Dan running out of his house, pulling on a shirt and zipping up his pants as he ran. He crossed the street to Donald's position.

"Did you get a look at the guy?"

"No, but he is on camera."

"Let's go check it out."

Annie met the two as they entered the house. Donald went to retrieve his personal laptop. When Donald pulled up footage of the burglar, he noticed the dark figure moving around the outside of the house.

"Whoever this guy is, he knows what he is doing," Donald said. "He seems to know about alarm systems."

"It looks like he is wearing gloves," Dan said. He got on his cell phone to call dispatch.

Lizzy sent a text to Annie. "What is happening? Is everything okay?"

Annie called Lizzy's cell phone to tell her what happened. Lizzy was up, dressed and over to Annie's house in a matter of minutes. She made sure to lock the front door as she left. She was not going to be left alone in Dan's house while a burglar was on the loose.

Dan and Donald continued to view the video footage from different camera angles. Apparently, the burglar was quick to pick the lock on the front door. This was no ordinary burglar. This person was a professional. Dan could not help but think it had to be Lawrence. He was motivated to get to the painting. Dan walked over to where Annie and Lizzy were standing.

"Annie, this might be a good morning to go to Ione's for coffee, donuts, and gossip."

Annie knew what Dan meant and nodded in agreement. Lizzy looked at Annie with a puzzled expression. Annie mouthed the words 'tell you later' to Lizzy. She motioned that she understood. Annie thought it might be a good idea to invite the Silver Sleuths for coffee and donuts. She looked at her watch and noticed that it was probably a bit too early to contact them.

Donald looked up from the computer and saw Laddie doing a dance around the kitchen door. He moved to let Laddie outside. Before releasing him, Donald made a quick look around. Deciding it was safe, he let Laddie out into his enclosed run. Laddie did his business quickly and made his way back to Donald in short order.

"I do not like that this guy can turn off alarm systems and pick locks so fast," Dan said.

"I will install added deadbolts to the doors today," Donald said moving the mouse on his computer to view more camera footage.

"One thing for sure, he will not be able to disengage my live alarm system. Laddie knew someone was outside before we heard the alarm turn off."

"Good boy," Dan said, patting Laddie on the head.

Dan heard a car pull up in front of the house. He looked out the window and saw a police vehicle parked outside. He exited the house and went to talk to the patrol officer.

"Now that we are all up so early, would anyone like breakfast?" Annie asked.

"I could eat," Donald said closing his laptop and moving it to the counter.

"I could really use some coffee," Lizzy said, reaching for a coffee mug in the cupboard. She pulled out a coffee pod from the glass jar on the counter and placed it in the coffee maker. In seconds, fresh brewed coffee filled her mug. She removed the coffee cup and set it on the counter after taking a sip. She then made a cup of coffee for Dan.

Annie was pulling items from the refrigerator to make a frittata for breakfast. She had cooked sausage, spinach, potatoes, onion, garlic, heavy cream, seasonings, and cheese. After spraying the baking dish with olive oil, Annie added the ingredients to the dish while Lizzy turned the oven on to pre-heat. When the dish was in the oven, Annie set the timer for thirty minutes.

Annie and Lizzy sat down at the kitchen table. Donald joined them with steaming cups of coffee for Annie and him. Dan came back from his meeting with the patrol officer. Patrol told Dan that they were unable to find anyone in the area. They would continue to drive around and look for anyone who looked suspicious.

As they waited for the frittata to bake, the four continued to discuss the possibility of the burglar being Lawrence. The painting had to be of great importance to him to break into a house in the early morning. Was there more to the painting than the letters revealed? Annie decided there was more to the painting and she wanted to find out what it was.

"I can stay here at the house while Donald goes to the hardware store and picks up what he needs to secure the doors," Dan said.

"Sounds good to me," Donald spoke up. "I want to spend time figuring out how the burglar disabled the alarm system."

"Could he have just cut the wires from the outside of the house?" Annie asked.

"An alarm should have notified me on my cell phone if that was done."

"Lizzy and I need to work at the shop today, but I was planning on coming home early to wait for Mom and Marie to arrive." Annie said, standing up from the table as the oven timer sounded that the frittata was ready.

♦ ♦ ♦

Lizzy and Annie walked into Ione's Bakery and Coffee Shop at eight-thirty on Saturday morning. As they ordered coffee and donuts, Annie turned to see Jacquie and John sitting at a table against the wall. They seemed deep in conversation. Annie was not sure she should interrupt them, when Jacquie looked up and noticed Annie.

"Annie, Lizzy, come over here and sit with us," Jacquie said, gesturing to the chairs across the table.

Annie and Lizzy sat down. After some idle chat, Annie asked Jacquie how she felt about going into the gallery. It had to be a bit unnerving for Jacquie. John was taking time off from work to be with her and make sure she was safe.

"At least I do not have to deal with Lawrence anymore," Jacquie said.

Annie looked at Lizzy and then looked down at her donut. She said, "You have new secure locks and hopefully you will be able to hire a new manager to take over soon. I know this may seem like a far-fetched idea, but have you asked Janette if she might want to manage the gallery?"

The idea had just popped into Annie's mind that instant. Maybe Janette wanted to stay in Bridgewater Harbor where she could work on her art. She has a relative here, and now she has friends. It seemed like a perfectly good idea. Annie wondered why she did not think of it earlier.

Jacquie and John looked at each other and then at Annie. Annie could tell they liked the idea.

"That is a great idea!" Jacquie said standing up from the table. "I am going over to the B&B and ask her."

John stood and followed Jacquie out the door. Lizzy set her coffee cup down and just looked at Annie.

"What?"

"It is a wonderful idea."

"It just came to me."

"Kind of like your class projects you design at the last minute?"

"Yes, as a matter of fact. Speaking of last-minute class projects, we should get to the shop. It will be time to open soon."

♦ ♦ ♦

As Annie's morning went along, she noticed Jacquie, John, and Janette walking from the B&B to the gallery. Jacquie saw Annie looking out the window and waved. She had a big smile on her face. Annie knew this was going to be a lovely working arrangement between Janette and the Spencer's.

Around ten o'clock, Annie saw Donald walking to town with LaVerne, Lorraine, Millie, and Elsie. He looked adorable surrounded by the senior ladies. As he walked past the shop, he looked inside at Annie smiling back at him. He shrugged and smiled back.

Annie noticed that Donald stopped to hold open the door to Ione's Bakery and Coffee Shop for the ladies. She suddenly remembered the comment that Dan made. Annie ran to her office and retrieved her cell phone and wallet. She might as well make it look like she was getting another donut.

"Lizzy, I will be right back," Annie said as she flew out of the door on the ocean side of the shop.

"Where are you going?" It was too late. Annie was out the door, but as Lizzy jumped up from the counter and made her way to the door, she noticed Annie quickly entering Ione's. Annie was thinking that Lizzy might be wondering what she might be up to. She made a mental note to fill Lizzy in on what Dan had asked her to do.

The Silver Sleuths were in line to order coffee and donuts. Annie stepped into line behind Millie. Lorraine was taking her time trying to decide what to order.

"Just order a black coffee and a donut," said an exasperated LaVerne. "We are growing old waiting."

"Oh, you were already old when we got here," Lorraine said, pointing to a maple bar. "I will take that one. No. No...the other one. Thank you."

"I was a brunette when I walked in here," LaVerne said to a second clerk at the counter. She giggled as she handed LaVerne a small coffee and a plain donut.

LaVerne turned to find a table and spotted Annie digging through her wallet.

"Annie, dear," LaVerne said approaching Annie in line. "Do sit with us when you get your coffee and donut."

"Thank you. That would be lovely."

Annie watched as LaVerne wandered off to find a table. She saw a young man sitting alone at a large table and stood next to him. "Oh dear," Annie heard from across the room. "I wonder if we will be able to sit down anywhere or just have to stand up and eat our donuts and drink our coffee right here where I am standing." At this point LaVerne was looking straight down at the young man. He got the hint and quickly stood, gathered his belongings, and moved to a smaller table. Pleased with herself, LaVerne sat down and summoned the other ladies to her table.

As Annie sat down with the Silver Sleuths, Lorraine leaned in and asked, "We saw the dark figure lurking around your front door this morning. We know he got away. Did anything happen inside?"

"We saw Detective Surely running across the street with no clothes on," Elsie added.

"He had clothes, but he was running while pulling up his pants and putting on a shirt," Millie said. "He was probably naked before he left the house," she said in a whisper.

"He did not need to get dressed for my sake," LaVerne announced.

Young girls at the next table began giggling. Annie was thinking about how to get this topic into a conversation over dinner. It would be amusing.

Annie told the Silver Sleuths what happened earlier that morning. She described the alarm being disarmed, the front door lock being picked, and how Laddie alerted them before the intruder made it all the way inside the house. Annie explained further that she called Dan first, and then called the police. That was why they saw him running out of his house and across the street.

"Such excitement!" Millie stated, "I wonder what the burglar wanted?"

"The painting," LaVerne spoke up. "I bet it was Lawrence."

"He wants the letters that were in the back of the painting," added Lorraine suspected.

"How...?" Annie began, but decided it was useless to try and figure out the mystery of why these particular elderly ladies knew everything going on in town. "Do you know why he would want the letters to Janette, Collette, and Suzette from their grandmother?"

"It is not the letters, dear," Millie stated. "It is the painting."

"I am a bit puzzled," Annie said. "What is so important about the painting?" She knew what was in the envelope that the letters were in, but wanted to find out just what these ladies knew. If they knew this much information, why had they not found Walter Smith? Annie was careful not to let her mind wander again. She did not want to miss Millie's answer to her question.

"It is not the bearer certificates that are important," LaVerne answered.

"It is the code," Millie said quietly.

"Code?"

"Yes," Millie said brushing crumbs from her blouse. "The code for what is hidden at the grandmother's home."

"How could you know this? Have you been talking with Janette or Suzette?"

"Oh, Annie," Lorraine exclaimed. "You would not believe us if we told you. We will just leave it at our being great sleuths."

"Oh, Lorraine," Millie said. "We saw something like it in an old movie."

"Quite clever, actually," injected Elsie.

With that last statement, the seniors gathered their trash and belongings and stood to leave. Annie just sat for a moment, not really knowing what to believe. Then it dawned on her that she did not finish what she originally came to tell the ladies. She watched them leave out the street-side door of the bakery.

Elsie held back from the group, then turned to Annie and said, "We will spread the word that the letters were found in the back of the painting. We can say they are safely tucked away in a bank safe deposit box if you want."

Flabbergasted that Elsie knew exactly what Annie was thinking, all Annie could do was slowly shake her head in acknowledgement.

"We will see you soon. Say hello to your mother and Marie for us." With those words, Elsie was out the door and joining the other ladies.

♦ ♦ ♦

Arriving home at three-thirty, Annie raced around to make sure the house was cleaned up. Stella and Marie would arrive soon by town car. She realized how much she missed the two of them over the past week. She was excited to hear all the stories they had about Disneyland.

At four o'clock, Donald walked out of the office with his coffee cup. He washed the cup in the kitchen sink and turned it upside down on the dish drying mat next to the sink.

"Are you planning something special for dinner," Donald asked Annie, "or should I pick up takeout from the Chinese restaurant?"

"Chinese sounds good. But we should wait until everyone is here and settled before we pick up food."

"Is everyone coming over tonight?"

"As far as I know, I do not think Dan would miss being here when Mom and Marie arrive."

"What time do you think they will be here?"

"Around five or five-thirty; depending on traffic."

♦ ♦ ♦

At five o'clock, Lizzy and Dan walked through the front door.

"Have they arrived home yet?" Lizzy asked.

Dan walked in carrying a bouquet of flowers. He set them down on the kitchen counter.

"Trying to get on Mom's good side?" Annie questioned.

"Lizzy made me get the flowers," Dan said looking a bit embarrassed.

A town car pulled up in front of the house. The driver exited the vehicle and opened the back doors. He then removed the luggage from the trunk of the car. Annie was the first to greet her mother and Marie with long hugs. Dan was next in line followed by Lizzy. Donald paid the driver and made sure all the luggage was on the sidewalk. Stella turned to give him a hug. Marie was all smiles when she hugged Donald.

"So how was the trip?" Donald asked.

"It was the best vacation I have been on in a long time," Stella answered. "But I am happy to be home again."

"I could live there," Marie added.

Donald and Dan picked up the luggage and made their way to the house. There was much chatter as the group settled inside. Donald took Marie's suitcase upstairs to her room. Dan set Stella's suitcase down by the front door.

"Dan, you can take my suitcase to my new apartment over the garage," Stella said. "I plan to move in immediately so you and Lizzy can have the house to yourselves."

"I think it would be best if you stay in the house for a while longer," Dan began. "A lot has been happening since you've been gone." Dan explained what he was currently investigating. He did not want to scare Stella and Marie, so he kept the information vague. Stella looked at Annie, but did not ask questions.

When Dan and Donald left to go pick up Chinese food, Annie, Lizzy, Stella, and Marie remained in the living room and talked about the trip to Disneyland. Marie did most of the talking about her many adventures in the parks. Stella passed around photos on her phone.

"Well, now we need to spend time on your wedding plans for next weekend," Stella said, changing the subject. "I am anxious to see the dress you bought."

Annie and Lizzy looked at each other. "Dress? Oh, yes, the dress."

"Have either of you even looked for dresses yet?"

"Well...I have thought about it," Annie replied.

"Oh, Annie! The wedding is next Saturday."

"I know, Mom. It has been so busy."

"You two close the shop tomorrow and go find dresses."

Annie and Lizzy nodded. Annie knew her mother was right.

"I have my flower girl dress," Marie joined in to the conversation. "It is a princess dress. I bought it at Disneyland. I have a princess crown, too!"

Marie proceeded to tell, in detail, all about her dress and how beautiful she looked in it. She had her part in the wedding all planned out. Annie loved that Marie was excited to be part of the wedding.

"And what type of dress do you think I should wear?"

"Oh, it doesn't matter. Wear anything you want," Marie answered.

Annie gave Lizzy a look of resignation.

♦ ♦ ♦

After dinner, Stella convinced Dan to take her suitcase to the apartment over the garage in Annie's backyard. The apartment was beautiful in its neutral tone colors, just as Stella had left it. All she needed to do was move in. Dan told Stella that he would help her move her clothes and other belongings in on Sunday. She could take her time deciding what to keep and what to get rid of later. Stella liked the idea. Dan inspected the kitchen and bathroom to make sure everything was in working order.

While Dan and Stella were gone, Annie and Donald cleaned up the kitchen. Donald put a soap pod in the dishwasher and pushed the start button. He then moved close to Annie and leaned in for a kiss. Annie wrapped her arms around Donald and breathed in the scent of his aftershave still lingering on his body. He was intoxicating in so many ways, she thought.

Drifting to the thought of them in the room outside of the vault, Annie began to feel all tingly inside. Would it be rude of them to slip away downstairs? She did not think it would take much coaxing to get Donald to agree. Would anyone miss them not being around?

Annie looked around the room. It was quiet. Lizzy was upstairs helping Marie unpack her suitcase. Annie took Donald's hand and hurried to the office. Pulling Donald inside, she locked the office door, and slid the bookcase open. The curtains had already been closed by Donald earlier. Annie guided Donald quietly downstairs to the secret room.

♦ ♦ ♦

Twenty minutes later, as they left the apartment to go back to the house, Dan inspected the locks Donald had installed during the remodel of the apartment. Satisfied, he closed and locked the door. Handing the keys to Stella, they descended the staircase and walked across the backyard toward the house.

Donald was on his way up the stairs to the second floor of the house when he passed Lizzy on her way down. She walked into the kitchen where Annie was looking in the refrigerator, and pulling out a bottle of water.

"Would you like a bottle of water?"

"No. I am not the one who just had a quickie in a house full of people!" Lizzy said with her hands on her hips.

"What?" Annie whispered loudly. "How do you know that?"

"Your clothes are untucked and your hair is messed up. Put yourself together before your mother walks back inside. And hurry up. She's on her way now." Lizzy said looking out the kitchen window.

Annie set her water bottle down and quickly straightened her clothing. She was pulling her hair back into a ponytail when Dan and Stella walked through the kitchen door. Annie picked up her water bottle and tilted it back for a drink.

One look at Annie's flushed face and Dan rolled his eyes at her. Lizzy knew what Dan was thinking and suppressed a laugh. Annie felt her cheeks heat up even more.

Donald came bounding down the stairs with Laddie close at his heels. The two entered the kitchen. Donald walked over to the refrigerator and pulled out a bottle of water. He slowly lowered the bottle when he noticed everyone looking at him.

"Anyone interested in a movie tonight?" Annie asked in a tone of voice higher than usual.

"That sounds like a great idea," Donald replied. "Let's set the movie up outside."

"I will make popcorn," Stella spoke up. "Dan, you go to your house and get the candy from the far-right cupboard in the kitchen."

Dan grabbed Lizzy's hand and looking at Annie said, "Yeah. We will be back in a few minutes."

It was Annie's turn to roll her eyes. Donald grinned at Dan. Stella turned to the cupboards to retrieve the box of microwave popcorn.

Marie came downstairs with a basket full of dirty clothes. She walked to the laundry room and set the basket on the washing machine. When she came back out to the kitchen, Annie asked her if she would like to watch a movie in the backyard. Excited, Marie went to the living room to look through the selection of movies.

CHAPTER 15

Sunday Morning

Annie lay with her eyes closed, feeling a slight breeze across her face. Where was the breeze coming from, she thought in her dazed state of mind? She slowly opened her eyes and realized that she and Donald were still outside on the lounge chairs, covered in blankets. Laddie was curled up at the foot of the large double-lounger.

Looking over at the nearby lounge chair, she noticed Dan and Lizzy cozied up together under blankets. Stella and Marie were gone. The projector was covered. It appeared that Annie, Donald, Dan, and Lizzy all fell asleep long before the movie ended.

Birds began their early morning chirping. The sky was getting lighter. Annie loved early mornings. There was something so clean and fresh about early mornings on the coast. She snuggled a little closer to Donald and fell back asleep.

It was six-thirty when Stella walked down the rose vine covered stairs from her apartment over the garage. She was just about to take the last step when she looked up and found four lazy adults still slumbering.

"Hey, sleepy heads!" Stella shouted as she took the last step. "Time to get up! I'll make breakfast. You kids clean up the backyard and put things away."

As blankets were being tossed aside, Laddie was the first to get up, stretch, and yawn. Annie and Donald sat up and looked around the area. Dan and Lizzy threw the covers back over the top of their heads. Donald threw a pillow at Dan.

Dan sat up and yawned. He looked around and then said, "Some action-packed movie. We all fell asleep in the middle of it."

Lizzy was straightening her hair as she sat up. "Wow! Those are noisy birds. Are they always this loud in the morning?"

"When you were a young girl, did you ever camp out in your backyard?" asked Dan.

"You are talking to a city girl."

"We have a house now. We should do some camping in the backyard," said Dan.

Lizzy gave a quizzical look at Annie. Annie laughed as she swung her feet over the edge of the lounge to stand.

Stella arrived with four mugs of hot coffee. She set the coffee on the side table between the two double lounges. Dan handed a steaming mug to Lizzy.

"Were the doors of the house locked during the night?" Dan's mind was on whether or not Lawrence might have made another attempt to retrieve the painting.

Stella picked up a coffee and handed it to Donald.

"Yes, I checked before I went to bed and told Marie to use the back-door code to get into the house when the movie was over. She was to make sure the door was locked after she went inside. I went to bed about three-quarters into the movie. For some reason I was exhausted."

Dan sat back, drinking his coffee, "Probably from all that vacationing at Disneyland."

"It was fun to get away. You four should try it sometime."

"I have a shop to run," said Annie.

"I used up my vacation when I came here after Aunt Helen's death."

"I just started work at Bridgewater Harbor Police Department. I haven't earned vacation yet."

"Looks like I am the only one who can go to Disneyland!" Lizzy announced.

Everyone stared blankly at Lizzy, "Well, it's not like I am packing to go at the moment."

Stella went back to the kitchen to get breakfast started. Dan and Lizzy went home to change their clothes. Donald and Annie went upstairs to do the same. They passed Marie on the stairs as they were going up.

"Good morning, Marie," Annie said.

"Good morning," Marie said barely looking up. "Are we going dress shopping today?"

"Yes, did you want to go with Lizzy and me?"

"Mom and I want to go to make sure you get a dress."

"You don't think I will come back with a dress for my wedding?"

"No."

Annie laughed and followed Donald up the stairs. Marie was probably correct. Annie had a tendency to be a procrastinator. At least with Lizzy, her mom, and Marie going with her, she was bound to find a dress and bring it home.

◆ ◆ ◆

The sun came out, after a few morning clouds, and the four women were on their way to Lincoln City Outlet Mall to find dresses for Annie and Lizzy. Annie was a bit excited. Getting a dress meant she was closer to marrying Donald. She was truly in love with Donald. Annie looked over at Lizzy, who was sitting in the front passenger seat of Annie's SUV. Lizzy seemed to be in deep thought.

"What is troubling you, Lizzy?" Annie said quietly. Marie and Stella were in the back seat talking loudly and laughing.

"Just thinking about you and Donald getting married, I wonder if I will ever get married."

"How about marriage to Dan?"

"He seems nervous about the subject of marriage." Lizzy turned her head to look out the window.

"When he decides to marry, it will be with you."

Lizzy's head turned to look at Annie. A contented smile appeared on her face. "I would marry him in a heartbeat."

After a twenty minute drive, Annie pulled into a parking spot close to an entrance of the outlet mall. The women exited the vehicle. As they did, they all started in different directions. Realizing what they had done, they stopped and looked at each other. Annie, Lizzy, and Marie met up with Stella.

"Okay. We need a game plan here," Stella said.

Annie suggested they follow Lizzy, as she knew what was fashionable and appropriate for an outdoor casual wedding. Lizzy signaled that they follow her to a dress store. Once inside, Stella suggested that they separate to find selections for Lizzy and Annie. Marie told Annie that she would find her the best dress, but it probably would not be as nice as her princess dress. Annie agreed with her and walked off to find a few dresses to try on.

Fifteen minutes later, Annie and Lizzy met at the dressing rooms and began trying on dresses they had found. Marie was next, bringing dresses to Annie. Stella came in last and separated out more dresses for Annie and Lizzy. She insisted they model the dresses for her and Marie before turning them down. There was a lot of excited chatter from Lizzy, who had a figure that fit into any dress. Annie, on the other hand, had to hold her tongue knowing her mother and Marie were nearby.

Both Lizzy and Annie announced they finally found the perfect dress. Stella told them to come out at the same time so she and Marie could see them. The doors of the dressing rooms opened and out walked Lizzy and Annie wearing the same exact dresses!

"Oh, dear." Stella exclaimed.

Marie giggled. "You have the same dress as Lizzy."

"And she looks so much better in the dress than I do," an exasperated Annie announced.

Lizzy laughed. "Annie, teal is not exactly a bride's dress."

"I know, but it is so pretty."

"Annie, try on the white dresses I brought to you." Stella insisted. "Lizzy, there is a beautiful lacey white dress that would be perfect for you."

Taking one last look in the mirror at her teal dress, Annie closed the door of the dressing room and changed into a sleeveless off-white lacy cocktail length dress. It had a satin belt and a scooped neck-line. The dress fit perfectly and made her look thin. At least that is what she thought. Once she opened the door of the dressing room and modeled her dress, she knew from the comments that this was the dress.

It was official; Annie thought as she handed a credit card to the cashier, she was getting married. There was no turning back now.

Shoes and other accessories were purchased and the women were ready to head back to Bridgewater Harbor. Annie was looking forward to getting back to her shop and catch up on work.

♦ ♦ ♦

It was eleven o'clock when Annie pulled the car into the driveway. She noticed Donald and Dan outside cooking something in a large pot on a propane burner. She pulled into the garage and everyone exited the vehicle.

Donald walked up to Annie and took her bags from her while giving her a kiss on the cheek. "We went crabbing!" he exclaimed.

"We limited out on crabs," Dan stated while taking shopping bags from Lizzy. "This is the last batch and then we can clean them."

"This looks like lunch," Stella said. "I'll get a table set up for shelling the crab after you boys clean them."

"Thanks, Mom," Dan said, pleased with the catch they got today.

Although Annie loved crab meat, cleaning and shelling two limits of crab was not what she wanted to do after dress shopping. She wanted to open her shop.

Stella advised that they should save some of the crab for later meals. She would bag it for the freezer. She also told the boys that they could take some of the crab meat to the ladies across the street. Dan grimaced and was about to say something, when Donald gave him a nudge on the arm. Donald told Stella that he would be happy to take the crab over to the ladies across the street.

With the table set up, the shelling of the crabs began. The clinking sounds of cracked shells as they hit the metal discard bowls filled the backyard. At each person's place was a bowl filled with fresh crab meat. Stella took a break and made up a crab meat spread and toasted some French bread with butter and garlic. She brought out a bottle of white wine, which Donald opened. Lizzy came out with wine glasses and the group toasted the upcoming wedding. By early afternoon, Annie had her fill of crab for a while.

CHAPTER 16

Sunday Afternoon

IT was late afternoon when Annie walked the few blocks to her shop. She was thinking about the activities of the past week. Janette's painting kept popping into her thoughts. Was there something else that made the painting so important? Her gut feeling told her there was more to Meredith's Garden.

As she continued to ponder the possibilities, Annie realized she was already at the door of her shop. She finished what her mother needed her to do in the morning. The dress was purchased and hanging in her closet.

Daisy was sitting on the bench just outside the door on the boardwalk. Annie had earlier sent a text message, asking Daisy if she wanted to work this afternoon. Daisy responded quickly, since she was eager to earn as much money as she could for college.

"Good afternoon, Daisy," Annie said digging through her tote bag to retrieve her purse and keys. She stopped and looked at Ione's Bakery and Coffee Shop. "I think we need chocolate and coffee. What do you think?"

"Sounds good to me," Daisy said standing up and following Annie to Ione's shop.

Daisy's brother, William, was clearing a table by the door when the two women entered. He looked up at his sister and smiled.

"William's first day of work is today," Daisy said.

"Looks like he is doing a great job," Annie remarked.

"You can sit here," William said making a last swipe of the table with his wet cleaning cloth.

"Thanks, William," Daisy said to her brother. "But we are just getting coffee and pastries to go. We're opening the shop late today."

William nodded and set off to clear the next table. The coffee shop had a steady pace of customers. Daisy and Annie got in line and soon departed the bakery with their goodies.

The day promised sunshine and finally the clouds were clearing to announce blue skies. Annie paused at her shop door and turned to look out over the ocean wall as a whale spouted in the distance. The smell of the ocean was intoxicating and the sunshine inviting. Annie envisioned Donald and her walking along the beach hand-in-hand without a care in the world. Is that what life was going to be like after she married Donald?

"Annie," a male voice interrupted her thoughts. "Stop daydreaming and open the shop door. I need to talk to you." Dan was standing directly in front of her with his usual look of annoyance.

Annie turned the key in the lock and opened the door. She held the door open as Dan signaled to Daisy to walk inside. He followed after her. Annie closed the door and locked it, as she would not open the store to the public for another hour.

"What can I do for you, Surely?"

"Detective Surely," Dan replied with a tone of annoyance. "Lizzy sent me here to pick up boxes from the storage room."

While Daisy was busy turning on lights, Annie set the chocolate pastries on the counter. Dan reached into Annie's bag of donuts and pulled out a chocolate cake donut and stuffed it in his mouth. She rolled her eyes at Dan, as that was one of her favorite donuts. Annie went to her office and set her purse on the desk. She walked out of her office and motioned for Dan to follow her to the storage room.

Once inside, Annie turned on the lights and was startled to find the room in disarray. Boxes were opened and turned over. Shelves appeared to have been ransacked. Large boxes of inventory were opened and product was strewn about on the floor.

"Why is this room such a mess?" Dan asked Annie.

She gave him an irritated look and said, "Because someone broke into my shop and did this!"

"Don't touch a thing," Dan said pulling his phone from his pocket. "I'll call dispatch and get a patrol unit over here to take a report. Ask Daisy to not touch anything in the shop until I check it out."

Annie went out to talk to Daisy. As she was telling Daisy about the burglary and mess in the storage room, Annie quickly walked to her office. Once inside, she surveyed the room. Her desk looked untouched, but she had the feeling all was not right with the office. Then Annie turned and saw it. The door on the cabinet which held her office safe was ajar.

"Dan!" Annie called out while exiting her office. She quickly walked to the storage room and found Dan ending a conversation with dispatch.

"What?" Dan said as he began texting on his phone. He was sending Lizzy a message that he was going to be detained.

"Someone may have broken into the safe in my office."

Dan moved past Annie, who was standing in the doorway. He entered her office and stood for a moment surveying the cabinet. Annie walked in and stopped at the doorway. The office looked untouched. The only thing out of the ordinary was the partially opened door on the cabinet.

Dan pulled out a pair of latex gloves and put them on his hands. He took photos of the cabinet with his cell phone. He also took photos of the desk and office area. Kneeling down, Dan took a close-up picture of the cabinet. There was a knock on the street-side door. Annie left the office to open the door for the officer on the sidewalk.

Annie greeted Officer Kathy Barrel as she unlocked the door. Kathy was a seasoned officer of ten years, with short dark brown hair, and an infectious laugh. Although physically threatening in a police uniform, she had a sweet side to her personality. Annie guided Officer Barrel to the office. Dan was opening the doors of the cabinet. The safe door was ajar. Annie's fears were realized. Someone did break into her safe. Dan was examining the lock on the safe. It appeared intact. Further investigation revealed a note from the burglar on a sticky note paper.

"Return the painting to the gallery or next time there will be no survivors!"

♦ ♦ ♦

Annie sat down in her office chair. She stared at Dan and asked, "What does he mean?"

"It is just a threat, Annie," Dan said. "You have never been bothered by threats before."

"But someone broke into my business and safe without a trace as to how they got inside."

"We will get this guy, don't worry," Dan said as he stood and gave Annie a hug. This was out of character for Dan, but Annie was comforted all the same.

Annie looked back down at the exposed contents of the safe. "Oh, no!" She said squatting down to get a better look at the safe. "Whoever did this took all of the cash from my register drawer."

While Dan and Officer Barrel did their investigation, Annie called Donald and told him she was closing the shop due to a break-in. Donald was quiet as Annie explained what she and Dan had found in the storage room and the shop.

"Annie, I would feel better if you let me come down there and walk you home."

"Maybe you should stay there with Mom, Marie, and Lizzy," Annie said. "I can ask Dan to take me home."

"Alright," Donald responded. "But I think we should all be more careful until Lawrence is arrested."

Annie and Daisy began cleaning up the storage room after Dan and Officer Barrel completed collecting evidence and left the shop. Annie was quiet as the two picked up product which was tossed about the room. Bottles of glitter were scattered across the room. Thankfully, they were not broken.

As Annie was picking up a jar of glitter, she noticed a piece of yellow note pad paper which had partially slid under a storage rack. She was about to throw it away when she decided to open the paper up and make sure it was not something important.

As Annie opened the crumpled paper, she discovered the code to her safe. The handwriting appeared to be the same as in the threatening note left in her safe. Only Lizzy and Annie had the passcode to the safe. How was this burglar able to get it?

"Annie?" Daisy asked as she looked up from her task of restoring packs of cardstock to their place on the storage room shelf. "Is everything okay?"

"I need to call Dan," Annie said standing up from her kneeling position on the floor. "I found a note that he should see."

Annie left the room and walked to her office, stopping in the doorway. As she looked down at the safe, she had a sudden intuition that someone had a camera hidden in her office and was able to see her and Lizzy punching numbers on the safe's keypad. Was it her imagination? A chill ran down her spine. She backed out of the room and closed the office door.

Annie pulled out her cell phone and pushed the button to call Donald. After several rings, Donald answered. He was transporting boxes over to Stella's new apartment with a moving dolly.

"Annie?" Donald answered. "Is everything okay?"

"Not really, Donald. I just found a piece of paper with my safe code. It was lying under the product rack in the storage room. It was written in the same handwriting as the threatening note."

"Dan just pulled up outside. Hang on and you can talk to him."

Annie waited as Donald walked outside and handed his phone to Dan.

"Donald said you found a note in the storage room," Dan stated in a serious tone. He was walking to the house while talking. Annie could hear Laddie barking in the background. "Try not to handle the note too much. I will be there in a few minutes." He handed the phone back to Donald.

"Donald, do you have anything in your vast array of electronics that would detect a camera signal in my office?" Annie asked.

"Give me a few minutes to go through my boxes in the office. I will get back to you."

Annie disconnected. Daisy walked out of the storage room to announce that everything seemed to be undamaged and back on the shelves. The two walked to the classroom area and determined that it had not been touched. Annie was thankful, because the equipment in the classroom area was expensive. She did not relish the idea of an intruder damaging her much needed crafting equipment.

While waiting for Donald to call back, Daisy and Annie went through each area of the shop looking for anything out of the ordinary. They searched the counter area and found it all as they had left it on Friday. Annie and Daisy sat down at the counter and chatted.

"I don't understand how this burglar got inside the shop," Daisy pondered. "Nothing is disturbed in the shop area, only the office and storage room."

Daisy's statement gave Annie an idea. She jumped up and quickly walked to the storage room. Daisy followed quietly. Once inside the room, Annie began looking at the ceiling for any sign of entry through the ceiling tiles. Was the burglar able to gain access to the shop through a concealed opening? She carefully walked through the room and around the shelving units. Daisy was close behind her, not quite sure why they were looking up. Both were mesmerized as they walked slowly through the area.

Annie stopped suddenly as something caught her eye. Daisy, looking up at the ceiling, collided into Annie, pushing Annie into a rack. The items on the rack fell over and Annie struggled to catch them before they fell to the ground. While grabbing the product, Annie could have sworn she heard a noise overhead. She stopped and listened. Daisy did the same, her eyes widening. They heard noises above moving away from the storage room area. Someone was in the crawl space!

Daisy and Annie both jumped as Annie's cell phone rang. It was Donald. Annie answered the phone while swiftly moving out of the storage room pushing Daisy out ahead of her.

"Donald," Annie said nervously. "I think there is someone in the crawl space above my shop. Would you ask Dan to come back here quickly?"

"We will be there in a minute," Donald replied. "Go to the coffee shop where there are other people around. We will meet you there."

Annie ran into the office and grabbed purses for Daisy and herself. The two left the shop and Annie locked the door behind them. They entered Ione's Bakery and Coffee Shop.

"Annie, what happened?" Ione asked as she wiped her hands on her apron. "You look as if you've seen a ghost!"

"Not a ghost, Ione," Annie commented. "A burglar was in my shop."

"Just now? Did you call Dan?"

"He and Donald are on their way," Annie said. Then she added, "I think I need coffee to calm my nerves."

"Coming right up," Ione grabbed a cup and filled it with coffee. She handed the steaming cup to Annie. Pulling a waxed paper sheet from a box, she slid open the donut display cabinet and grabbed a chocolate croissant. She handed it to Annie.

"You know me all too well, Ione."

"On the house, Annie," Ione said. "If it wasn't for you, there would be no excitement around here. Daisy, what can I get for you?"

Daisy gave her order and after being served the two women walked to a table. Dan and Donald entered the bakery just as Annie sat down.

"Do not ask me to go back inside the shop until I have had my coffee and chocolate," Annie ordered Dan.

"Just give me the key. Donald and I can check out the place. Officer Barrel is on her way back."

Annie proceeded to tell the men the details of what transpired while she and Daisy were cleaning up the back room, and the feeling she got when she walked into the office. She relayed hearing noises in the crawl space above the storage room. She spoke of the area where she suspected the burglar may have gained entry.

As Donald and Dan left the shop, Annie realized Ione was sitting next to her soaking in all of the information Annie had given to Dan. This was sure to be today's main gossip. Annie stared at Ione, Ione caught her eye and began wiping the table with a wet cloth. She stood and moved to another table. Making a few swipes with her cloth, without a word, she moved on to the front counter.

Donald sent a text to Annie to come over to the shop. Annie and Daisy quickly finished their pastries and took their coffees with them. As Annie arrived at the shop, she found Donald using a small boxy gadget with an antenna. He scanned the area of the office. The gadget made a lot of noise when Donald guided it next to a crafting book on the bookcase across the room from her safe cabinet.

"Don't touch it," Donald warned. "Let Dan take a look first."

Annie nodded, trying to get a closer look without touching the book. It appeared to be a cleverly hidden camera pointing directly at the safe.

"Wait a minute!" Annie said in an irritated tone of voice. "This is one of my crafting books, one of my expensive crafting books!" Now Annie was mad. This guy had to be caught and soon.

Daisy escorted Officer Barrel to the storage room where Dan was investigating. Donald and Annie joined them. Donald pulled Daisy aside and asked if she would keep an eye on the office. He left the office door open and asked her to stay at the counter. She agreed and immediately left to stand guard over the office.

Dan found a ladder in a closet of the storage room. He took it over to where Annie said she suspected the burglar entered the room. Officer Barrel handed a flashlight to Dan, who cautiously lifted the ceiling tile. As Dan raised the tile up about six inches, it was suddenly pushed back down, causing Dan to wobble on the ladder. Officer Barrel quickly placed both hands on Dan's butt, attempting to keep him from falling. Realizing where her hands were, she immediately removed her hands. She pushed past Dan on the ladder, and hurried to push open the tile with surprising force. Dan tossed the light up to her and she was into the crawl space in seconds.

"I see him!" Officer Barrel shouted down to Dan.

"Why didn't you let me go ahead of you?" Dan asked Officer Barrel as he hurried up the ladder and lifted himself into the crawl space.

"Because I have a vest on and you don't."

Annie heard a blood curdling scream from Daisy. Donald and Annie raced out of the storage room in time to see Lawrence turn the lock on the shop door and exit. He ran down the boardwalk. Donald and Annie ran after him. They neared the end of the boardwalk and they heard an engine engage. Squealing car tires indicated Lawrence was leaving the area.

Lynda Wooster cautiously peered out the door of her upholstery shop when Donald and Annie were running back to Ocean Loads of Paper.

"What is going on out here?" Lynda asked, wiping her hands on a paint rag. Lynda was in her shop early to finish a painting project on a piece of old furniture.

Annie stopped running and turned back to Lynda. Donald ran inside the store to check on Detective Dan Surely and Officer Barrel.

"Hi, Lynda," Annie said attempting to catch her breath. "Did you happen to see a guy running past here?"

"I heard a lot of commotion coming from the crawl space above. Then I heard a scream. I was walking to the door when I think I saw

Lawrence from Spencer's Gallery running by my shop. What's going on? Should I be worried?"

"It was Lawrence. He broke into my shop and my safe!"

"Oh, my goodness!"

"Keep your doors locked for now. Detective Surely will want to talk to you about what you saw." Annie said as she turned to walk back to her shop.

CHAPTER 17

Sunday Evening

I t was late in the afternoon when Donald and Annie finished securing and cleaning the shop. Donald enlisted the help of Fred, from the hardware store, to secure the opening in the wall between Annie's shop and Hermitage Furniture through the crawl space. Apparently, Lawrence had been in both shops, lowering himself through access panels in the ceiling. The question remained: How did Lawrence gain entrance into the shops?

Dan Surely left hours ago after locating evidence and speaking to local shop-owners. Officer Barrel left shortly after Lawrence's exit to take a reported burglary call at the senior living apartment complex. Fred left once he completed his repair work. Annie asked Daisy to go home earlier in the day. The shop was quiet now.

Sitting in her desk chair, Annie gazed at the bookcase which had concealed the camera in one of her craft books. She was still irritated that Lawrence used one of her crafting books to disguise a camera. It was one of her favorite books. Now it was ruined and she was not sure whether she would be able to find another one. She would check online to look for a replacement book, she thought to herself.

Annie knelt down to her safe and punched in the code. She turned the handle and pulled out the cash register tray. Every bit of money was taken, even the coins. Annie shook her head. She made a mental note to go to the bank the next morning to restock the starter cash for the register.

As she set the register tray down, Annie looked back inside the safe for Saturday's sales receipts and money, not expecting to find it. Papers inside the safe had been rifled through. As she pulled out the papers, she noticed the handmade pouch she kept in the safe for cash and credit card receipts. She grabbed the bag feeling the cash and papers inside. She opened it to find everything intact. Lawrence had taken the empty bank bag, but not the decorative pouch she made for the purpose of storing cash and receipts to record for a later bank deposit. Annie was elated.

Donald entered the office, "You will want to change the passcode on the safe before we leave."

"Oh, good idea. I should have thought of that earlier," Annie said, digging through her desk drawer to locate the instructions for changing the safe's code. The instructions were filed under a secret code-named file. She kept the actual password in a secured application on her phone. Annie read the instructions and entered a new passcode. She tested it and then closed the safe. After entering the code and re-opening the safe, Annie put the instructions back in her drawer. Closing the safe, she grabbed her purse and left the office with Donald.

♦ ♦ ♦

Donald and Annie returned home and after a quick snack, they helped Stella, Marie, and Lizzy finish moving things to Stella's new apartment over the garage. Annie told Stella and Lizzy about the burglary in her shop. They were both shocked and surprised by the events Annie relayed to them.

"Annie it might be time to get an extensive alarm system in place in the shop," Lizzy said. She was concerned about the safety of any one of them being at the shop alone.

"I agree," Annie said. She would talk to Donald tonight and see what type of alarm they could set up soon.

By six o'clock, Stella announced she was stopping the work on her apartment to start dinner. Annie and Lizzy offered to help, but Stella told them to take a break and relax outside on the patio. Donald excused himself and went to his office. Marie said she would make iced tea for everyone. The sky was partly cloudy and there was a cool breeze coming off the ocean. It felt chilly, so Annie got sweatshirts for her and Lizzy.

Marie came out with a tray of iced tea and cut up vegetables with a salad dressing dip. She set the tray on a glass table in front of Annie and Lizzy. Annie and Lizzy leaned forward and began eating from the plate of vegetables.

"Marie, I thought you might be interested in knowing that William is working at Ione's Bakery and Coffee Shop now," Annie said dipping a sliced carrot into the dip. She looked up at Marie. Marie was blushing.

"Do I still have a job at your shop?" Marie said, dipping a carrot in the bowl of dressing mix on the tray.

"Of course, you do," Annie and Lizzy said in unison. They looked at each other and laughed. Marie smiled.

In a moment of silence, footsteps were heard approaching the backyard. All three ladies listened. As the footsteps drew nearer, Annie heard the familiar voices of the four women living across the street. LaVerne, Lorraine, Millie, and Elsie appeared in view.

"There they are, Millie," LaVerne announced. "I knew they would be in the backyard and it appears they are not busy at all."

"I still say we should have knocked on the front door," Millie stated politely.

"Good evening, ladies," Annie stood and signaled for the women to be seated.

"Would you like some iced tea?" Marie asked.

"You are such a dear, Marie," Elsie answered. "Yes, but I would like my tea hot with a dash of milk. No sugar. Thank you. You're a love."

"Hot tea for me too!" LaVerne spoke up. "I don't want anything in my tea."

"I will have the same as LaVerne," added Lorraine.

"It is beginning to get chilly outside," Millie said. "I believe hot tea would be nice, with sugar. Thank you."

Marie left the patio and entered the house. While she was gone, LaVerne leaned forward toward Annie and Lizzy. She looked at the other seniors and signaled they all do the same. Annie and Lizzy leaned in as well.

"We heard there was a bit of trouble in your shop this afternoon," LaVerne started. "We also know it was Lawrence. We saw him today around the senior apartments."

"We tried to follow him, but he is too fast for us," Lorraine injected.

"Elsie took pictures," Millie stated.

"You have photos of him around the senior apartments?" Annie asked Elsie. "Can I see them?"

"You can have them, just as soon as I get them back from the photo developer."

Annie tried not to look disappointed, but wanted so desperately to remind the ladies they had a camera on their cell phones. She held her tongue. Glancing at Lizzy, Annie knew she was thinking the same thing.

"Someone tried to break into Bart Jones' apartment today," LaVerne said. "We suspected it might have been Lawrence. That is why Elsie took pictures. We saw him nearby the apartment complex."

"Lawrence has to be staying somewhere, but where?" Annie said, thinking out loud. She noticed everyone staring at her. "Has anyone noticed what car he drives?"

"I think he steals cars," Elsie said.

"But Dan would have said something about car thefts," Lizzy spoke up. "It is a small town after all. Car theft would be a big thing."

"And we would have heard about it," Lorraine injected.

"He is either getting around on foot or someone is driving him around," LaVerne said.

All were quiet for a moment. Marie broke the silence as she exited the house with the screen door slamming behind her. Everyone sat up straight as Marie set a tray of hot teas, a small pitcher of milk, a bowl of sugar, and spoons on the table.

"Mom said you can add your own sugar and milk as you want it," said Marie as she pointed to the milk and sugar. She returned to the house.

Annie smiled at the sweet way Marie referred to Stella as 'Mom'. Her mind wandered to her new family. Dan was back in town, Marie was now like a sister to her, and Stella seemed the happiest Annie had seen her in a long time. Annie was jolted from her daydream suddenly.

"LaVerne!" Elsie shouted. "I thought you didn't want anything in your tea?"

"I don't," LaVerne stated. She opened the flask she took from her pocketbook and poured a dash of golden liquid into her hot tea. "I am just toning down the bitterness of the tea." She took a spoon from the tray and stirred the steaming fluid. She set the spoon down on the tea cup saucer.

Lorraine pointed to her tea, "Add a bit to mine while you are at it." LaVerne did as instructed. She tightened the lid and stuffed the silver flask into her purse.

"Well, ladies," LaVerne began. "We know who the troublemaker is around here. Now we need to concentrate on helping Detective Surely find him. Annie, we will work on a plan and let you know."

The group sipped their tea and discussed setting up a town network of people to keep an eye out for any 'Lawrence' activity. Annie and Lizzy were fascinated by being involved in the Senior Sleuths discussion.

The kitchen door opened to the patio and Dan stepped out carrying a beer. He stopped short when he saw the senior ladies. He quickly turned and began to walk back into the house.

"Oh, Detective Surely," Lorraine shouted in a high-pitched voice. "Please come join Annie and Lizzy. We were just leaving."

Dan stopped, turned and eyed the ladies suspiciously.

The four women gently placed their tea cups on the tray and stood.

"Annie, Lizzy," LaVerne spoke. "We thank you for your hospitality." She leaned close to Annie, "Let's just keep this discussion to our little group, shall we?"

"Yes, I agree," Annie said as she and Lizzy stood.

Dan walked over to Lizzy and kissed her on the cheek. He nodded as the ladies left the patio and walked down the driveway. When he was certain they were out of earshot, he growled, "What are they up to?"

"They came for tea," Annie said walking to the back door. She opened the door and entered, leaving Lizzy alone with Dan.

The aroma of garlic, onion, and Italian seasonings filled the air. Stella was adding tomato sauce to the meat mixture. Spaghetti, Annie thought. Her favorite.

"Can I help?" Annie asked Stella.

"The bread is already sliced. Check the oven to see if it is up to temperature."

Annie did as her mother instructed. She could smell the scent of seasoned butter and parmesan cheese as she placed the foil wrapped bread on the oven rack and closed the door.

♦ ♦ ♦

Annie hung the dish towel up to dry. It was eight o'clock in the evening. Dan and Lizzy left to go home across the street. Stella was tired from moving her belongings to the apartment and now she had the task of unpacking. Marie wanted to go to her room early so she could watch a show on television. That left Annie and Donald alone.

"Looks like we have the evening to ourselves tonight," Donald said as he leaned against the kitchen counter. "Is there anything special you would like to do?"

Annie thought for a moment. Was there anything she would like to do with a spare couple of hours? And then it dawned on her. The painting. She wanted to view the painting again. There was something about the painting that was important to Lawrence. The painting had to hold a secret that was far more valuable than the bearer stock hidden behind the canvas.

"Donald," Annie said suddenly. "I want to go downstairs and take another look at that painting."

"I would love to get you downstairs again," Donald said, as he moved toward Annie and wrapped his arms around her waist. Donald began lightly kissing Annie's neck.

Annie was getting all tingly inside. She snuggled in closer to his chest. He was warm and she could still smell the intoxicating scent of the masculine shampoo in his hair. She breathed in deeply and exhaled slowly.

Donald took Annie's hand and guided her to the office. He locked the door behind them, and slid the bookcase to the side, revealing the lit stairway down to the hidden room. When they reached the bottom of the stairs, Donald placed his hand on the switch to dim the lights. He walked over to a side table and turned on a small stereo unit. It played soft romantic music. Annie took Donald's hand and walked to the sofa where they embraced in a long passionate kiss.

♦ ♦ ♦

It was after eleven in the evening when Donald woke Annie. "Hey," he said in a whisper voice. "It is getting late. We should go upstairs to bed."

Annie was trying to wrap her mind around where she was as she slowly woke up. She was snuggled up against Donald's chest. It was so warm and comfortable. She did not want to move.

"Oh!" Annie exclaimed as she sat upright. "We forgot about the painting."

"We can take a look at the painting tomorrow after work. Let's go to bed." Donald stood up and held out a hand for Annie. She took his hand and lifted herself off the sofa. After straightening the room, the two climbed the stairs to the office above. Donald slid the bookcase back into place. They walked to the office door and Donald unlocked the door, stopping to give Annie a kiss. Annie wrapped her arms around Donald and kissed him back.

CHAPTER 18

Monday Morning

Early morning fog drifted in across the ocean. Annie sat on her bedroom sofa with her hands wrapped around a hot cup of coffee. The air seemed chilled, even as she sat in a warm, cozy room. A slight breeze moved the branches on a tree in the front yard. Annie's thoughts were of the painting. There had to be a message or something in the painting itself. She was eager to check it out, but Donald wanted to wait until later this evening.

Turning her thoughts to work, Annie placed her coffee cup on the side table and picked up a small yellow pad and pencil. She began making a To Do list. It was about time to get her mental To Do list in writing. She was marrying Donald in less than a week. Even though it was only a small group of people attending the wedding outside in the backyard, Annie wanted to make sure everything was in order.

As she stared at her yellow pad, Annie realized she had completed the most important task, which was buying her dress. She and Donald opted for plain gold bands as their wedding rings. Hers would be welded to her engagement ring at a later date. The flowers were being designed by Donald's mother, and Lizzy made arrangements for Patty to work with Myra on the floral designs at the local floral shop, Bonnie's Belle-Flower Florist. Ione was making the cake. Annie's mother sent out a few invitations. Donald and Annie wanted a simple ceremony. She did not want to make a show out of the wedding.

Annie placed the yellow pad and pencil on the side table and picked up her coffee cup. Taking a sip, she stood and walked around the corner to the bedroom. There lay Donald, sound asleep. His alarm would wake him in less than thirty minutes. Annie quietly left through the bedroom door, closing it behind her. As Annie was about to walk down stairs, she heard soft scratching at the bedroom door. She turned and quietly opened the door for Laddie, who exited quickly and ran down the stairs and waited for Annie at the back door. Callie appeared at her kitty door in the hallway and followed Annie down to the kitchen, expecting canned food.

After taking care of Laddie and Callie, Annie made herself another cup of coffee. She stood in the kitchen looking out into the backyard. Her mother's apartment was dark. It was quiet in the house. Marie was still sleeping upstairs in her room. This was a good time to go check out the painting, Annie thought to herself. It would not take long and in doing so now she could concentrate on projects at the shop without thinking about Meredith's Garden all day.

Setting her cup down on the kitchen counter, Annie made her way to the office. She decided not to lock the door, but after sliding the bookcase open, she slid it closed behind her. Descending the stairs, Annie stopped at the large painting on the wall and pulled it open toward her. She punched in the safe code and turned the wheel to open the door into the vault.

Lights automatically illuminated the vault room as Annie entered through the doorway. She stopped to once again ponder the vast wealth that appeared before her. Sculptures, paintings, safes, file cabinets, bookcases, and a counter that ran the width of the room. The long counter had a white Formica top. Below were sets of wide shallow drawers. The type one would see in an engineering office. Annie was wondering why she had not noticed the counter with all the drawers before. She continued to walk along the counter toward the other side of the room. Not all the drawers were the same size. Some were narrower and deeper in size.

Annie spun around and walked back to the wide, shallow drawers. She was too curious not to take a quick peek. It all belonged to her anyway. What harm would it be to look? She knew she would eventually need to spend time in the vault and inventory everything it contained. As organized as Helen was, Annie pondered the idea that there may already be a complete listing of items in this room.

With both hands outstretched, Annie paused a moment. What was she expecting to happen? Nothing was going to jump out at her. She shook her head and took hold of the drawer handle and pulled. It was locked. She tried another. Again, the drawer was locked. She looked at the drawer for a key hole. There was none. Just handles. How was the drawer locking? She grabbed the handles and pulled with all her might. She lost her grip and fell backwards onto the floor. The drawer did not budge.

Realizing she was wasting time, Annie decided to tell Donald about the drawers and let him figure out how to open them. She was about to lift herself off the floor, when she looked up and noticed a button hidden underneath the overhang of the counter. It could not be that simple, she thought to herself. She stood and moved her hand along the underside of the counter until she reached the button. She pressed firmly on the button and heard a mechanical click.

Placing her hands on the top-drawer handles, she again pulled on the drawer. To her surprise the drawer opened. Inside were black velvet covered lids with a ribbon-like tab used to raise the lid. She reached out to one of the tabs and lifted up the lid. Annie gasped and staggered backward. She stood open-mouthed at the sight of sparkling diamonds carefully displayed in a black velvet tray. She had only opened one of six sections of one drawer. Not wanting to disturb anything, she quickly closed the lid and closed the drawer. She heard a mechanical click and hoped that the unit had locked itself.

Annie felt being in the vault seemed like she was imposing on Robert and Helen's personal property. She had to keep reminding herself that Helen had left the property to her. What was Helen thinking Annie would do with all this wealth? Annie was so happy to not have to deal with this dilemma by herself. She had Donald to help her. Yes, Donald was a blood relative after all. Maybe he could find out the story behind the vault and the secret room under the cottage.

Moving away from the counter of drawers, Annie walked over to the painting, which was hanging on a display in the center of the vault with other paintings. She took a quick look at her watch and decided she still had time before Lizzy would be ready to walk to the shop.

Annie moved in closer to the painting. Beginning at the top, she carefully scanned the surface, following the brush strokes and trying not to look at the painting as a whole. She reached an iron bench in the garden with a wooden seat and intricate scroll work. The pattern was almost unnoticeable. She looked away and then raised her eyes to gaze upon the bench.

"Numbers," Annie said out loud to no one in particular. Numbers were carefully painted into the scroll work as highlights. She never noticed the characters before. She was not sure anyone would notice the intricate scroll unless they were looking for actual numbers. Is this why Lawrence wanted the painting? Of course, it was! The numbers had an importance. Lawrence was willing to kidnap, maybe even kill for those numbers!

Annie stood still for a long moment. She was on to something so important that she needed Donald's advice. Maybe even Dan's advice. She needed to tell one of them and soon. She looked around the room for something to write down the numbers. Not finding any scraps of paper, she made a mental note to bring a pad and pen downstairs later.

As she exited the vault room door, Annie turned and stopped to take a look at the drawer with a tray containing loose diamonds. "Wait until Donald sees this," Annie said aloud. She left the room, closed the vault door and secured the painting hiding the vault door back in place. Climbing the stairs, she pulled the bookcase open just in time to see Donald enter the office.

"There you are," Donald said as he walked through the office doorway carrying a cup of coffee. Laddie followed close behind him and walked up to Annie. He used his nose to lift her hand and she scratched him behind the ears.

"Donald," Annie said with excitement in her voice. "Come downstairs with me. I need your help with something."

"Will it take long? I have a meeting in fifteen minutes."

"I will be quick."

"I like quickies!"

"Oh, Donald," Annie said. She pulled open a drawer on the desk that stood in front of the bookcase. Locating a small notepad and pen, she closed the drawer and headed down the stairs.

Donald set his coffee cup on his desk and locked the office door. He followed Annie downstairs and pulled open the large painting. Annie entered the code into the safe keypad. Donald turned the handle and swung the door open. Lights again illuminated the vault room. Annie dashed over to the painting.

"Take a look at the wood and iron bench sitting in the garden of this painting," Annie said, pointing to the area of the artwork. "There are numbers painted in the scroll work."

Donald bent over to look more closely at the painting. After taking a few moments of inspection, he said, "I can see the numbers now. How in the world did you find them?"

"I was scanning the painting up close. I had no idea what I was looking for, but then I saw the numbers in the bench scroll work."

"I am amazed none of us saw this earlier when we were looking at the painting."

"What do you think the numbers mean?" Annie asked Donald.

"Hard to say at the moment. Let's write the numbers down and I will do some research."

Annie handed the pad and pen to Donald. She read off the numbers. They switched places and he read the numbers off to her. They wanted to double-check that the numbers were written down accurately.

"My meeting is going to start in five minutes," Donald said as he tore the piece of paper from the notepad and handed the notepad to Annie.

"There is one more thing to show you," Annie told Donald. "I found a tray of diamonds in that top drawer in the counter."

Donald moved over to the counter and attempted to pull the drawer open. Annie stepped to the side of Donald and pushed the hidden button. A mechanical click was heard and Annie signaled to Donald to try the drawer again. This time the drawer slid open with ease.

Annie pulled the ribbon tab on the black velvet lid. Diamonds sparkled in front of them. There were probably a dozen diamonds at first glance.

"Wow!" It was the only thing Donald could say at the moment. He closed the lid and pulled open the section next to the diamonds.

"Rubies?" Annie said in surprise. "I was expecting more diamonds." Annie opened the third section in the front row. There before them were sapphires, a deep dark blue stone.

"Wow!" Donald again said.

"Was your uncle a precious stone collector?"

"I am beginning to believe I hardly knew my uncle and aunt."

Donald looked at his watch and closed the lids of the stones and then slid the drawer closed. Again, the sound of a mechanical click was heard, indicating that the locking mechanism was in place.

After securing the vault room, Annie and Donald returned to the office. Donald logged into his meeting on the computer and Annie left to get ready for work. Neither of them said a word to each other. They were both in deep thought over what they had found... another, in the long list of mysterious finds in the lives of Robert and Helen Harper.

♦ ♦ ♦

Annie unlocked the shop door and walked inside. She stopped suddenly, listening for sounds of a possible intruder. She was still on edge about Lawrence invading her shop the previous day.

"Annie!" Lizzy exclaimed as she abruptly stopped behind Annie. Lizzy was attempting to keep the coffee cups upright.

"Sorry!" Annie said as she turned and took her coffee from Lizzy's hand.

Annie entered the shop and set her purse and coffee on the counter. Lizzy and Annie walked through the shop together, clutching their cell phones in case they needed to call for help.

"Oh, this is silly, Lizzy," Annie remarked as she returned to the front counter of the shop. "Donald made sure the place was secure."

Lizzy laughed and pulled a donut from the bakery bag on the counter.

While they were discussing the upcoming meeting with the tenants of the two buildings, which Lizzy had set up days ago, Daisy knocked on the ocean side door of the shop. Lizzy jumped up to unlock the door. Daisy entered and hesitantly looked around.

"We checked it out already," Annie said with a reassuring smile.

"Have you heard whether Lawrence has been caught?" Daisy asked.

"Not yet, but we are keeping an eye out," Annie replied. "And with the Silver Sleuths investigating, he should be caught soon!"

"Don't say that around Dan, Annie," Lizzy cautioned. "You know how he feels about those sweet ladies interfering with his work."

♦ ♦ ♦

Two o'clock rolled in slowly for Annie. She wanted to go home and research the numbers she and Donald copied down from the painting. At some point she would need to talk to Janette and find out what she knew about the numbers. Keeping this information from Lizzy was a struggle for Annie. She told Lizzy everything. But it was important to keep this information between Donald and her for now.

A small group of tourists arrived for a pre-scheduled class on box making. Today's design was a small pizza-style box with a decorative paper rose adorning the top. Annie had after-dinner mints to add in the finished box. The classroom was set up and ready to begin instruction, and Daisy was excited to be today's instructor. Annie was so pleased to find Daisy taking on prepping and teaching the classes. Marie, who arrived at noon, was also available to help with the class.

The weather outside was misty and gray. Annie suspected it was keeping tourists from spending time on the boardwalk and visiting the shops. She was contemplating closing her shop after the class ended. Annie was sitting at the counter thumbing through email when her cell phone rang. Startling her, she nearly dropped the device as her hands attempted to get a firm grip on the phone. Looking at the caller ID, Annie noticed it was Donald. The phone had rung for the third time before she was able to answer it.

"Hi, Donald," Annie said, nearly laughing at her antics of juggling the phone.

"Hi, Annie," Donald paused. "I may have figured out a possible reason for the numbers, but I don't want to discuss it over the phone. What do you think of having a dinner party this evening with the usual people and inviting Janette, Suzette, Jacquie and John?"

Annie figured the 'usual people' meant Dan, Lizzy, Stella, and Marie. With Donald and herself, the count was now up to ten people.

"I think I should order Chinese take out for dinner," Annie stated. "It will feed ten people easily."

"Good idea. You order the food and I will drive over and pick up you, Marie, and Lizzy. What time would you like me to leave here?"

"How about five o'clock?"

"Perfect." Donald disconnected.

Annie turned to Lizzy, who had just settled on a stool at the counter. She was logging into her computer laptop and checking inventory on the store spread sheet she designed.

"Donald is picking us all up at five o'clock today," Annie began. "We are having Chinese take out for dinner. I thought we could invite Janette, Suzette, Jacquie and John."

"A party? I'm in. Should I send a text to Dan?'

"Yes, and I will contact the others." Annie picked up her cell and began texting her mother. A minute later Annie's cell phone rang. It was Stella.

"Can I do anything to help with dinner?"

"I was thinking of keeping it all very informal," Annie explained to her mother. "How about paper plates and cups?"

"Easy clean-up for us. See you later." Stella hung up.

Annie contacted Janette, who accepted Annie's invitation and offered to ask Suzette, Jacquie and John.

"Annie," Janette started, "Have you heard anything about Lawrence or his whereabouts?"

"I will explain all of that this evening," Annie said. "Donald and I have some questions about your painting."

"I am happy to talk about the painting," Janette said. "I will see you this evening."

With the evening plans arranged, Annie turned her attention to the classroom activities. Everyone seemed to be enjoying their crafting experience. Annie heard lots of chatter and laughter. Daisy and Marie seemed to be having a good time. Straightening up a few shelves, Annie returned to the counter to help a customer. The remainder of time at the shop seemed to fly by, when at 5:00 PM Donald walked into the shop. Annie had ordered the food for dinner just before he arrived.

"Taxi's here!" announced Donald. "I am parked in front of the Chinese restaurant. Did you order the food yet?"

"Ordered and ready to pick up in a few minutes." Annie jumped up from the counter to help lock up the store.

Lizzy was already in the office locking up the day's receipts and cash. With purses and bags in hand, Lizzy turned the light off in the office and closed the door behind her. She handed Annie her purse.

Marie and Daisy were standing by the front door talking when Annie, Lizzy, and Donald approached. Annie was relieved when Daisy offered that she had plans with her friends tonight. Annie would have loved to have Daisy come for dinner, but since the group was discussing the painting, Annie felt the discussion should be kept to the group for now. The fewer people who knew about the situation the better. As the last person out the door, Annie locked the door and the group, minus Daisy, walked over to the Chinese restaurant to pick up dinner.

CHAPTER 19

Monday Evening

The weather was a bit cool this evening, so Stella suggested setting up food in the dining room. Annie quickly agreed, thinking that she did not want anyone to overhear the group's conversation about the painting. Annie planned to ask some important questions as to why the numbers were painted into the artwork. What did the numbers represent? What did Janette know about the numbers?

Donald set bags of food containers on the dining table. As Annie opened and set the boxes of food in the center of the table, Stella placed napkins out in several stacks for people to help themselves. Marie brought out chopsticks and plastic forks.

"I set up the office to view the painting photos," Donald said, taking out a box of fried rice from one of the bags. He handed it to Annie. "I connected the laptop to the television. That will enlarge the photos, making it easier to see the numbers in the scroll work."

"I never thought of that," Annie said, scanning the table to make sure everything was set out. She turned to Donald, "The office is a more private area. Let's take Laddie with us. He will alert you if anybody is trying to listen at the windows."

"We should keep the dinner conversation light for now."

"I agree."

All heads turned to the front door as Dan entered the house. He had used his key to gain entry. Annie scowled at Dan for a moment, letting him know she was a bit irritated for his entering without knocking first.

"I thought you might be in the backyard, so I let myself in with the key you gave me," Dan said sheepishly. He knew from the look on Annie's face what she was trying to convey to him.

"Take your jacket off and come inside," Donald spoke up walking into the foyer.

Dan looked into the dining room and said, "Glad to see we are eating inside. It is getting chilly out there."

Dan walked into the kitchen. Lizzy was setting up drinks for everyone. Dan leaned in to give her a kiss. Lizzy smiled at Dan.

"How was work today?" Lizzy asked as she handed Dan a cold bottle of beer.

"No sign of Lawrence if that is what you are hinting at."

Lizzy offered a glass to Dan. He waved it off.

The front door bell chimed and Annie walked up to the door and peered through the peep hole. She turned and smirked at Dan as if to say, 'Notice how one rings a door bell before entering someone's home'. Dan, noticing the smirk, attempted to ignore her.

Annie welcomed Suzette, Jacquie, and John into the house. Janette was on the front porch ending a phone call. She quickly walked up to the front door and entered the house.

"You have no idea how much I am looking forward to eating Chinese food tonight," John said as he handed his coat to Jacquie, who was hanging hers on a coat rack near the front door.

"Food is on the table," Stella announced. "Let's eat while it is still hot."

As the group was settling in around the large dining room table, Janette pulled Annie aside.

"Did you see the email I forwarded from my mom with the photo of the wedding certificate of my grandmother and Walter Smith?" Janette said showing the photo to Annie. "I sent it to you earlier. Would you be able to print it out so we can show it to everyone here? Maybe someone will see something I have overlooked."

Annie looked at her phone and noticed that she indeed had a new email. When she opened it up and saw the photo of the wedding certificate, she excused herself and walked into the office to make several enlarged copies of the photo.

Returning with the photos, Annie handed one to Dan and one to her mother. She sat down next to Lizzy, who was leaning in to look at the print in Annie's hand. Everyone had dished out food on their plates and were eating.

"Something does not look right," Stella remarked as she put her fork down and held the photo with both hands. "Would you mind if I kept this until tomorrow?"

"No, not at all," Annie said.

"I want to contact the county office in California and verify this information."

"What are you saying?" Janette asked. "Are you thinking it may not be a real wedding certificate?"

Everyone stopped eating, waiting for Stella's answer. Dan expressed a knowing smile and took a drink from his beer bottle.

"That is exactly what I am saying," Stella replied. "The seal on the paper is not right. Something is off."

Donald pulled out his phone and began searching for the State Seal of California. Annie set the paper down in front of Donald. He zoomed in on the area of the state seal in the graphic on his phone.

"She's correct," Donald pointed out to Annie. "This state seal has the wrong date on it."

"And the county seal looks as if someone cut it out of another document and copied it on a poor-quality copying machine," Annie pointed to the county seal. "See where the image is cut and notice the jagged edges around the image."

"Good catch, Donald," Dan said stuffing an eggroll in his mouth. He chewed and swallowed and then said, "Nice job, Mom. You should have been a detective. I saw the incorrect date immediately."

"What about me?" Annie asked Dan. "I noticed the copy of the county seal."

Dan rolled his eyes at Annie. He picked up his chopsticks and began lifting food to his mouth.

Lizzy nudged Dan and then said, "Annie caught the forged emblem, because she is a superb crafter. Crafters notice detail."

"Annie, you did notice an important detail," Stella said. "I must admit I focused on the state seal as being suspicious, because of how quickly Walter and Meredith married in secrecy. After death, Walter disappeared suddenly before Janette and her mother arrived at her grandmother's home."

"He also had Meredith's body cremated before anyone could object," Dan announced between bites of beef and broccoli. "He may have had something to do with her death."

"The police report said it was a heart attack," Suzette joined into the conversation.

"Appearances may be deceiving," Jacquie said.

John nodded in agreement.

The room was quiet until Marie broke the silence, "I think she was murdered."

Again, the room fell silent. Annie could see Janette's eyes appear watery. Janette was attempting to keep her head down. She pushed the food around on her plate, but was not eating.

"Let's not talk about this anymore," Stella said.

"After everyone is finished, we will go into the office and take a look at the photos Donald enlarged of the painting," Annie said, attempting to change the subject. "I have a theory about the numbers."

Annie's announcement sparked new interest in Janette as she finished eating the food on her plate. "I am sorry if I still get emotional over my grandmother's death," Janette stated. "I can except her poor health, but I still have a hard time accepting she was happily married to this Walter fellow."

"Once a spouse has passed away, the emptiness is deep and sometimes unbearable," Stella interjected. "Having someone around as a companion helps ease the loneliness."

Annie noticed Dan had stopped eating and was looking down at his plate. She assumed he was concerned if his leaving to work in Portland, after Richard Weston's death, had an effect on Stella. She was, after all, the mother who raised him. Dan left for Portland so soon after Richard's death. Annie was in college at the time. He is back now, Annie thought, and she did notice her mother was much happier now that Dan was back.

Across the table, Annie saw John take Jacquie's hand, which was resting on the table between their plates. They were such a cute couple. It was obvious to Annie that the two were very much in love. Annie hoped that she and Donald were like that twenty years from now.

Donald sat in quiet contemplation. Was he thinking about his Aunt Helen, Annie wondered? Now that he knew Helen was his biological mother, was he wondering if he should have kept in better contact with her? It was difficult to second guess what people thought. Just because she did not keep in constant contact with friends and family was not an indication that she thought any less of them. Annie was thankful she had her mother and Marie close by. Now she had Donald. Even Dan was back in town. She felt blessed to have her family close.

"If everyone is finished eating," Annie began, "we can go to the office and begin." Annie stood from the table and began clearing the food containers. As people stood, they began to help clear the table. Since there was very little food left, Annie tossed the containers in the garbage and Marie helped wash down the table.

While people filed into the office, Annie noticed Marie standing in the kitchen. , She watched the group heading to the office. Annie stopped and walked back to the kitchen.

"Are you coming, Marie?" Annie asked.

"I was not sure you wanted me to be there," Marie replied.

"Of course, I want you there," Annie said. "You may see something we are missing."

Marie smiled and followed Annie to the office, where they found chairs among the group already seated. Donald dimmed the lights and began the introduction of the photos. He explained that the intricate scroll of the bench in Meredith's Garden appeared to be a number. The first photo that appeared on the screen was of the entire painting. Donald pointed out the bench in the painting.

"It's such a beautiful painting, Janette," Jacquie announced sitting up in her chair and looking at the photo of the painting on the large television screen. "I was so captivated by the colors when I first saw it in the shop."

"It is almost as if you could walk through the garden and smell the flowers," John added.

"Don't get your nose too close, John," Donald laughed. "There's a bee on that flower."

There was a rumble of chuckles throughout the room.

"I am not seeing anything unusual about the painting," Suzette commented, squinting at the screen and trying to find something that looked suspicious.

"Let me go to the enlargement of the bench," Donald said, switching to the next photo.

There was a gush of excitement from the group as the next photo appeared on the screen. It was of the intricate scroll work on the bench. There were definitely numbers noticeable.

"I never painted those numbers on the bench," Janette proclaimed. "How did they get there? Who altered my painting?"

"The question is 'why' did someone alter the painting?" John spoke up.

"Does the backyard look like this now?" Dan asked Janette.

"No," Janette responded. "It looks a bit different now. Flowers come and go, trees grow, pathways change, that sort of thing."

Minutes ticked by as the group pondered the meaning of the numbers. Donald set up a white board near the group and the numbers were copied down. Various ideas were brought up, but none seemed to make sense. What was the reason for the numbers?

"I do believe the numbers are of importance," Annie spoke up.

"Like a treasure map," Marie injected.

"Or a combination to a safe," Lizzy added.

"I have never seen a safe in my grandmother's home," Janette said. "Then again, I have never looked for one."

"The Silver Sleuths believe the numbers are a code of some kind," Annie said, turning to see Dan roll his eyes at her upon the mention of the Silver Sleuths.

♦ ♦ ♦

Not coming up with any solid ideas, Annie's guests decided to call it a night. Suzette wanted to get back to the Bed & Breakfast, as she had an early morning the next day. John and Jacquie said their good nights and grabbed their coats before exiting the house behind Suzette.

Janette held back and pulled Annie aside. She told Annie that she was thinking about making a trip to her grandmother's home in California for a couple of days. She could search the house and see if she could find a safe. Annie asked Janette to stay a while longer and they could talk more.

Dan and Lizzy were the next to leave. Dan had court the next morning and wanted to review his case. Lizzy said goodbye and told Annie that she would walk with her to the shop in the morning.

Stella said goodnight and left out the kitchen door and down the pathway to her apartment above the garage. Donald watched as she entered the apartment and closed the door. Donald then turned the lights off in the backyard. Laddie had just returned from his enclosed dog run outside and was ready for bed. He stood at the bottom of the stairs and looked at Donald.

"Donald," Annie said. "Janette thinks it might be a good idea to fly back to her grandmother's house and try to find a safe or any other reason for the numbers."

"That's a great idea," Donald said. "Let me get my laptop and I will help you make arrangements for a flight out tomorrow morning." Donald walked to the office with Laddie close at his heels.

Marie opened the refrigerator and looked inside. "Mom made chocolate cake with chocolate frosting for dessert," she said pulling the untouched block of chocolate goodness from the shelf.

Annie looked at Janette.

"Well," Janette said, knowing what Annie was going to ask. "Maybe a small slice."

Marie set the cake on the counter and brought out plates and forks. She cut slices from the cake. Annie suggested she cut the slices in half, as Marie was being too generous with the portions.

Donald came back to the kitchen with his laptop and set it on the counter. He spied the chocolate cake. Annie placed the plate of cake in front of him.

"Is there any ice cream?" Donald asked, looking at Annie.

Marie laughed and opened the freezer. She pulled out a container of chocolate ice cream. It was Annie's favorite.

While the ice cream was being dished out, Donald helped Janette book a flight to California. It would leave Portland in the late morning. That would give Janette plenty of time to drive to Portland and return her car to the rental office. Without her knowing, Donald booked Janette in first class and paid for her ticket. She and Annie were deep in conversation, so he did not want to interrupt her. He wrote down the reservation number and printed out her ticket and boarding pass. Janette slipped the papers in her purse and thanked Donald, all while continuing to talk with Annie.

"I will make a complete search of the house," Janette said with an excited tone in her voice. "I can do a live video chat with you and maybe you will see something of interest. It is getting late and I still need to pack."

With that said, Janette thanked Annie and Donald for dinner. She then thanked Marie for dishing up a delicious dessert. Donald waited for Janette to get into her car before closing and locking the door. He turned on the alarm, turned off the lights and followed Annie and Marie to the second floor. Laddie was pushing his way past everyone to reach the top of the stairs first.

♦ ♦ ♦

Annie was brushing her teeth and preparing for bed, all the while thinking about the painting and its meaning. She turned the lights off and crawled into bed. Donald was fast asleep on his side of the bed. Laddie was softly snoring in his bed next to Donald. Callie ate at a private food station near the top of her cat tree, built where Laddie could not bother her or get into her food.

Annie sat up in bed with copies of the photos Donald had printed out. She took a pencil and darkened in the numbers. She was hoping that darkening the numbers would give her an inspiration as to what they meant.

At midnight, Annie turned off the light and fell sleep. As she turned over, the copies fell to the floor. Callie jumped down from her cat tree and stood on the papers. She batted them around before losing interest and walking off.

Fog surrounded Annie as she felt the dampness of the night. A yellowed parchment paper dropped at her feet. She bent down to pick it up. It was old and weathered. There were markings on the paper. She had a difficult time trying to see the markings. It was so foggy. She called out to Donald. He was nowhere to be seen. She looked again at the parchment. Now there appeared to be trees and flowers. What did they mean?

In the distance she could see a pirate ship leaving the area. "Pirates?" Annie questioned. The fog engulfed the pirate ship and it was gone.

"What do pirates have to do with this parchment?" Annie asked herself. She stared at the map. "It's a treasure map!"

CHAPTER 20

Tuesday

At seven o'clock in the morning, Annie was awakened by a heavy cat sitting on her chest. Callie was staring at Annie, willing her to open her eyes. Annie had overslept and Callie was not about to miss her morning canned food.

Annie sat up and was about to get out of bed when she noticed the photos scattered across the floor. She stared at the photos. Suddenly an idea came to her.

"That's it!" Annie said out loud.

"Meow."

"Callie," Annie said as she jumped out of bed. "I think I have figured it out!"

"Meow."

"I need to hurry and get dressed," Annie told Callie. "I hope it is not too early to contact Janette."

"Meow."

Callie took that to mean she was not getting her canned food anytime soon. She got up and walked over to her cat tree by the window. Just as she was about to jump up onto the tree, she turned to see Annie enter the bathroom and close the door. Miffed, Callie hopped up to her feeding station and began to munch on her dry food.

Annie exited the bathroom with a towel over her wet hair and a toothbrush sticking out of her mouth. She walked to the nightstand on her side of the bed. She picked up her cell phone and typed a text to Janette. After hitting the send button, she stood staring at the phone awaiting a response.

Reviewing the message in her head, she wondered if she might have been too cryptic. Was Janette taking so long due to not understanding Annie's text? She reread the message again. No, it was just enough to pique Janette's interest. Still not getting a response,

Annie put her phone down and returned to the bathroom to finish getting dressed.

"Of course," Annie said out loud to herself in the mirror. "Janette is on her way to Portland and can't look at her cell phone while driving. She will see the text later."

♦ ♦ ♦

At eight o'clock, Annie was downstairs in the kitchen making a cup of coffee. While the coffee was brewing, she cleaned Laddie's dishes and filled them with food and water. She did the same for Callie. She tossed a load of clothes in the washing machine and then opened the cupboard door to find she was out of laundry detergent.

Oh, great," Annie said to Callie, who was eating her much loved canned food. "I need to go grocery shopping. I hate grocery shopping. I buy too much junk food." Callie continued to eat without lifting her head to comment.

Donald walked into the kitchen. He handed Annie her coffee and placed his cup under the coffee dispenser. After setting up the coffee and pressing the flashing 'go' button, Donald turned to Annie. She was standing at the kitchen counter with both hands on her coffee cup, soaking in the warmth of the fresh brewed dark liquid.

Donald set his coffee cup down, reached for Annie's cup and placed it on the counter. He then pulled her into his arms and they hugged for a long time. Annie kissed him and then pulled away, taking a sip from her cup of caffeine.

"Sleeping in on purpose today?" Donald asked with a teasing smile on his face.

"Long night of pondering what those numbers mean." Annie again snuggled into Donald's arms.

"Get a room," came a voice from the stairway. Marie walked into the kitchen still dressed in her pajamas and wearing fuzzy pink slippers. Her hair was reaching out in all directions on her head.

"We have a room," Donald said, still holding Annie in his arms.

Annie laughed and pulled away to talk to Marie.

"Are you planning to work at the shop today?"

"Yes."

Hearing her cell phone chime, Annie checked her text messages. Lizzy was outside and ready to walk to the shop.

"Lizzy is ready to walk to the shop," Annie said. "You come when you get ready."

Marie nodded as she was peering into the refrigerator for something to eat.

"Donald," Annie began. "I think I figured out a possible idea for the numbers."

"I am listening."

"I want to contact Janette and have her do some looking around at her grandmother's house first."

"Now I am curious."

"It is a long shot, but what else do we have to go on right now?"

Annie kissed Donald goodbye, grabbed her purse and was out the front door to meet up with Lizzy.

♦ ♦ ♦

Annie spent the better part of the morning preparing a fun box idea for the afternoon class that she had been procrastinating over. It was nearly mid-summer and she needed to come up with some end of summer ideas. Meredith's Garden kept creeping into her thoughts. She had to concentrate to stay focused for the class of paying customers.

Instead of cards, Annie was designing a handmade box for a small gift. She would begin with plain cardstock for the base and then cover the sides with designer paper in coordinating colors. The top of the box would be layered with die cut images and embellished with glitter and sticky-backed pearl bits.

Just as Annie was hoping that Marie would show up in time to help her make enough kits for the class, Marie and Stella walked in the shop.

"Perfect timing!" Annie exclaimed. "I have about twenty kits to make up for the class. Anyone game to help?"

I can help," announced Marie as she pulled up a chair next to Annie in the classroom.

"Count me in," joined Stella.

It took the better part of an hour to finish packing the kits for the class. Annie was covered in glitter, as usual, and glue was sticking her fingers together. She was not sure how the glue even got on her hands, since she was not using glue when preparing the kits. Annie was glad Donald was not there to see her in her current disheveled state. He would certainly have had a good laugh.

No sooner had she finished her thoughts when Donald walked in with his mother, Patty. He stopped abruptly upon seeing Annie covered in glitter. Since his mother and Stella were present, Donald held back any comments. He just smiled and shook his head. Annie could feel the heat of blush expanding across her face.

Annie stood and walked over to give Patty a hug. Glitter flew through the air and on anyone near Annie. Patty tried to be discreet when brushing the sparkly stuff from her shirt.

"Mom wanted to meet with Stella about the flowers for the wedding before the end of the day," Donald informed Annie. "We thought it would be easier to meet here. I need to get back to work."

"What?" Annie questioned. "No comment about my messiness?"

Donald leaned in and whispered in Annie's ear, "I am saving that for later." Donald was about to continue, but was interrupted by a group of people entering the shop.

"Patty, let's go to the flower shop and talk to Myra about the floral arrangements for the wedding," Stella suggested. "We can get out of Annie's way since she has a class starting in a few minutes."

"Mom," Annie paused her activities. "I feel bad not helping out with all the arrangements. Should I be doing something?"

"Nonsense. We have it all planned. Unless you wanted to be involved in the planning."

"No, not really. I trust you know; I want to keep it simple."

"Simple," Patty nodded to Stella with a smile.

"Yes," Stella responded. "Simple." She took Patty by the arm and the two walked out of the shop.

Annie stared at the door for a moment, wondering what 'simple' meant to them. She turned her attention to her classroom, which was beginning to fill up with students. She had fifteen students registered, but usually ended up with a few more last-minute attendees. Class was to begin in a few minutes, so Annie walked to the back room to get a bottle of water from the small refrigerator.

♦ ♦ ♦

The afternoon had raced by and Annie was anxious to close the shop and head home. Rand and Patty would be there, and she was excited to catch up on their news. Annie also thought about contacting Janette as soon as she got home to discuss the 'treasure map' idea. She had not heard from Janette all day and was wondering if she had arrived at her grandmother's home. She made a mental note to send a text message to Janette later this evening.

The weather was calm and the sun was shining brightly when Annie and Marie made their way home. As Annie and Marie approached their new home, Annie noticed the large bus-sized recreational vehicle backing slowly into the backyard. She and Marie quickly made their way through the house, by way of the kitchen, to the backyard. Annie could hear Donald's voice from where he was guiding Rand into the parking space next to the garage. Rand stopped the large vehicle upon Donald's command and turned off the engine. This was a massive bus, Annie thought to herself.

There was much excitement and chatter as Annie, Marie, Donald, and Rand looked at the monster in the backyard. Annie could not imagine driving something that large through the streets of Bridgewater Harbor. As large as this mobile machine seemed to be, it fit within the confines of its parking spot and seemed at home with the yard. Annie was impressed. She wondered what it would be like to travel the country in a motor home. She made a mental note to talk to Donald about his thoughts on the matter.

Stella and Patty arrived home a few hours earlier than Annie. They were in Stella's apartment making wedding plans over coffee. As they made their way down the stairs from Stella's apartment over the garage, Stella stopped suddenly at the sight of the behemoth in front of her.

"My goodness," Stella exclaimed, continuing down the stairs. "That is larger than my apartment."

"This is our home away from home," Rand said, giving the side of the motor home a gentle pat.

Annie approached Rand and gave him a hug. "I think it is wonderful."

Rand looked down at his shirt and brushed away a few specks of glitter. "The wedding day must be near. You are sparkling with joy."

Annie stepped back, turned and grimaced at Donald, who was standing behind her laughing.

"I had a bit of a glitter incident today at the shop," Annie apologized. "I guess I should go change."

"Nonsense," Rand said with a warm smile. "It just shows you are working hard in your shop."

Donald offered to help Rand hook up the amenities for the motor home. Annie followed the two men along the side of the garage to the back of the vehicle. As Rand continued around the back and to the other side, while Donald stopped and looked at the back of the garage. Annie followed his eyes, not sure what caught his attention. Rand called out to Donald, and the two continued around the back of the motor home and to the other side where they met Rand. Annie approached Donald and asked about what caught his attention when looking at the garage.

"I can't put my finger on it, but something looks out of place," Donald replied, as he placed chocks behind the rear wheels of the RV. "Remember when we were looking for a secret door in the cottage?"

Annie nodded.

"It is something we should check out when we get a chance."

"Maybe we should keep this to ourselves for now, Donald," Annie stated.

♦ ♦ ♦

Annie, Stella, Patty, and Marie prepared a scrumptious dinner. Dan and Lizzy joined them just as they were all sitting down at the dining room table. The conversation began with the travels of the Harpers. There were questions about the various locations and stops Rand and Patty made. Annie thought it would be fun to take a driving trip to California next year.

The topic then turned to the events in Bridgewater Harbor since Annie and Donald returned from California. Annie and Donald explained about the painting Meredith's Garden, Janette the artist, the kidnapping of the three women, and Lawrence Smyth.

"We know that the wedding certificate of Janette's grandmother and Walter Smith is fake," Stella noted. "Janette believes he came to Bridgewater Harbor a few weeks ago, after her grandmother's death."

"If he is here," Dan began, "He is hiding or using another name."

"We should ask the Silver Sleuths to be on the lookout for this guy," Lizzy injected.

Dan snapped a disapproving look at Lizzy.

"They really do know what is going on in this city, Dan."

"I do not want the Senior Snoopers involved in this mess." Dan grabbed the platter of meat and forked a serving onto his plate. Donald passed the vegetable bowl to Dan. He waved it off.

"Annie," Dan snorted. "Do not let those busybodies get in the middle of this kidnapping case. Lawrence is a dangerous criminal."

The table was quiet. Annie was about to open her mouth to say something to Dan, when both Lizzy and Donald gave her cautioning looks. She sipped her iced tea instead. Annie listened to the scraping of forks on the dinner plates. The silence was nerve-racking.

"There is something you can do for me tomorrow, Dan said in a lowered tone of voice. "Contact Janette and see if she has discovered anything at her grandmother's house. See if she will do a video of each room. Find out if there is a photo of Walter Smith. I do not believe Walter Smith came to Bridgewater Harbor without good reason."

"We were going to live chat with the camera, but recording it is a good idea," she replied. Then she added, "Do you think he is looking for another wealthy wife?" Annie questioned.

"Anything is possible. If he is, then I need to find out who he is before another woman dies."

CHAPTER 21

Wednesday

Translucent waves of teal exploded over the rocky point stretching out into the ocean. Eagles were perched high on top of the fir trees drying their feathers while overlooking the salty sea. A light breeze was evident in the swaying trees. The sun was making its morning appearance.

Annie took a last sip from her coffee and set the cup down on the end table next to her loveseat in the small room off the master suite. Often now, she thought about the lonely mornings she had spent at her mother's home across the street when she would watch the ocean in the early morning hours just as the sun began to rise over the mountains behind her. She stood, stretched, and walked over to the bed she now shared with Donald. It was six o'clock and he was waking up. Laddie seemed to be asleep, but opened one eye to watch Donald stand up.

Donald stretched after standing. He spotted Annie watching him, "Good morning, early bird."

"Good morning to you too!"

"How about breakfast?"

"You get dressed and I will start the preparations for a skillet hash with sausage and eggs."

"I love you so much right now," Donald said as he hurried to the shower.

Annie headed down the stairs and wondered if the smell of food cooking would wake Marie early today. It was worth a try. She would love it if Marie walked with her to the shop today.

Annie was lenient with Marie's schedule at the paper craft shop. Marie was eager to work and make her own wages. Annie helped Marie understand the value of money by setting up a bank account. Marie was watching her money grow at the moment, but Annie wondered how long that would last. Marie often wanted to buy unnecessary things and Annie and Stella would sometimes talk her out of her extravagance. Other times, Annie would remind Stella it was Marie's money to spend as she wanted. After all, Annie was able to provide for Marie's immediate needs since Helen had left her with a home and a fortune.

"Meow!" came the urging voice of Callie. Annie bent down to pick up Callie. Her cat had lost a bit of weight after the arrival of Laddie, but Annie did not feel Callie was suffering just yet. The fluffy Maine Coon was a bit overweight and losing a pound or two was not concerning at this point. Callie was adjusting to the giant canine at her own pace. At least she was making more appearances when family members were present. Laddie seemed to ignore her after she swatted him a few times, letting him know who was going to be the boss around the house.

Annie gently placed Callie on the counter in the laundry room at her feeding station set up out of the reach of a nosey dog. After placing some canned food in a clean dish, Annie measured out dry food and added it to the second dish on the counter. She cleaned and refilled Callie's water dish and gave the fluffy furball a soft pet before entering the kitchen.

♦ ♦ ♦

It was eight-thirty when Lizzy, Marie, and Annie entered Ione's Bakery and Coffee Shop. Once inside, the three stood behind a long line of customers. Annie was debating changing her order today. A bear claw looked particularly good, but did not have the chocolate she so desired in the morning. As she made her way to the cash register to order, Annie heard herself giving her usual order.

"I think I am going to need a couple more to help me get through this day," Annie said, leaning over the counter whispering to Ione.

"Better be careful not to add on too many pounds," Ione whispered back, eyeing the line to see if anyone was listening in to their conversation. "The wedding is only a few days away."

"Oh, Ione," Annie said. "I am not nervous about the wedding. In fact, I am very excited and ready to walk down that aisle, even though it is just a sidewalk to the front of the cottage in my backyard."

Ione laughed and said, "Donald is a wonderful man, Annie. Watching the two of you together brings joy to my heart." Ione handed the bag of donuts to Annie and took the money handed to her, placing it in the cash register.

Annie paid for Lizzy and Marie's orders and the three of them walked to Ocean Loads of Paper to enjoy their goodies.

♦ ♦ ♦

It was after eleven o'clock when Annie heard her cell phone ringing from her desk in the office. She picked up the phone and noticed the caller ID showed Janette's name.

"Good morning, Janette," Annie answered.

"Oh, Annie," Janette said. "I am so sorry I did not call yesterday. My mother wanted me to help her with errands and it took all day. We did not stop until after eight last night."

"You and your mother must be exhausted." Annie said, sheepishly realizing that she promised Dan she would contact Janette in the morning. Since she got sidetracked, Annie was relieved that Janette called her.

"I had a good night's sleep and I am ready to begin the search. Where should I begin?"

"Dan wants you to video record the search," Annie began, "If you do that in our video chat, I can see what you see."

"Between the two of us, we might find something important," Janette added.

♦ ♦ ♦

Annie waited with excited anticipation for Janette to set up the video chat. She nearly jumped as her thoughts were jolted by the ringing of her phone. Janette appeared on Annie's screen.

"Let's begin with a walk-through of the house." Annie suggested.

"I can point out anything that seemed out of place when mother and I arrived."

Janette walked through the entryway and pointed out where Meredith's Garden once hung on the wall. It was located in the foyer where anyone could see it as they entered the house. Beneath the vacant spot on the wall Annie could see a small table with a framed photo of Janette with her grandmother. It was as if Janette's grandmother was making a statement as to how much she loved the painting her granddaughter had created.

Moving through the living room proved ordinary. Nothing seemed out of place according to Janette. Janette pointed out the coffee table where she first noticed the note pad and discovered the notation Walter had made of Bridgewater Harbor. The coffee table was now clear of the note pad. A small crystal dish with hard candies sat on a doily in the center of the table. A walk-through the guest room and office brought similar results.

"Annie," Janette paused walking and turned the camera to her mother. "This is my mother." A tired looking woman quickly waved and turned to open a door.

"I am walking to my grandmother's bedroom now," announced Janette.

Annie could see Janette's mother walking ahead through the now opened door. She stood for a moment, taking in the recent loss and the emptiness of the room. Janette stopped behind her, but giving Annie a full view of the room. It was dark due to the curtains being drawn. Janette's mother walked to the windows and began opening the blinds. Janette reached for a switch and when she pressed it, light filled the room.

Janette walked into the bedroom. "It seems so cold in here," she said as she scanned the room with the phone camera.

Annie could see various items on the dresser and dressing table. Meredith was very neat and organized. Nothing seemed disturbed or knocked over. It did not appear that anyone had searched the room.

Discouraged, Janette sat on the edge of the bed next to Meredith's nightstand. Annie could see a framed photo, a fancy dispenser of tissues, a telephone, and a notepad with a pencil.

"Janette," Annie had a sudden thought. "Look under the bed. Is there anything there that might have fallen from the nightstand?"

"Let me get a flashlight from the kitchen," Janette said, placing the phone on the bed. "I will be right back."

Annie stared at the ceiling for what seemed like an eternity. The camera then moved about in a jerky motion as Janette positioned herself on the floor, pointing the camera under the bed. The flashlight illuminated an area under the bed void of any objects. Annie could tell by the jostling of the camera that Janette was trying to get as far under the bed as possible.

"I don't see anything," Janette said as she was attempting to back out from under the bed.

"Wait!" Annie shouted. "I saw something lying next to the nightstand in the far back by the wall."

The camera moved and what appeared to be a prescription bottle came into view. Janette's hand could be seen reaching for the bottle. The camera lurched about again as Janette scooted herself out from under the bed. As she was moving, she bumped into the nightstand, knocking over the framed picture.

Not realizing she was focusing the phone's camera on the photograph, Janette picked up the photo frame giving Annie a close-up view of the picture. It had slipped in the frame to where Annie could swear there was another photo behind it.

"Oh no!" Janette cried. "I broke my grandmother's beautiful frame."

"It doesn't look too bad," Annie said still looking at a close-up of the frame. "I think it can be fixed. Can you remove the photo? It looks like there is another photo behind it."

Janette sat the phone down on the nightstand while she fumbled with the photo frame. Annie could see the frame coming in and out of view in the camera.

"Oh, Annie!" Janette exclaimed. "There is another photo. It is of my grandmother and a man."

Janette picked up the phone, showing the photo to Annie. It indeed was a picture of a beautiful older woman with an older man standing next to her.

"The back has handwriting on it. It reads 'Walter Smith and I on our wedding day'. Annie, this is the only photo we have of Walter Smith, and my grandmother was hiding it for some reason. Why?"

"It is possible she suspected him in some way."

"There is another notation in pencil," Janette continued. "It's very light. I can barely make it out. It reads, 'The secret is in Meredith's Garden'. My painting is titled Meredith's Garden!"

"Janette, those numbers in your painting are the answer to the secret."

"I believe you are right," Janette said, now pointing the camera to the bottle she found under the bed. "And by the way, the prescription bottle I found on the floor was filled the day before my grandmother died. It was her heart medication. The bottle is nearly empty."

Annie asked Janette to send her photos of the pictures in the frame, the back of the photo with the messages, and a photo of the bottle's prescription label. Janette disconnected from the video chat and in a few minutes, Annie received several photos from Janette. Janette sent a text message that she and her mother were heading to the pharmacy where her grandmother's prescription was filled so they could talk to the pharmacist.

Annie sat quietly in her office for several minutes. She thought about why Meredith would hide the only known photo of her and Walter. Why would Meredith hide the photo unless she became suspicious that Walter was up to something unthinkable? Then there was the message of 'The secret is in Meredith's Garden'. It had to mean the painting of Meredith's Garden. It also had to be referring to the numbers that Annie discovered entwined on the bench. What do the numbers mean? Annie made a mental note to discuss the findings with Donald, Dan, and Lizzy tonight over dinner. Right now, she needed to get to work.

Annie filled Lizzy in on the conversation she just ended with Janette. They both agreed the secret was in the numbers found in the painting. But what did the numbers mean?

♦ ♦ ♦

Usually, hours seemed to race by in the afternoon when Annie had classes to prepare, crafts to create, and new product to test out. Today, the clock seemed to be in slow motion as Annie kept checking it to see if it got any closer to quitting time. Finally, four forty-five rolled around and Annie began cleaning up and start closing procedures while Lizzy dashed over to Ione's Bakery and Coffee Shop to pick up dessert for dinner.

Annie called her Mom to ask if she should bring anything home for dinner. Stella was just entering the kitchen door when Annie called.

"I am making stuffed chicken breasts," Stella said. "I was hoping you would make the Brussels sprouts when you get home."

"Sounds wonderful," Annie said, realizing she was suddenly hungry. "Lizzy is bringing dessert."

Annie talked to her mother for a few minutes longer before disconnecting.

"There is a line up at Salty's for burgers tonight," Lizzy remarked as she entered and locked the ocean side door of the shop. She set the large boxed cake on the counter and walked over to the street side of the shop to lock the door.

"I think there is a new movie playing at the theater tonight," Annie said, closing the cash register and moving the till drawer to the safe. "There is always excitement when a new movie comes to town."

Marie began sweeping behind the counter around Annie, as Annie locked the office door and handed Marie and Lizzy their belongings. "Sweep tomorrow, Marie. Mom has stuffed chicken breasts for dinner and we do not want to be late."

Marie placed the broom handle against the wall and took the coat and tote bag handed to her.

♦ ♦ ♦

Annie was just finishing up sautéing the Brussels sprouts with sliced almonds and fig infused balsamic vinegar. She scooped them from the pan to a glass serving dish and slid it down the counter toward Marie, who picked it up and walked to the dining table. Stella walked behind Marie holding a platter of chicken breasts stuffed with a sausage, vegetable, and bread stuffing. Gravy made from cream of chicken soup was poured on top of the chicken. Annie followed her mother, carrying a pitcher of ice water.

Dan burst through the front door, kissing Lizzy on the cheek, and rushing to the downstairs bathroom, located in the archway under the stairs. A short hallway connected the kitchen with a small sitting room just off the dining room. The sitting room had built-in bookcases stretching across the end wall of the room.

Within seconds, Dan was back and entering the dining room. "Something smells really good."

Donald stood from his chair and pulled out a chair for Stella. He was about to reach over and do the same for Annie, but she sat down too quickly. Lizzy stood by her chair as Dan walked around her and sat down. Everyone stared at Dan. Realizing what he had done, he slowly stood and looked at Donald as he pulled out Lizzy's chair.

"You are responsible for this," Dan said to Donald.

"What can I say?" Donald said shrugging his shoulders and raising his hands, palm sides up. "I'm a nice guy."

"Sit down, Dan," Stella said. "Annie has some exciting news to tell us."

CHAPTER 22

Thursday Morning

S itting on the loveseat in the cozy cove of her bedroom, Annie glanced at her watch. She had plenty of time to just sit and think. It was only five-thirty in the morning. She needed to think and absorb everything that had happened so far. She took a sip from her steaming coffee mug and set it down on the side table. Already on the table was a pad of paper with the craft designs she had spent two hours working on after every one left for the evening. It was so difficult to be creative when the mysterious painting kept creeping into her thoughts.

Last night at dinner, Annie explained the walk-through she and Janette had performed on Janette's grandmother's home. She ran the group's conversation through her mind once more. The discovery of the photo of Meredith with a gentleman and the inscription on the back of the photo proved to be the highlight of the conversation.

"Annie," Lizzy said nearly dropping her fork. "You've found Janette's grandmother's murderer!"

"I would not get too excited, Lizzy," Dan said, taking a second helping of Brussels sprouts. "A photo of a man standing next to Meredith does not prove murder."

"Yes," Annie spoke up. "But now we may have an idea of who Walter Smith is, and if he is one of the three gentlemen who arrived here at the same time in Bridgewater Harbor."

"It does seem to be an exciting discovery," Stella added.

"We still do not have any proof that Walter killed his wife," Dan said, signaling for the platter of chicken to be passed to him. "An ideal situation would be for Walter to confess he killed Meredith."

"Dan is right," Donald said. "You have no idea how the pills went missing. Maybe Meredith spilled them."

Annie recalled giving Donald a scowling look. Maybe she was getting too excited over nothing. But then again, there seemed to be no one by the name of Walter Smith in town.

"That's right!" Annie said out loud. "Walter Smith is using another name." He may still be one of the three men who showed up at the same time.

♦ ♦ ♦

Annie heard Donald getting out of bed and walking to the bathroom. Laddie groaned and turned over in his bed.

It was six o'clock and the sun was up and shining brightly over the ocean. Annie took it as a sign that she was on to something important about Meredith's death, the painting of Meredith's Garden, and the puzzling numbers in the painting. She decided to print out the photo of Meredith and Walter and show it to her four favorite ladies. If anyone knew who this man was and if he was currently in town, it was the Silver Sleuths.

♦ ♦ ♦

At six-thirty in the morning, Stella walked into the house through the kitchen door. Annie met her in the kitchen.

"Everyone should be here in fifteen minutes for breakfast," Stella said, quickly grabbing bacon and eggs from the refrigerator. "I cannot believe I overslept. You have me thinking about the painting and Walter Smith. I had a dream that I was walking through a back-yard maze. It was terrible. I could not get through the maze, yet I could see it in the yard. My feet were stuck somehow."

"Mom," Annie whispered. "I think you are on to something. I have always thought the numbers in the painting were steps to a goal. Meredith's Garden is a painting of Janette's grandmother's backyard garden. I hope it is not too early to text Janette and ask her to walk through her grandmother's backyard when all of us are here to watch."

Annie pulled out her phone and began to text Janette. It was a few minutes before she received a response. Janette was up and dressed and waiting for Annie to call. Annie responded back with a message that she was waiting for Donald, Dan, and Lizzy to show up for breakfast before she made the call.

The numbers on the bench in the painting were now on her phone. She jotted the numbers down on a pad of paper. Annie was ready…now where was everyone? Annie ran up the stairs to check on Donald. He was coming from the bedroom when she arrived at the top of the stairs.

"Excited to see me?"

"No," Annie started. "I mean, always. It's just that I wanted to get everyone moving this morning so we can call Janette and watch her walk through the backyard on a video chat."

"I can set that up so we watch it on my larger screen," Donald offered.

"That sounds perfect," Annie said, turning to knock on Marie's bedroom door. Annie was not sure if Marie would want to miss the excitement. As it was, Marie came to the door dressed and ready to go downstairs.

"You are up early," Annie remarked.

"I want to go to work today."

"There is always work to be done," Annie said, waving Marie to go ahead of her down the stairs.

As they descended the stairs, Annie noticed Donald bringing his personal laptop to the dining room. He set it up at the end of the table so the group could gather around it.

Dan and Lizzy knocked on the front door. Marie answered and let them inside. As Stella was carrying a platter of scrambled eggs, ham, and bacon to the table, Dan swiped a slice of bacon.

"Dan," Stella admonished. "Go sit down and wait until we are all seated to eat. Annie, bring the bowl of fruit, please."

Annie did as her mom asked and Marie brought a pitcher of water to the table. Lizzy was taking coffee orders. After everyone was seated and plates filled with food, Annie announced her plan for a video chat with Janette. Donald was all set with the laptop. Conversation was quiet as everyone, even skeptical Dan, ate breakfast.

Annie kept running the plan through her mind. Could this really be it? Are the numbers in the painting steps to a treasure? What was the treasure? Annie hoped it would be something great and not a disappointment. What if Walter already found the treasure? She was sure Lawrence had not beat them to it, as he would not still be in Bridgewater Harbor looking for the clues.

"Annie?" Donald said as he placed a hand on Annie's shoulder. "Are you finished? Can I take your plate to the kitchen?"

She was in deep thought again. "Oh, yes. Thank you."

"Leave the dishes, Donald," Stella said. She stood and walked to the end of the table where the laptop was. "I can get them later. I want to get the show on the road."

Donald smiled and sat down in the chair by his laptop. He asked Annie to text Janette and let her know they were ready. With a couple of minutes, Janette was signaling a video chat with Donald.

Janette's face appeared on the computer screen. "Annie, Mom and I are here and ready to follow your plan."

Dan rolled his eyes and exhaled loudly at the word 'plan'. He had no idea what Annie was searching for, and was certain it was not treasure. Lizzy nudged him to listen.

"Janette," Annie began. "I had a thought that the numbers were footsteps. Then Mom told me this morning that she had a dream of taking steps through a maze in a backyard. So, I got the idea that the numbers are measured footsteps in your grandmother's backyard."

Dan's cell phone chimed. He pulled it out to look at the text message. "I need to go. I have real detective work to do." He kissed Lizzy and exited through the front door.

Everyone looked at Lizzy. "Continue, Annie," Lizzy said, with excited anticipation. "Don't pay attention to Dan. He really is interested in the numbers and what they mean."

As Janette moved her phone camera further in front of her, Annie recognized Janette's mother. After polite introductions, Annie continued with her plan. "Janette, if we could begin at the door leading to the backyard, I want to see what the backyard looks like."

Janette and her mother walked through the house and exited the back door. Standing on the patio made of red brick, Janette focused the camera on the vast expanse in front of her. She slowly turned the camera so the view showed various flower beds, pathways, fountains, ponds, trees, and shrubs adorning the yard. Two steps led down to a sidewalk which branched to the left and right, and directly ahead through bordering flower beds.

Annie placed the paper with the numbers on the table for the group to see. The numbers did not make sense. Where do they begin? Left? Right? Straight ahead? There was no hint of a starting point.

Donald ran to his office to get a copy of the bench photo he made earlier. He enlarged the photo to show the intricate scrollwork and the numbers. As he walked back to the dining room, he noticed that the numbers were stretched out along the scrollwork design.

"Does this appear to be directional?" Donald asked the group.

Heads moved closer to the copy of the bench and the elaborate design.

"Can you hold the photo up to the camera so I can see what you are looking at?" Janette asked.

Donald held the paper up and Janette stared at it for a few moments. She and her mother were looking out into the yard, and then back at the photo.

"I think it starts that way," Janette's mother said, pointing to the left of where they were standing. "Look at the pattern in the scroll and the numbers seem to be making turns."

"I agree with Janette's mom," Lizzy said. "It appears to be telling the viewer to take six steps to the left, and then five steps straight ahead and then turn right."

"Let's see what happens if I follow those directions," Janette stated.

Annie set down her notes and the photo. She gave the first set of instructions. Janette stopped. Annie gave the next set of instructions. Janette counted out the steps. Stella, Marie, and Lizzy were counting along with Janette in soft voices. Excitement was building.

"I am still on either a pathway or sidewalk," Janette announced. "Let's continue."

Annie gave the next set of steps, at the same time examining the photo of the bench to determine which direction to walk. She watched as Janette made concise steps, counting with each foot fall. So far, their plan was working. Janette had maneuvered around shrubs, flower beds, and a small pond.

Looking ahead, Annie noticed only a few step instructions were left. It did not seem like there was anything indicating treasure. Annie felt a pang of disappointment. They may be no further than when they started. She read off the next set of numbers, then the last.

"It leads to a bench in the garden," Janette exclaimed. "It is a different bench than what is in the painting. The bench in the painting was actually in my mother's yard. I used it as subject matter when I originally made the painting. Grandma's bench here is different. In fact, Grandma designed this part of her garden after my painting."

"Show us what is around the bench," Annie suggested.

Janette panned the camera around the bench area. Behind the bench was a mature tree. To the right side of the seat was a cinder block wall. It was covered in ivy in sections. The ivy seemed to be cut away from the carved panels depicting garden scenes attached to the wall. One scene showed a pond with fish springing out of the water. The camera moved to the carved panel nearest the bench.

"Stop!" Annie shouted.

Janette stopped and held the camera on the panel. She walked up to the panel to get a better view. The panel was a bronze copper plaque with a carving of a garden bench. Below it appeared the words 'Meredith's Garden'.

"That is the same plaque that is shown in the photo of your grandmother and Walter Smith!" Annie said, as she contained herself from jumping up and down.

"You're right," Janette nearly shouted. "The back of the photo said that the secret was in Meredith's Garden. Annie, it has to be behind this panel."

"That would make sense, Janette," Donald said. "It looks like this panel is different from all the rest we've seen so far."

"Janette," Annie asked. "See if the panel moves."

Janette handed her phone camera to her mother. The group could see Janette attempting to pull and tug at the panel. It did not budge.

"Try sliding it to one side," Lizzy offered.

Janette tried as Lizzy suggested. Nothing happened as she pushed on the right side. As she pushed the panel to the left, it began to move. She pushed further until it opened as far as it would go, exposing a metal door with a lock.

"We found it!" Janette cried. "I cannot believe we actually found it."

The camera jostled about as Janette and her mother seemed to be hugging each other. While they did, Stella, Marie, Lizzy, Donald, and Annie all stood in amazement at the scene they just witnessed.

"Did we just solve the mystery of Meredith's Garden?" Annie asked Donald.

"Possibly, but you do not know what is behind Door #1 yet. It could be nothing at all and it is locked."

"What would someone keep in a garden wall?" Stella asked.

"I think it is gold and jewels," Marie spoke up.

"Do you think it is the ashes of Meredith's first husband?" Lizzy pondered. Every one stopped and looked at Lizzy with expressions of curiosity.

"What would the secret be?" Annie asked. "The back of the photo of Meredith and Walter said that the secret was in Meredith's Garden. This panel said it was Meredith's Garden and it has a locked door behind the panel. I would think it contained something valuable."

By this time Janette and her mother had regained their composure and the camera was pointed at the locked door.

"Janette," Annie asked, bringing her thoughts back to the discovery. "Have you discovered a key somewhere in your grandmother's belongings?"

"No."

"Let's give this a try," Donald said, scooting his chair up closer to the computer screen. "Move the camera in close to the side of the panel. I want to get a good look at it."

As the camera moved to the left side of the panel, Donald noticed that there was ample room for someone to place their fingers to the inside of the panel. He instructed Janette to do so.

"Ew," Janette complained. "What if there is a spider in there?"

Donald looked at Annie with a knowing smile.

"I know what you are thinking," Annie said to Donald. "That is not something I would say in the middle of finding treasure." At least not out loud to Donald.

Janette's mother handed the phone to Janette and proceeded to place her hand behind the panel. She moved her hand around in various spots. Suddenly she pulled out a small key box with Velcro attached to the back. She slid the box open and produced a key in the camera view.

"This is it, folks!" Donald shouted as the group moved closer to the computer screen.

There was some movement of the camera when Janette handed the phone back to her mother and took the key.

"Here is the key," Janette said as she held the key in front of the lock. "Anyone want to guess what is inside this locked door?"

"Open the door!" Marie spoke up first. "Open the door!"

Annie was thinking the same thing, but did not want to say it out loud.

Janette chuckled and then placed the key in the lock. She turned the key and took a step back as she pulled open the panel door. The sun was shining brightly now and illuminating the contents of the safe. Inside was a jewelry box, what appeared to be a journal, and a plastic pouch containing papers.

The group watching could see Janette's hand shake as she pulled out the jewelry box. She moved to the bench and sat down, placing the jewelry box on her lap.

"My mother's pearls and diamond necklace and earrings," exclaimed Janette's mother. She kept the camera on the jewelry box as Janette lifted a pearl necklace from the container. With her other hand she pulled out another piece of jewelry.

"It appears that my grandmother hid her most valuable jewelry in this safe," Janette finally spoke. "She must not have trusted Walter Smith."

"What is the book we saw in the safe?" asked Donald.

Janette set the box down on the bench and walked back to the safe. Her mother followed with the camera. Reaching inside, Janette pulled out the book and opened it to the first page.

"It is a journal written in my grandmother's handwriting."

"That book may give you plenty of reasons why your grandmother hid the jewelry in this safe," Annie remarked. "Once you have had a chance to process it all, I would be interested in knowing if there is anything in the book linking Walter Smith to your grandmother's death."

"In other words," Donald added. "We hope you are willing to share what you find out."

"Of course," Janette answered. "We never would have found this without your help."

♦ ♦ ♦

After Janette and her mother thanked the group for their help in locating the missing jewelry and the journal, Janette announced that she would be making arrangements to fly back to Portland and drive to Bridgewater Harbor in her rental car. She was not about to miss Annie and Donald's wedding. She told them that she would try to catch a flight out the next day. Annie invited her mother to come along, but Janette's mother declined stating she needed to finish settling her mother's estate. She wished the two a lovely wedding. Donald and Annie said goodbye and disconnected.

"That reminds me," said Stella. "You two have a wedding to attend in two days. Are you both ready?"

"Of course, we are," Annie chimed, wondering what she might have forgotten.

"Do you have the rings?"

"Do we need rings?" Annie asked.

"Yes," answered Donald. "I want everyone to know I am marrying the most wonderful woman in the world."

"And who might that be?" came a male voice from behind the group.

CHAPTER 23

Thursday Mid-Morning

Annie, Donald, and the rest of the group all turned at the same time to see Detective Surely standing behind them.

"Funny, Dan," Annie said as she smirked at Dan. "Why are you back?"

"I wanted to find out if you found treasure."

"As a matter of fact, we did."

Dan paused for a moment with a look of disbelief on his face. "What did you find?"

Annie relayed the process of how they found a safe embedded in the cinder block wall that bordered the backyard. She told Dan of the journal and jewelry.

Dan's phone chimed and he looked at the message. "I need to get back to the office." He kissed Lizzy on the cheek and was out the door.

♦ ♦ ♦

The morning was spent designing and mocking up a new design for a box. Annie was inspired by a paper craft artist in the United Kingdom by the name of Linda Parker. Linda's style and use of color impressed Annie. Although Annie had made boxes in the past, they never looked or felt sturdy enough. With lessons learned from Linda Parker, Annie now created beautiful, well-made, sturdy boxes. Once she knew the basics, Annie was able to calculate the dimensions for new projects she imagined. Sample boxes were now everywhere in the shop. She just could not stop making them.

Annie looked at the clock on the wall. It was eleven-thirty in the morning and the shop was quiet. Tourists would be crowding the streets and shops by the afternoon. Annie thought it might be a good time to take a break and eat lunch.

"Anyone hungry for lunch?"

Annie noticed Marie working on a display stand, making sure the product was neat and tidy. She had a basket of product next to her. She was restocking shelves.

Marie looked up and nodded with a smile.

"I could eat," Lizzy said, not bothering to look up from her computer screen.

Annie suspected Lizzy was working on inventory or ordering supplies. She would spend hours perusing the online catalogs. For someone who did not actually craft, Lizzy had a vast knowledge of the materials used in crafting. Annie believed Lizzy was a closet-crafter.

"We have three choices," Annie said as she stood and stretched. "Chinese, deli sandwiches, or Old Salty's hamburgers?"

"Hamburgers!" both Lizzy and Marie said in unison.

"Hamburgers it is. One with the works, two with ham, cheese, lettuce and mustard only, fries for all, and one vanilla shake, one strawberry shake, and the best of all...one chocolate shake."

Annie walked to the office to get her wallet and jacket. Although it was sunny and warm in appearance, the breeze off the ocean was cool. As she was leaving the shop through the ocean side door, she noticed LaVerne and Lorraine entering the shop through the street side door. Annie made a mental note to print out Walter's photo to show to the Silver Sleuths when she returned. It would not take that long, and she figured the ladies would still be in the shop.

Old Salty's was a candy shop that made salt water taffy, Caramel corn, and chocolates. After the shop next to it was vacated, Salty, the owner, merged the two business locations by opening up the wall and adding an ice cream and hamburger counter. Salty made the best burgers in town. On occasion he would sell hot dogs. Fries or chips were the only choice of side items. Salty kept choices limited. It made his life simple.

After placing her order, Annie turned, noticing that the once nearly empty restaurant was now packed with townspeople hurrying to get their lunch orders before the tourists came. She saw Lynda Hermitage behind her, the owner of Hermitage's Furniture. Lynda created beautiful hand-painted pieces of furniture. Much of her business was in reupholstering old furniture, a task she learned from her grandfather. Hermitage Furniture was located next to and north of Annie's shop at the end of the building housing all of the shops on the boardwalk.

Once Lynda placed her order, she walked over to where Annie stood waiting for her food. Annie and Lynda were discussing how quiet the morning was when Annie's order was called. She picked up her order of burgers and fries, attempting to balance the tray of milkshakes, and walked back to where Lynda was standing by the door. Annie was about to ask Lynda a question, when she spotted Dan walking into the shop from the street side of the restaurant.

Dan had his eye on someone who was waiting in line to order food. Annie tried to see who it was, as she scanned the crowd. Her eyes stopped on a tall, good looking man with dark hair. Lawrence!

Lawrence spotted Dan and made a dash to the ocean side door of the restaurant. Lynda noticing the man dashing toward her, stepped aside, putting Annie directly in his path. Lawrence bolted full force for the door, knocking Annie against the wall. As Annie fell to the floor, her milkshakes went flying through the air, cascading down on innocent bystanders waiting in line.

"Are you okay?" Dan said as he leaped over Annie, not stopping for an answer. He bounded through the door and Annie could see through the glass that Dan was headed south down the boardwalk.

Attempting to stand, Annie slipped and fell down again. Someone offered her a hand up. She did not see who it was, but gladly accepted the assistance. Milkshake was everywhere on the floor and on the people still standing in line, wondering what had happened.

Salty was running around with paper towels trying to clean up the mess. The patrons were in a state of shock. It had all happened so fast. One of Salty's employees brought out a mop and was attempting to clean the floor, sloshing an overly wet mop across the feet of customers.

Annie looked at Lynda standing frozen next to the door. Her hair was covered in chocolate milkshake and dripping down onto her shirt. Whipped cream slid slowly down the right side of her head.

"Oh, Lynda!" Annie winced. "Are you okay?"

Lynda gave a slight nod. A clump of milkshake fell to the floor in a splat.

Salty approached Annie. "You scraped up your shoulder, Annie. Let me call the paramedics."

"No, Salty," Annie said feeling her shoulder. "I will be fine. I am more worried about everyone here. Let me pay for their meals. Just bring the bill over to my shop later."

"You do not need to do that. It was not your fault."

"I insist," Annie said, looking at the scrape on her arm. Good thing she had a first aid kit at the shop.

Just then the cook tapped on a bell and yelled, "Order up for Lynda".

Lynda looked at the counter where her food was sitting in a bag. She looked at her clothing and touched her hair. Annie watched as Lynda turned with a groan and walked out the door without her food.

Annie felt terrible. She carefully walked through the slosh of milkshake and picked up Lynda's order. She would run it over to her immediately. She was about to leave when Salty brought over another tray of milkshakes.

"Do you need help getting this to your shop?" Salty asked.

"No, I will be fine. I have Lynda's order. She left to go get cleaned up. I will drop it off for her."

♦ ♦ ♦

After taking Lynda's lunch to her and making sure Lynda was uninjured, Annie walked through the doors of her shop. She took care to set the milkshakes down on the counter in front of Lizzy. Lizzy looked up and noticed Annie.

"I'm afraid to ask what happened."

"Lawrence was in line at Salty's," Annie began after taking a sip from her chocolate shake. "Dan spotted him and came into the shop. Once Lawrence saw Dan, the chase was on. That's all I am saying at this point."

"I got a call from Ione," Lizzy said with a smile. "The word is out."

Annie groaned. She really did not need people gossiping about how her milkshakes ended on up on everyone at Salty's. This time it really was not her fault. She took a bite from her hamburger. Pickles! Ugh!

Lizzy leaned over to look at Annie's shoulder and arm. "Marie, can you bring the first aid kit here?"

"What did Annie do now?" Marie asked from the back room.

"I just have a small scrape on my arm. Nothing serious."

Lizzy picked up a fry and dipped it in sauce. "LaVerne and Lorraine were here to sign up for your latest class. I told them that we would be closed on Friday, Saturday, and Sunday for your wedding. They said that the entire Senior Center is making a gift for you and Donald, but it won't be ready until after your wedding."

"How sweet," Annie said as she looked up. She was attending to her wound. "I wanted to have them look at the photo of Walter Smith. I should print out a few copies of him to spread around. Someone may have seen him in town."

Annie, Lizzy, and Marie finished with their lunch. After having the milkshake, Annie was thinking she needed coffee to wash it all down. Lizzy knew what she was thinking and offered to go to Ione's for coffee and maybe just a bit of dessert.

When coffee and dessert arrived, and since the shop was unusually quiet, the three ladies sat at the counter and talked away the next hour. Annie had lost all desire to work today.

"Dan wants me to move in with him on a permanent basis," Lizzy proclaimed. "He wants me to give up my apartment."

"Is that what you want?"

"I love Dan," Lizzy began. "But I have had that studio apartment since I moved to Bridgewater Harbor. It is a sign of my independence. I do not want to be dependent upon Dan."

Annie took a sip from her coffee cup. Was she dependent upon Donald? Of course not, she thought. She had her own money, her own business, and her own house. All of which Donald would be sharing with her shortly.

"First of all," Annie said. "You are not dependent upon Dan. He is more dependent upon you. You have two jobs, working here and working as the manager for R&H Enterprises." Annie stopped and thought for a second. "When are we going to work on R&H Enterprises?"

The door chimed and several customers entered the shop. Annie, Lizzy, and Marie all looked at each other as if customers were a bother today.

♦ ♦ ♦

"Did anyone remind Daisy that the shop is closed this weekend?" Annie asked.

"I did," Lizzy responded. "She is going to your wedding and then spending the rest of her time off with friends."

"Tomorrow is going to be a busy day," Annie announced. "Mom and I were thinking about having the chairs set up the night before. The weather has been great, so having the yard set up and decorated the day before should be okay. Saturday morning, we can put the table cloths on the tables and set up the cake Mom ordered. It is just a small backyard ceremony. We are keeping it simple."

Was it Annie's imagination? Did Lizzy just give her a funny look? Lizzy quickly looked away and began straightening papers on the counter.

The door chimed again and Jacquie Spencer walked through the door carrying a baseball bat.

"Did you hear?" Jacquie shouted as she walked to the counter where Annie and Lizzy were standing. "That Lawrence is still around. He made a mess out of Salty's place. If he dares to come near me again...well, I have a baseball bat and I am not afraid to use it."

Annie stared at Jacquie and her bat. She was sure Jacquie meant business with that bat.

"Did he come to your shop?" Lizzy asked.

"No," Jacquie set the bat down, leaning it against the counter. "If he does though, I am ready for him."

Annie and Lizzy looked at each other. Annie wondered if she, too, should have a baseball bat.

"Anyway," Jacquie said, calming down and gaining composure. "John wants to take the guys out for dinner and beers at the Bridgewater Brew House tomorrow night. Sort of a bachelor party. Do you know if they have any plans yet?"

"Donald never mentioned any plans," Annie said. Then looking at Lizzy, Annie asked, "Has Dan mentioned anything?"

"Come to think of it, no."

"Good," Jacquie said. "I will tell John to contact Donald. What are the girls doing?"

Annie and Lizzy looked blankly at each other. Annie never really thought about it.

"Actually," Annie said. "It is such a small wedding that I did not think about it."

Annie caught Jacquie and Lizzy looking at each other like they knew something was going on and they were not telling Annie.

"I guess we should do something for you, Annie," Lizzy said after a moment of silence. "After all, you are the bride and as best woman, it is my responsibility to host...something."

"Great!" Jacquie said, picking up her bat. "I will be there at seven tomorrow night. Should I ask Suzette and Janette? I would suggest the party at the B&B, but Suzette has it ready for customers coming soon."

"I thought Suzette was not opening for at least a week yet," Annie stated.

"Um, well, she is still working on it, but has the majority of it ready to go." Jacquie said her goodbyes and left the shop without looking back.

Both Annie and Lizzy watched her with curious expressions. At least Lizzy seemed as confused as Annie about Jacquie's comments.

Annie left Lizzy at the counter and walked to her office. She did not want to forget to make copies of the photo of Walter Smith. She would go over to Millie's house on the way home to show the picture to the senior ladies.

As Annie waited for the photos to come out of her printer, she sat at her desk thinking about being married in two days. She thought she should be nervous, but in reality...she was calm. She thought about how excited she was to be marrying Donald. She felt comfortable with Donald. Donald was her match in every way.

As the last photo finished printing, Annie gathered them up and placed them into her purse. She walked out of her office and announced that it was closing time to Lizzy and Marie. Annie had printed a note explaining the closing of Ocean Loads of Paper on Friday, Saturday, and Sunday for the wedding weekend. She taped the notices on both doors and turned to look at the shop. Marie had done a marvelous job restocking shelves and straightening up the classroom area.

Lizzy and Marie walked to the center of the shop where Annie was now standing and looking around.

"The next time you walk into this shop, you will be Annie Harper," Lizzy said with tears forming in her eyes.

"Annie Weston Harper," announced Annie, tears forming in her eyes.

"Get a life!" Marie said, interrupting the sappy moment. "Let's go home."

Marie walked to the office to get her jacket and tote bag. Annie and Lizzy were still standing in the middle of the room.

"Lizzy," Annie said, ignoring Marie. "I am getting married!"

Laughing, Annie walked to the ocean side of the shop and locked the door. She had already locked the street side when she put up the notice on the door. Lizzy began counting the till. Marie, being done with her closing chores, began turning off lights. Fortunately, the light over the cash register stayed on and Lizzy was able to complete her task.

Annie opened the safe for Lizzy to put the tray inside. She closed and locked the safe door. Remembering the camera Lawrence installed in a vintage crafting book on the bookshelf, Annie turned to examine the entire bookcase for any further invasion of privacy. Seeing nothing disturbed, she grabbed her purse and jacket and closed and locked the office door. She was making a point to lock the office door, not that it mattered to Lawrence, but maybe it would deter any other burglar.

Lizzy had her purse and was putting on her designer jacket when Annie exited the office. One last check of the rooms in the shop and the three ladies were out the door. There was a slight breeze with stronger gusts of wind as Lizzy, Marie, and Annie walked the short distance home.

"What is for dinner tonight?" Lizzy asked Annie.

"I have no idea," Annie remarked.

"How about soup?" Marie said, zipping up her jacket and holding her tote bag close to her body. The wind was beginning to feel cold. Annie wished she had brought a warmer jacket.

As the women turned the corner to their street, Annie noticed LaVerne and Lorraine up ahead. She wanted to call out to them, but they were a half a block away. She quickened her pace to catch up. Lizzy and Marie followed Annie. The mature ladies were walking at a slow pace.

When Annie was within fifteen feet of the two members of the Silver Sleuths, she called out their names. LaVerne and Lorraine stopped and turned to see Annie approaching quickly. Annie stopped in front of the ladies. She was out of breath from practically running to catch up.

"Well, if it isn't the bride-to-be," Lorraine said.

"Hello, Annie," LaVerne added.

"I am so glad I caught you today," Annie said between breaths. "Janette found a photo of Walter Smith at her grandmother's house. She sent me a copy and I printed it out hoping you could show the photo around and see if anyone recognizes Walter Smith."

Annie dug through her purse and pulled out the stack of photos she had just printed at the shop. She held up the photo for LaVerne and Lorraine to view.

"Oh no!" Lorraine exclaimed.

CHAPTER 24

Thursday Evening

Both LaVerne and Lorraine turned and quickly walked to Millie's house. Annie looked at Lizzy with concern. Marie, who was now ahead of the women, walked across the street and climbed the steps to Annie's front door. Annie noticed Donald exiting out the front door with Laddie on a leash. She ran across the street to talk to Donald and met him at the sidewalk.

"I just showed the photo of Walter Smith to LaVerne and Lorraine," Annie said. "I think they know who it is."

"What did they say?"

"They said 'oh, no' and hurried to Millie's house," Annie said, anxiously looking for any sign of activity outside of Millie's house.

"Laddie needs to take a quick walk," Donald said pulling back on Laddie's strained leash. Laddie was in a hurry to relieve himself. "I will meet you at Millie's."

Annie crossed the street and met Lizzy in front of Dan's house. Seeing Dan's car in the driveway, Annie asked Lizzy to get Dan and take him to Millie's house. Annie explained that she thought something disturbed LaVerne and Lorraine when they saw the photo of Walter Smith.

Reaching the front door of Millie's house, Annie listened for a moment, being careful to stay to the side of the door. LaVerne was calling out to Millie while searching the dining room, living room, and hallway. Not getting a response from Millie, LaVerne called up the stairway. Annie leaned on the door so she could hear better, when the door slowly opened, revealing her standing in a near crouched position. She straightened up in time to see the man in the photo walk from the kitchen area and stand in front of the fireplace in the living room.

"Millie is resting," said the elderly man. He appeared tired or troubled, Annie thought.

"Bart Jones," LaVerne said, taking a step down from the stairway. "Or should I say Walter Smith?"

Walter did not answer LaVerne's question directly, but replied, "I go by a lot of names."

"Where is Millie?" Lorraine asked.

"Sleeping." Walter said. "She is taking a nice long nap."

Chills radiated throughout Annie's body. Wishing Dan were here to protect her and the ladies, Annie also prayed Millie was not dead.

Lorraine started for the stairs, "I want to see her now."

"My wife does not wish to be disturbed," Walter said, raising his voice.

"Your wife?" LaVerne questioned.

Walter produced a wedding certificate and handed it to LaVerne. She looked at it. Annie walked over and stood behind LaVerne. The certificate looked genuine and it had the seal of the State of Oregon, but Annie's gut feeling was that the document was a fake.

"May I see that?" Annie asked, taking the paper from LaVerne's hands. "This signature...on the line of 'Person solemnizing the marriage' is the same as the one on the California wedding certificate of Walter and Meredith, Janette's grandmother. This marriage document is a fake!"

"How clever of you, Miss Weston," came the voice of a tall, dark haired, person walking from the kitchen. He stood in the doorway holding a gun.

"Lawrence!" Annie shouted, realizing she could see the back door from her vantage point, where she caught a glimpse of Dan. She tried not to look directly at Dan. He appeared to have heard Annie shout out Lawrence's name. He gave Annie the 'OK' sign. Annie stared directly in Lawrence's eyes. She took a deep breath to calm her nerves.

"So, you and Bart or Walter, whatever his name is, are working together," LaVerne said. "Did you kill Millie too?"

Lorraine could be heard sucking in air.

"What are we going to do with three more of them?" Walter asked Lawrence. "There are too many witnesses. Let's just get out of here."

"Quiet, old man!" Lawrence bellowed at Walter.

"I told you we were moving too fast," Walter reprimanded the man holding the gun. "I had it under control."

"Well," Lawrence said, pointing the gun at Annie. "If Miss Weston had left well enough alone, I would still be in possession of the painting and the clues to where that old bat hid her jewels."

"You know about the numbers in the painting?" Annie moved deliberately to the middle of the opened front door with the purpose of handing the marriage certificate to LaVerne. She could hear Donald and Laddie just outside the opened door. She was trying to figure out a way to signal them not to enter the house.

Lawrence explained that he had connections on the black market and found out that Meredith had hired a skilled restorer of vintage paintings to add the numbers to the painting. The word got out that the numbers led to a treasure. It was later learned through Walter that Meredith had removed her finest jewelry from her safe in the bedroom and hidden them. Lawrence thought that the clues to the jewelry location were in the painting. When Walter got Meredith to agree to marry him, Lawrence pretended to be a clergyman and forged a wedding certificate. Lawrence stole the painting and took it with him to Bridgewater Harbor, where he was hired as a manager at Spencer's Gallery.

"It was the perfect place to fence my stolen paintings," Lawrence began. "Then that stubborn woman decided to work at the gallery full time. She sold Meredith's Garden to you of all people after discovering it with a load of paintings I had in the back room. They were stolen paintings I was arranging to sell to private buyers."

"Did you kill Meredith?" Annie asked Lawrence.

"I may have suggested the old lady be given extra medicine to help her rest," said Lawrence, giving Annie an evil smirk. "You see, she was quite shaken when she discovered a burglar had stolen her precious painting."

Annie was trying to breathe evenly and keep calm. Lawrence continued to explain how clever he was in his plans. As he spoke, Annie could see the hair of a person outside walking under the window toward the back of the house. Walter was standing with his back to the window, blocking Lawrence's view outside.

"Now what?" LaVerne asked Lawrence.

"You should take Bart's suggestion and get the heck out of here while you can," Lorraine advised.

"Shut up, old woman!" Lawrence yelled, aiming the gun at Lorraine.

"Put the gun down, Lawrence," Annie shouted in alarm.

Hearing Annie shout out, Laddie, who was outside near the front door, broke from Donald's grasp and made a dash inside the house. Spotting Lawrence with a gun, Laddie made a flying leap through the air and grabbed the arm holding the gun. Lawrence dropped the gun and at the same time was tackled to the floor by Dan, who had burst through the kitchen door. Laddie was on the floor eye to eye with Lawrence, growling and baring teeth. Both Lawrence and Dan stopped a moment and froze. Dan could hear Donald giving Laddie commands. Laddie held his position while Dan continued to handcuff his prisoner.

Walter made a move toward the gun on the floor. Annie pushed him back and picked up the gun. She handed the gun to Donald, who was now standing next to Annie. He unloaded the weapon.

Seeing Officer Kathy Barrel, who had entered with Dan through the kitchen, Donald crossed the room and handed the gun, ejected bullet, and clip to her. Annie moved to LaVerne and Lorraine who were hugging each other.

Dan secured and pulled Lawrence up off the floor and handed him over to Officer Barrel. Walter was handcuffed by another officer and walked out behind Lawrence. Donald gave Laddie a command and the dog moved to his side.

"This is the second time in a month that I have had to rescue you," Dan growled at Annie.

"You did not rescue me," Annie said with her hands on her hips. "Laddie tackled Lawrence first. He's my hero."

Laddie let out a low woof and growl directed at Dan. Dan stopped and looked down at Laddie, then rolled his eyes at Donald as he continued.

"Hey," Donald said, patting Laddie's head. "He's still in training."

"I am the good guy," Dan said to Laddie as he walked out the front door. Laddie groaned and repositioned himself on the floor.

♦ ♦ ♦

"Millie!" Lorraine cried, realizing they forgot about Millie.

LaVerne began up the stairs with Lorraine close behind her. Millie appeared at the top of the stairs on the landing. Behind her was Elsie.

"Oh my," Lorraine whispered to LaVerne. "We completely forgot about Elsie."

"Millie," Annie cried out. "Are you all right?"

"Of course, I am fine," Millie responded. "Unless I look like I am floating above the floor like a ghost." Millie pinched herself and laughed, "Nope. I am alive as can be."

Annie asked Millie if she knew Bart Jones was Walter Smith. Millie told her that she and her group suspected him when he tried to push a serious relationship on her. After discussing it with the ladies, they decided to try and trap him on their own. They even suspected Lawrence had a connection to Bart Jones.

Millie explained that Bart tried to get her to take some pills, saying that they were her medication.

"The only medications I take are vitamins pills, but he didn't know that," Millie said. "I happened to mention to him that I was taking pain pills for my back. Of course, I really don't take pain pills."

Elsie explained that Bart thought the pills in the made-up prescription bottle were real and was trying to get Millie to take them. Millie pretended to swallow the pills, but then spit them out when Bart was not looking. Elsie was hidden away in the closet where she could see Millie. Millie pretended to fall asleep and Bart went downstairs.

"We placed cameras around the house and were waiting to see what would happen when Bart went downstairs," Millie said. "My grandson installed the cameras a few days ago. Elsie and I watched the whole ordeal on our phones."

"If things got bad," Elsie spoke up, "I was to call the police immediately."

"Things did get bad," Annie stated loudly.

"We were so worried about you," Lorraine said to Millie.

"I'd say the plan worked," LaVerne said, slapping her hand on the stairway rail. "Another case solved by the Silver Sleuths."

"Excuse me?" Dan questioned as he had re-entered the house through the opened front door.

Annie jumped when she heard Dan speak up. He was standing directly behind her. She had no idea he was there. "Are these cameras recorded?"

"Oh, yes, Detective Surely," Millie said matter-of-factly. "We intend to watch them over and over."

"I don't think so, ladies," Dan said. "Those recordings are evidence at the moment."

"But we were going to show them at the next Silver Sleuths meeting," announced Elsie.

"We're going to have a talk about the Silver Sleuths." Dan said in a lowered tone of voice.

"Is that Lizzy standing outside?" LaVerne said, attempting to change the subject. "I understand you and Lizzy are quite the item."

"She is so pretty," Lorraine said. "If you don't marry her quickly, someone else will."

"Don't start...," Dan began, but was interrupted by a commotion outside.

Dan turned to look out the door. Lawrence was breaking loose from Officer Kathy Barrel's grip. Even though Lawrence was handcuffed, he was able to break loose and began sprinting down the street.

Laddie sprang from his position next to Donald and seemed to fly down the street, barely touching the pavement with his paws. He reached Lawrence just as Lawrence turned to see teeth baring down on him. Lawrence let out a terrified scream as Laddie knocked the escaping prisoner to the ground and sat on top of him. Officer Barrel was a split second behind Laddie. She stopped and began laughing.

"We need to sign this dog up as an officer," Kathy Barrel said.

Several other officers reached the scene. They bent down to lift the cuffed escapee and stopped when Laddie refused to move.

Donald signaled Laddie, and the dog obeyed immediately, leaving the scene and returning to Donald's side. Dan could see Donald giving Laddie a treat and patting him on the head. Dan moved back into the house and turned his attention to the ladies on the stairs.

"Now where is the recording of the camera feed?"

"It is right here," Elsie said as she walked down from the top of the stairs. She was carrying a recording device that looked like a small

DVD player. She handed it to Dan who took it and tucked it under his arm.

"I will be watching you ladies. Stay out of trouble." Dan said walking out the door.

"We have a copy," Elsie whispered to the group with a smile after she made sure Dan was not in ear shot. "Millie's grandson set it up to make an automatic copy on her laptop."

Boy, Annie thought, she was glad to be friends with these ladies. She wanted to make sure to stay on their good side.

♦ ♦ ♦

Hours later, Donald, Stella, Marie, Lizzy, Laddie, and congregated around the kitchen table each stunned and silently wondering what to do next. It was Marie who broke the stillness.

"I am hungry. Are we going to eat?"

"Let's order pizza," Donald suggested, pulling out his cell phone and looking up the pizza restaurant in his contacts list. He turned and walked to another room to make the call.

"I'll make a salad," Stella said. "Annie, you and Lizzy get plates, utensils, and napkins. We'll eat in the living room."

"I can get a movie to watch," Marie offered.

♦ ♦ ♦

By the time the movie ended, Dan had arrived and took what was left of the pizza. He grabbed a cold beer from the refrigerator and sat down next to Lizzy.

"I don't know how you fumble into these situations, Annie," Dan said taking a bite of pizza. "But you managed to expose a couple of serious felons. Walter Bartholomew Jones and his son, Lawrence Smith Jones, have multiple felony warrants in the United States. They are big-time swindlers and very persuasive."

"Swindlers?" Annie asked. "What about Meredith? Was she murdered?"

"I will know more as the investigation continues."

"At least Janette's mother found the jewels before Walter and Lawrence," Lizzy spoke up.

"It has been a long day," Annie said, standing up and beginning to tidy the living room. "I am ready for bed."

Agreeing with Annie, every one stood, stretched, and began to take their plates to the kitchen. Stella said she would clean up in the morning. Marie said goodnight and climbed the stairs to her bedroom.

Donald let Laddie outside in the back-yard dog run. He waited at the door while Laddie sniffed around. He watched as Stella made her way to her apartment over the garage. Laddie ran through the opened door, nearly knocking Donald over, drank water from his water bowl and headed upstairs to bed.

"I guess he was tired," Annie said to Donald as she began turning off lights. "I hope you don't mind, but Dan and Lizzy took the rest of the pizza home."

"Too bad," Donald said, as he and Annie walked up the stairs. "I was looking forward to cold pizza in the morning."

CHAPTER 25

Friday

Morning light was filtering through the window blinds. Annie opened her eyes, staring into the big green eyes of Callie, her Maine Coon cat. Callie was perched on Annie's side, as Annie lay with her head on Donald's chest. She raised her head up to look at Donald. He was awake. Looking across Donald's body, Annie saw Laddie sprawled out lengthwise next to Donald. Laddie's front leg was stretched across Donald's chest. Donald lay on his back, eyes open, staring at the ceiling.

"Good morning," Annie said with a slight giggle in her voice.

"Can I just point out that we are in a king-sized bed," Donald remarked. "Why is it that everyone is piled on top of me?"

"It must have been a chilly night."

"I am going to invest in heating pads for the pet beds."

Callie slowly stretched and yawned, taking her time moving off of Annie's side. Annie rolled over onto her back and looked up at the ceiling.

"Do you realize that this is the last day we will both be single?" Annie said, continuing to stare at the ceiling.

"Tomorrow's going to be a busy day," Donald said, still staring at the ceiling.

Annie looked over at him. "If you are going to back out, do it now or forever stay married to me,"

Donald grinned. "Forever married to you sounds perfect to me." He rolled over and kissed Annie.

♦ ♦ ♦

The kitchen was a buzz of activity as Annie sauntered down the stairs. She was thinking about the decorations for the ceremony in the backyard. A few chairs on the grass near the cottage entrance, maybe a couple of flower pots flanking the porch area of the cottage, she could scatter some rose petals along a path to the cottage area where the pastor would perform the ceremony. Yes, she thought, a nice quiet, small, beautiful ceremony. Afterwards, her family and a few friends could sit around the table and have steak from the grill and wedding cake for dessert. It would be fun and relaxing.

As Annie reached the bottom of the stairs, she realized that her mother looked frantic, she was still in her nightgown and robe, her hair was messy, and she was missing one slipper. Lizzy and Marie were sitting at the kitchen table eating breakfast. Patty Harper was outside on the patio plucking rose petals from stems on the patio table. She waved at Annie. Annie raised her hand and waved back, still confused as to why her mother was looking the way she did.

"Mom, what is the deal here?" Annie asked.

"You are getting married in one day," Stella said. "We have so much to do and very little time to do it."

"Mom, it is just a small group of people," Annie said, grabbing a coffee cup from the cupboard. "We have larger barbecues that take no time at all to prepare."

Stella stood frozen staring at Annie.

"What?" Annie asked.

"Nothing," Stella said returning to her cleaning. "I need you and Lizzy to walk to Ione's and pick up three dozen donuts."

"I can do that, Mom," Marie said, jumping up from the table.

"No!" Stella looked sharply at Marie. "Annie and Lizzy need to go get the donuts. I need your help here." Stella seemed to calm down after taking a deep breath.

"Okay, I will go on one condition," Annie said, taking a sip of freshly brewed coffee. "You go take a shower and get properly dressed."

"Oh, dear," Stella said raising a hand to her hair and looking down at her clothes. "What time is it?"

"Almost nine o'clock," Annie said looking at her watch. "I guess I fell back to sleep after Donald got up for work."

Lizzy stood up from her seat at the kitchen table and pulled her purse strap off the back of the chair. "Let's go, Annie," she said, "I think they want us out of here for a bit. Let's get coffee and the donuts at Ione's."

As Lizzy and Annie exited out the front door, Annie turned to see her mother leaving out the kitchen door in a rush. She suspected her mother was going to get dressed as she had requested. It was a bright and sunny morning. There was a coolness in the air, but the sun made it warm enough.

"Donald's parents came home late last night," Lizzy said, making small talk as they walked. "They had a wonderful time at the B&B in Wheeler."

"It was nice of Donald to loan them his truck," Annie said. "They wanted to explore the area up north."

"Patty said they stopped by the Tillamook Cheese Factory and had large ice cream cones."

"I should take Donald up north," Annie said thinking out loud. "I love Tillamook ice cream and he would love Cannon Beach."

Annie and Lizzy walked past Ocean Loads of Paper. They both made it a point to peer in the windows. Seeing that all was in order, they continued to Ione's Bakery and Coffee Shop. There was the usual line-up of townspeople inside Ione's waiting to order coffee and a pastry. The buzz of voices suddenly stopped as Annie and Lizzy walked inside. Polite greetings were made as the two found their way to the back of the line.

"Maybe we should get some breakfast while we are here," Annie suggested. "I don't think Mom wants me messing up the kitchen this morning."

"I had a bowl of cereal and coffee already," Lizzy responded. "I could use a donut. I seem to be nervous for you and I am not the one getting married."

There were several coughs in the crowd.

"Did you hear that?" Lizzy whispered to Annie. "Were those coughs a statement of my not being married?"

"Don't be ridiculous," Annie replied. "They were probably commenting on you wanting a donut after eating breakfast."

"So, you're saying they think I'm fat?" Lizzy scanned the dwindling crowd.

"Lizzy," Annie said. "This is my wedding. You have nothing to feel nervous about. I am not nervous."

"I just have a feeling something is going to happen."

"Now I am nervous."

"Next!" Ione called from the counter.

Annie and Lizzy walked up and ordered three dozen donuts, plus two donuts to eat in the bakery, and two cups of coffee. Ione pulled three already filled boxes of donuts in front of her. William, who was now helping at the counter, pulled the two ordered donuts from the trays in the display case and poured the coffee.

"Your mother called earlier." Ione said placing money in the cash register and returning the change to Annie.

"Thanks."

"So, the wedding is tomorrow," Ione stopped what she was doing. "Are you nervous?"

"No, but Lizzy is nervous enough for me."

Ione stared at Lizzy for a moment. Someone cleared their throat behind Annie and Lizzy, indicating they wanted the line to move. Taking the hint, Annie and Lizzy found a table and sat down.

"Did you see that?" Lizzy immediately said as she sat down.

"See what?" Annie asked, taking a sip of coffee. She placed her donut down on the napkin at the table.

"Ione," Lizzy said in a whisper, looking back at Ione. "It was a pity look...at me!"

"Seriously?"

"You will be married and I will be the woman everyone looks at sadly while shaking their head. My dad said I would end up like this. He was right."

"What has gotten into you?" Annie set her coffee cup down and looked at Lizzy.

"They are right. I am pathetic."

"Would you stop? There is nothing pathetic about you. You work two jobs, one being the manager of R&H Enterprises. You are beautiful, successful, and talented."

"That's right!" Lizzy sat up straight in her chair. "I am very successful."

"Now eat up and let's get back to the house and get the backyard decorated. It should not take more than an hour."

"Yes, boss."

♦ ♦ ♦

Fifteen minutes later, Annie picked up two boxes of the donuts and Lizzy picked up the third. They walked out into the bright sunshine which was making a bold show on the streets of Bridgewater Harbor. Annie set the boxes down on a café table outside the bakery to readjust her purse strap on her shoulder. Diane and Fred from Fred's Hardware Store walked quickly past the two women outside.

"Hello Diane. Hello Fred," Annie said, suddenly noticing who was walking by her. Was it Annie's imagination, or were Fred and Diane purposely trying to pass by her without being noticed? Good grief! Annie thought she was beginning to act like Lizzy.

Stopping, Fred and Diane turned around to face Annie and Lizzy.

"Oh, look Fred," Diane stated in a high-pitched voice. "It is Annie and Lizzy. Good morning, Annie and Lizzy."

The four people stood and stared at each other for several moments. Annie thought it was a bit strange.

"Annie," Diane said, now using her regular voice. "Are you ready for the wedding tomorrow?"

"Yes," Annie said, still trying to figure out why Diane was acting so strangely.

"Lizzy...oh, Lizzy...," Diane started, in what sounded like a pity voice.

Were those tears welling up in Diane's eyes? Before she could get a closer look, Fred put his arm around Diane, said a quick apologetic good-bye, and dashed into Ione's café.

Annie began walking up the street toward home. Lizzy hurried along behind, attempting to catch up to Annie. Lizzy had to practically run to keep up with Annie.

"Did you see that?" she huffed at Annie.

"Lizzy, I'm sure it's not what you think."

"Lizzy...oh, Lizzy...," Lizzy imitating what Diane said. "How is that not what I think?"

"Donald and I are going to have a nice, quiet, calm, small wedding ceremony tomorrow. Afterwards we will have a relaxing steak dinner. By Monday, everything will be back to normal."

Lizzy stopped dead in her tracks. Annie, realizing Lizzy had stopped, turned and looked at Lizzy. She turned back to look at a chaotic scene unfolding before her.

"Where does the moving van fit into a quiet and calm wedding?" Lizzy asked, still standing and staring at the commotion before her.

Annie and Lizzy entered the house through the front door. They set the donut boxes and their purses on the kitchen table and walked to the kitchen door window with mouths agape. Before them was a yard transformed into a large outdoor wedding venue.

"There must be at least a hundred chairs out there," Lizzy whispered. She turned to Annie, "I told you I thought something was going to happen."

Without saying a word, Annie left Lizzy at the back door and walked to Donald's office. She opened the door and entered a room darkened by lack of lights and curtains drawn tight. Donald was sitting at his desk staring at the computer screen.

"Do you know what is happening outside?" Annie asked.

"Why do you think I'm here in the dark?" Donald responded. "My boss gave me the day off to get ready for the wedding, and I am hiding from your mother under the guise that I am working."

Donald stood as Annie approached his desk. She wrapped her arms around him. They embraced and Annie did not want to let go.

You know...," Annie smiled coyly at Donald. "We could lock the office door and escape downstairs."

Donald walked to the office door, locked it, and they both moved the bookcase, sliding it sideways. The stairway lit up, guiding them downward to the finished room off the vault room. Donald stopped to close the bookcase. As Annie reached the room at the bottom of the stairs, she suddenly realized that it was perfectly quiet. She began to relax...even more considering where Donald was now placing his hands.

♦ ♦ ♦

It was an hour later when Donald and Annie emerged from the hidden solitude of the secret room downstairs. They secured the office and walked into the kitchen to find Lizzy sitting at the table chomping down on a sandwich.

"Is it lunch time already?" Annie asked Lizzy.

"I could eat," said Donald as he walked over to the counter and pulled a couple of slices of bread from the loaf on the counter.

"There is tuna already made in the refrigerator," Lizzy said between bites. She turned to Annie, "Where have you been?"

"I needed to talk to Donald," Annie said, moving to the counter and getting bread out to make a sandwich.

"Well, this is the last time you can 'talk' until after the wedding," Lizzy stated. "You need to deal with your mothers now. Look at me! I am stress eating, because your mothers are going nuts with the simple, small, backyard wedding. There are twenty people out there taking orders from both your mom and Donald's mom...at the same time!" She ate another large bite, chewed, and then swallowed. She drank half a glass of water and set the glass down.

Both Donald and Annie stared at Lizzy.

"Lizzy," Annie announced. "This is Donald's and my wedding. Look at us. We are not nervous. You have no reason to be nervous."

"Speak for yourself," Donald injected. "I think I just got my first gray hair."

Annie stood straight and walked to the door. "I am going to have a talk with our mothers. Are you coming, Donald?"

"I love you very much, but nothing is going to get me out there right now."

"Fine," Annie said, determination setting in. "I will just happen to let it slip that you have the day off today."

"I thought you would wait until after we were married before you throw me into the lion's den," Donald said, setting his sandwich down and following Annie out the door.

Spotting Stella on the cottage porch, Donald tapped Annie on the shoulder and pointed her out. They made their way through the sea of folding chairs set up in rows throughout the yard.

"Mom," Annie stood with her fists sitting tight at her hips. "We need to talk about this."

"Oh, Annie," Stella began. "Isn't this just the most beautiful setting for a wedding?"

"But, Mom, we talked about a small wedding."

"Oh, this is small by wedding standards."

"There must be a hundred chairs set up out here," Donald said, appearing to be counting.

"Yes," Stella agreed. "The rest of the guests will have to stand. It isn't a long ceremony."

"Mom!" Annie tried to get Stella's attention, but a helper was placing flowers in the middle of the walk way and Stella ran to instruct the poor fellow to move the blooms.

"Annie," Donald said placing his hands on her shoulders. "Let's get Lizzy and go over to Dan's house to escape for a bit." Donald signaled Laddie to follow.

Annie knew Donald was right. She just needed to get away from all the confusion and regroup. It might not be as bad as she thought. She needed to keep telling herself that. Annie felt Donald moving her to the kitchen door. They walked inside, grabbed sandwiches, and made their way to Dan's house across the street.

♦ ♦ ♦

Lizzy, Donald, and Annie were sitting in silence at the breakfast bar eating their sandwiches when Lizzy's cell phone rang. She picked it up and saw it was Dan calling.

"Hello, Dan," Lizzy answered in a happy tone of voice, though she felt as if it took all of her strength to muster up enough cheer.

"When I called Mom, she said you, Annie, and Donald disappeared," Dan said, almost laughing. "She said Annie was upset over the wedding set-up. She did not know where you went."

"We are hiding at the moment."

"I got a text of the alarm being turned off at our house by someone using your code," said Dan. He seemed to be amused by the whole thing.

"We just can't hide, can we?"

"Is Annie really upset?"

"Well...," Lizzy started.

"Look, remind Annie that she is the only daughter and her mother really wants a wedding to remember. Donald's mother is probably thinking the same thing about her only son. Let them have their moment. It is not about the wedding ceremony for Donald and Annie. It's about a couple who love each other and want to spend the rest of their lives creating their own moments."

"This is why I love you so much," Lizzy gushed. "You have your romantic moments."

"Do not spread that around," Dan said firmly. "I will deny it if asked. I have to get back to work. I will be home around five o'clock. Find out what the guys are doing tonight and text me. Love you. Bye."

Annie noticed the look on Lizzy's face as she set her cell phone down. What was that comment about Dan having romantic moments?

"Did Dan have anything important to say or was he just calling to make you blush?" Annie asked.

"He wants to know what the guys are doing tonight for Donald's bachelor party."

"I thought we would just sit around, drink beer, and watch an action-packed movie," Donald responded. "Maybe I should text Dad to stop hiding in the RV and sneak over here. We can plan something before Dan gets home." Donald began typing on his cell phone.

"Dan will be home at five o'clock," Lizzy said.

Annie asked what they were going to do all afternoon while hiding from her mother. Lizzy told Donald and Annie what Dan had said about the ceremony. Annie was quiet for a bit, but decided it was best to just let it all happen and not worry. Donald agreed.

"Dad is watching a ball game and does not want to be seen leaving the RV," Donald said, reading the text message. "Plans have been made for the guys to meet at Bridgewater Harbor Brewery at six o'clock for dinner and suds. John Spencer is picking up the tab. Well, that is nice of him."

Lizzy sent a text to Dan informing him of the time and place to meet. He sent a message back that he would be home to change clothes. He would walk to town with Donald and Rand.

"That leaves us," Lizzy said turning to Annie.

"You know, having everything planned is really not so bad," Annie said as she got up and placed her coffee cup in the dishwasher. "Let's go back over to the house and see what Mom has arranged for us this evening."

♦ ♦ ♦

"Nothing," said Stella, stopping long enough to answer Annie's question.

"Nothing?" Annie questioned. "You didn't plan anything for my bachelorette party?"

"Nope," Stella said. "That's up to your best woman."

Annie looked to Lizzy. Lizzy's face went white.

"Oh, Annie," Lizzy said apologetically. "I thought about it earlier, then completely forgot."

"Actually, it worked out great," Annie said, smiling at her friend. "It will be you, me, Marie, and the moms tonight. We will drink wine, eat pizza, and watch a romantic comedy movie."

As it happened, twenty people showed up at seven o'clock with wine, squeezing into Annie's living room to celebrate her last night as a single woman. She was overwhelmed by the friendship.

CHAPTER 26

Saturday Morning

"Sniff, sniff, sniff." Annie woke to a cat nose, up close in her face. Callie was standing on Annie's chest attempting to wake her.

"Is your food dish empty?" Annie asked Callie.

As if to answer Annie's question, Callie jumped off the bed and hopped up to her feeding station. She peered into the empty bowl and looked at Annie.

"Yes, I know," Annie said sleepily. "Just let me wake up."

"It's about time," came Lizzy's voice from the sitting area of Annie's master suite. "I am surprised you did not wake up to the coffee I was brewing. I was hoping you would be up already, so I let myself in and made coffee." She had her hands wrapped around a steaming mug of coffee.

"How much wine did I have last night?" Annie asked as she swung her legs over the side of the bed. "I feel terrible."

"It's called a hangover. Have some coffee. I would get it for you, but I am afraid to move or my head will explode."

Annie looked at the clock. It was seven in the morning. At least she thought it was morning. After brewing a cup of strong coffee, Annie sat down next to Lizzy on the sofa. They sat in silence for a few moments. Annie's head hung over the steaming cup.

"Do you think the guys are better or worse than us?" Annie asked.

"I don't know. I don't care."

They fell back into silence.

Stella burst through the bedroom door carrying a small tray of food. "Good morning! Stella greeted the two women. "Happy wedding day!"

"Good morning, Mom. Could you turn the volume down a bit?"

"I knew you would both be hurting this morning," Stella announced in a quieter voice. "Which is why I made dry toast and bacon. You should eat something and take some aspirin. I brought the bottle for you both."

"Bacon?" Annie asked as she sat up to view the breakfast tray her mother was presenting. "I could eat bacon." She got up to brew another cup of coffee.

"Pass me the dry toast and aspirin," Lizzy said, setting her coffee cup down and reaching for the toast on the tray that Stella had placed on the coffee table.

"I want you both ready by ten-thirty so we can take photos," Stella instructed. "Rand will be our photographer today. The wedding is going to be so beautiful. One to remember forever." Stella left the bedroom as quickly as she entered.

"Remind me...who is getting married?" Lizzy asked making crunching noises as she bit into the toast.

"I just wanted a quiet little wedding and to spend the night wrapped in my wonderful husband's arms," Annie said. "What happened?"

"You let your mother happen, that's what," Lizzy said. "Then Donald's mother happened. Then they told Ione. Then the town happened. Need I say more?"

"You are saying that Donald and I should have gone to a justice of the peace at the courthouse and got married without telling anyone?"

"No!" Lizzy sat upright from her slouching position on the sofa. "If you did, I would not be best woman and walking down the aisle with Dan."

"But you are not the one getting married."

"True," Lizzy stated. "But don't you think he might get the idea that marriage would be good for him as he walks me down the aisle?"

"Very subtle, Lizzy." Annie said as she stood up and walked to the coffee machine. She pushed the button for strong coffee and watched the steamy liquid pour into the coffee mug.

Annie sat down next to Lizzy on the sofa. Lizzy gave Annie a questioning look and then looked at the coffee in Annie's hands. "How many cups of coffee have you had this morning?"

"I need this to calm my nerves," Annie said, taking a small sip.

◆ ◆ ◆

Annie looked at the clock. It was eight-fifteen. Both Annie and Lizzy were looking and feeling better. They decided they had another hour to procrastinate until they needed to get ready. Lizzy and Annie spent the time reflecting over the last two weeks, the painting and its secrets, the new friends they now had, and what the future held.

After getting their hair and make-up done, Annie and Lizzy decided to wait on getting into their dresses until the last minute and put on robes for the moment. They still had plenty of time and needed a distraction. Hearing more and more voices in the backyard, they decided to find a better vantage point to watch the action in progress.

Annie and Lizzy sneaked downstairs to peer out the kitchen window and watch the seats fill up in the backyard. Annie noticed LaVerne, Lorraine, Elsie, and Millie making their way to the second row behind where Stella was to sit in the front row. Donald's parents were to be seated across the aisle from Stella. Annie noticed Lois, Dan's biological mother, sitting in the third seat in from the aisle of the front row. She thought her mother, Stella, arranged for Lois to be close to Dan, who was the best man. The next two seats in the front row were reserved with signage. Annie could not see who they were reserved for from her vantage point in the kitchen.

"Annie, Lizzy, get upstairs and get ready," Stella barked as she walked into the kitchen, spotting the two women peering out the window. "The wedding will be starting soon. Rand wants to get photos of you and Lizzy." Stella herded both Annie and Lizzy to the staircase and then turned to rush back outside.

A half an hour later, Annie looked stunning walking down the stairs in her wedding dress followed by an equally beautiful Lizzy in what almost appeared to be the exact same dress. The difference in the dress was the light blue satin ribbon belt that Lizzy wore.

Annie's dress was adorned with a creamy white satin ribbon belt around her waist. Both dresses were mid-calf length for an afternoon wedding.

Rand, Donald's father, was waiting in the living room with a camera on a tripod and filter lights set up on each side of the fireplace. He signaled for Annie and Lizzy to stand in front of the fireplace for photos. Ten minutes, and what Annie thought were thousands of photos later, Rand finished the photography session. He explained what he had planned for the rest of the photos after the ceremony. Annie agreed and told Rand about some additional photos she wanted taken.

"Well, Annie," Rand asked. "Are you ready to walk down the aisle?"

"I've been ready," Annie answered with a smile.

"Are the guys in place?" Lizzy asked Rand.

"They should be by now," Rand answered, removing his camera from the tripod. He grabbed his camera bag, making sure he had all of his equipment to capture the following moments.

Ione entered the living room with bouquets of flowers for the bride and best woman. She announced that she was helping Annie's mother by getting the two young women in place. They were to exit out the front door and make their way around the house and down the driveway to the backyard. Lizzy was to walk ahead of Annie.

"Where is Marie?" Ione asked frantically.

"I haven't seen her in a while," Annie answered.

"Just look for the only princess in the crowd," Lizzy offered.

Ione tapped out a message on her cell phone and waited for a response. Within seconds the phone chimed and Ione was told Marie was standing in place waiting for the bride.

"Okay," Ione stated. "It's go-time!" She escorted Annie and Lizzy to the front door and directed them to the staging place in the driveway.

Once Annie rounded the front corner of the house, she saw Marie twirling in her princess dress and Dan standing in front of her watching the crowd. As Annie and Lizzy approached, Dan turned and smiled at Annie, but his attention was soon diverted to Lizzy. He lit up with a passionate smile and approached Lizzy, giving her a kiss on the cheek.

"Get a room!" said Marie.

"What?" Dan asked.

"Never mind, Dan," Annie said, stepping up to Marie and putting her arm around her. "You look beautiful, Marie."

"I look like a princess," Marie responded and twirled around to show Annie her dress. Marie's head was adorned with a tiara atop her neatly styled hair. Her pink dress flowed to an ankle length, showing off her sparkling shoes. Marie carried a basket containing rose petals of pink and white.

"A simply beautiful princess."

"You look beautiful too," Marie said, giving Annie a quick look.

"Thank you, Marie," Annie said.

Taking a few steps ahead of Dan to view the crowd, Annie said, "Where did all these people come from?"

"They have been arriving for at least an hour," Dan said surveying the large gathered group of friends and neighbors talking happily amongst themselves. Dan motioned for Annie to follow him across the driveway.

"What happened to my small, intimate wedding in the backyard?" Annie asked no one in particular. She turned to follow Dan.

"I talked to Donald earlier...actually, last night over beers," Dan began the conversation. He paused, expecting Annie to say something, but realized he had not finished what he had to say. "Annie, I want to propose to Lizzy."

"So, Dan, what is the problem?" Annie asked. She made a side glance to see if Lizzy was listening. "If you are serious, why not propose now?"

"Now?"

"Yes, after you walk her up the aisle," Annie whispered. "It would be so romantic to propose in front of everyone here."

"That's what Mom thought," Dan said, suspecting Annie of having already planned the timing of his proposal.

"What are you waiting for, Dan?" Annie realized that her mother was aware of Dan wanting to propose to Lizzy. What was her mother planning? Her mother probably told Dan not to say anything to her until just before the wedding. Annie's mother knew Annie could not keep something as exciting as Dan proposing a secret from Lizzy.

Dan paused in thought, and then motioned Annie to get ready to walk down the aisle. He moved next to Lizzy, who was re-tying Marie's bow on her basket of rose petals.

"Are you upset?" Lizzy asked, noticing Annie looking at the crowd of people gathered in the backyard.

"No," Annie admitted, now smiling at her newfound secret. "I guess it is endearing to see so many people care about Donald and me getting married."

"Kind of sweet when you think about it," Lizzy said, trying to peer past Annie who moved in front of her for a quick look over the crowed.

"Are those police officers on Donald's side of the seating area?" Annie asked.

"I may have asked a few friends from the department to come," Dan replied. "They had nothing better to do on a Saturday afternoon. Besides, I was thinking it would even out the sides. Donald doesn't have a lot of friends here yet."

Annie turned to Lizzy with a look of bewilderment and then walked back to her position behind her best woman.

Stella ran up to the waiting group. "Are we ready?" She was giddy with excitement. Giving Annie a kiss on the cheek and long hug, she hurried down the aisle to her seat in the front row. There was a hush in the crowd.

"All ready," Annie stated as she watched her mother walk away. Were those butterflies that just flittered in her stomach? A wave of nervousness suddenly hit Annie. She slowly inhaled and exhaled. That didn't help. She tried again. Did she know what she was doing? Yes. Did she really love Donald? Yes. Was she ready to marry Donald? Absolutely.

The music began.

CHAPTER 27

Saturday Afternoon

Marie started down the aisle, tossing rose petals high into the air. The soft floral bits floated down on those seated near the walkway. Annie watched and laughed as Marie slowly made her way to the front row and sat down next to Stella after a dramatic twirl to show off her dress. A puff of rose petals suddenly appeared high in the air where Marie was seated. She apparently had more petals in her basket. Annie noticed her mother directing Marie to place the basket under her seat.

Annie took a deep breath and looked skyward at the clouds directly overhead. She thought about her father and wished he were there to walk her down the aisle. Just as she finished that thought a flash of light caught her attention. The light appeared to come from the house behind Annie's house. She looked again at the house, which sat up on a sloping hill about fifty yards from her back fence.

"Dan," Annie said, tapping on Dan's shoulder just as he was beginning to move forward to walk down the aisle.

"What?" Dan responded. "Are you getting cold feet?"

"No, of course not," Annie said, a bit irritated that Dan would suspect she was thinking of stopping the wedding. "Did you see the flash of light coming from the house up there?"

Dan looked up toward the house and said, "The house is vacant, Annie. Maybe you saw a ghost."

A ghost? A chill went down Annie's back. She was just thinking about her Dad. Could that flash of light be a sign that he was with her? Yes, Annie thought...her Dad was with her, walking her down the aisle.

"It is our turn to go," Annie heard Lizzy saying to Dan.

Dan held his arm out and Lizzy placed her arm around his. They began the slow march down the aisle. Annie watched, realizing how perfect the two were together.

Ione signaled Annie to move forward. Just as she took her first step, she again glanced up at the vacant house on the hill. Did she just see someone in the window watching her? As she moved forward, she could not help but look again at the house. She was certain she saw a figure.

Colliding into a chair, Annie caught herself before she stumbled into the lap of a guest. She stood straight and admonished herself for not paying attention. Annie made her way, now half-way to what she thought was a long walk to get to Donald.

Annie kept her focused ahead as Dan and Lizzy made their way to the front porch of the little yellow cottage in the backyard. Pastor Paul stood straight and still holding a bible in his hands. He smiled and nodded as Dan and Lizzy approached.

Lizzy began to turn to the left where she would be positioned next to Annie during the ceremony. Dan softly took her hand and pulled her back toward him. Feeling a tug on her hand, Lizzy turned to face Dan, who was down on one knee holding a ring box in his other hand. He released her hand and opened the box. Displayed inside was a beautiful diamond ring. Annie stopped just five feet from the porch and stared at the two, tears stinging her eyes.

"Lizzy," Dan began.

"Speak up!" came a shout from a guest seated in the far back.

Dan looked up at Lizzy, "When I planned this, only family and a few friends were going to be here. Half the town is here now."

Lizzy smiled at Dan.

"Lizzy," Dan said in a louder voice, turning toward the guests with an exasperated look on his face. Dan then turned to face the beautiful woman before him. "The first time I saw you, I knew we could have something special together. I knew that I could not spend the rest of my life without you. I love you with all my heart. Will you marry me?"

"Oh Dan...," Lizzy began, glancing over Dan's head to the sight her parents sitting in the first row, on the far side of the aisle. She had not noticed them before, because Donald's parents were sitting next to the aisle and Dan's biological mother, Lois, was sitting next to Donald's mother. Lizzy's mother was next to Lois, and her father in the last seat on the end. "Mother! Dad!" Lizzy shouted and walked past Dan to where her parents were seated. "What are you doing here?"

"Elizabeth," Lizzy's father stood to talk. "This fine gentleman approached your mother and I by telephone and politely asked for your hand in marriage. I told him that you were old enough to make your own decisions. Your mother and I are proud as peacocks of the life you have made for yourself. I was wrong to try and get you to marry someone you did not love. Daniel assures me that the two of you are in love. In my opinion, you would be foolish not to marry this man, but as my wife, your mother, points out...my opinion does not matter."

"Of course, it matters, Daddy," Lizzy said with tears streaming down her face, as both remembered her father once demanding she marry a business partner's son, who she did not love, and her escape to her own life.

"Then agree to marry this fellow before he changes his mind!" Lizzy's father demanded. With a smile on his face, he sat down.

Lizzy stepped back to Dan, who was now standing, and pulled him in for a long, passionate kiss.

"You have not answered my question."

"YES! Yes, I will marry you right now!"

"Now?" waivered Dan.

"Wasn't he supposed to ask her to marry him before they walked down the aisle?" asked an elderly lady sitting behind LaVerne.

"Shh!," reprimanded LaVerne, turning around to quiet the woman. Chuckles were heard throughout the guest seated in the area.

"We don't have a marriage license to get married right now," Dan continued, oblivious to the distraction among the seated guests.

Stella jumped up from her seat in the front row and hurried over to Dan and Lizzy waving a large white envelope in the air. She brushed past Annie, who took a step back to avoid bumping into her mother. Annie looked at Donald questioningly. Donald shrugged his shoulders in reply. He then mouthed to her that she looked beautiful. She mouthed back "I love you."

Stella stood next to Lizzy and Dan, opening the white envelope and producing a document. She handed the document to Dan, who took the paper and glanced at its written contents.

"Well," Stella explained. "I was helping Annie and Donald by picking up their marriage license, so I thought while I was there, I might as well get one for you and Lizzy. You never know and it is always better to be prepared."

There were whispers of agreement throughout the attendees gathered for Annie and Donald's wedding. Stella turned to acknowledge the people agreeing with her.

"Well?" LaVerne stated to Dan and Lizzy. "What's the hold-up?

"Annie and Donald," Lizzy began. "Shouldn't we continue with their ceremony first?"

"Ladies and gentlemen," Pastor Paul announced. "We will have two weddings today. Let us begin with Annie and Donald. I have your license in my hand. Are we ready to begin?"

Dan and Lizzy stepped to the side of Annie and Donald. Laddie quietly stepped in between Donald and Dan. He was wearing a black bow tie on his collar. Annie leaned over to see Laddie. He appeared to have a smile on his face.

Stella took the license from Dan and handed it to Pastor Paul. She quickly took her seat. Pastor Paul tucked it under Annie and Donald's license and began the ceremony, "Dearly beloved..."

Fifteen minutes later Donald kissed his bride and cheers erupted from the crowd. An explosion of rose pedals blew into the air from the front row. Annie could hear her mother asking Marie to save some for Dan and Lizzy.

Annie was now Annie Weston Harper. She felt giddy inside. Life was good. She stood aside and was about to hand Lizzy her bouquet when Myra came rushing up the aisle with a large floral bouquet in her hands.

Surprised, Lizzy exchanged her 'best woman' arrangement and took the bridal bouquet. She stepped up next to Dan.

"Are you sure you want to do this now?" Lizzy asked Dan.

"Unless you are wanting to plan a large wedding to please your mother, I would prefer to marry you now so you do not have a chance to change your mind."

"We can let them throw us a huge reception later," Lizzy responded. "That will make Mom and Dad very happy, and we won't have to lift a finger."

"Let's do this," Dan said.

Dan and Lizzy turned to face Pastor Paul. As he proceeded through the vows, Dan and Lizzy smiled at each other. Lizzy had tears forming in her eyes.

"Do you," Pastor Paul asked. "Daniel Andrew Surely Weston, take thee Elizabeth..."

"Wait a minute!" Dan interrupted.

Gasps could be heard across the backyard. Annie leaned over to give a sharp look of concern and irritation to Dan.

"My name is Daniel Andrew Surely, not Weston."

"Well...," Stella jumped up and moved to Dan and Lizzy's side. "That's not entirely true."

"What?" Dan looked to his biological mother. Lois stood and walked to Dan's side.

"It is what Stella says," Lois began. "You were legally adopted by Rich and Stella when you were seven years old. I had to do what was in your best interest at the time. Stella and Rich insisted that I remain part of your life. I wanted you to be in a loving home, and at the same time stay a part of your life. I am really more of an aunt figure than a mother. Stella is your mother. She and Rich raised you to the wonderful person you are today. Please do not be mad at Stella."

"I'm not upset," Dan said. "I have always felt like I was a Weston, just not in name. I really am a Weston. I have you to thank, Mother. Thank you!" Dan hugged Lois. She clasped Stella's hand and squeezed it before returning to her seat.

Lizzy turned to Annie. Annie saw tears moving down her cheeks.

"I hope those are tears of joy, Lizzy."

"Yes," Lizzy said carefully wiping her eyes. "I am going to be Lizzy Weston, not Lizzy Surely. Have you any idea how difficult it is to say Lizzy Surely?"

The two women laughed until both of them were wiping tears from their faces.

"May we continue?" Pastor Paul asked, looking at his watch.

Moments later Dan and Lizzy were pronounced husband and wife. Dan kissed Lizzy and they faced the guests who cheered for the two couples. This time as Annie and Donald, Lizzy and Dan walked back down the aisle they were bombarded with rose petals blasting out from standing guests along the aisles. It seems that the people sitting in the aisle seats were previously given bags of rose petals to toss at the bride and groom.

Once the two newly married couples finished their walks down the walkway, people stood and began to gather chairs and move them around tables that were set up near the garage. This left room for people to mingle on the lawn in the backyard. Instead of a reception line, Annie and Donald chose to circulate among the crowd. Annie looked around and saw Lizzy and Dan chatting with Lizzy's parents. Lois was cheerfully chatting with Stella. Marie was twirling with a friend of hers. Patty and Rand were making their way through the crowd. Annie signaled Donald, who was bending down to straighten Laddie's bow tie. He stood and smiled as his father and mother approached.

"Congratulations to you both," Rand said, giving his son a hug. Patty hugged her new daughter-in-law and then hugged her son. She had tears in her eyes.

"I am so happy right now," Patty said. "I will miss seeing my son every day though."

"That little house in California is yours as a wedding gift if you want it," Rand offered.

"Thanks, Dad," Donald said. "But I think we belong here in Bridgewater Harbor."

"Well, you will end up with it eventually."

"I hope we can stay in your guest room when we come to visit," Annie added. "Laddie will want to visit his grandpa and grandma from time to time."

Both Rand and Donald laughed. Patty was not sure she wanted to be a grandmother to a dog. Annie changed the subject before Patty asked about grandchildren.

CHAPTER 28

Saturday Evening

Stella announced that it was time for the brides and grooms to cut their cakes. Annie looked to the table where she noticed two three-tiered cakes placed side by side. One was chocolate on the outside with tiny purple flowers entwined around golden strands encircling the cake. A bride and groom kissing stood on the top of one cake. Beside the bride was a calico cat and beside the groom was a Labrador dog.

The second cake was white with delicate frosted flowers adorning each layer. Ione explained to the couples that while Annie and Donald's cake was chocolate with ganache filling, Lizzy and Dan's cake was white with a strawberry whipped cream filling. Topping the cake was a bride and groom handcuffed together. It was meant to be funny, but Lizzy chose to view it as blissfully handcuffed together for life.

"Do you get the feeling that everyone in town, except us, knew that Dan and Lizzy were getting married?" asked Donald.

"That must be why people were acting so peculiar yesterday," Annie answered.

Dan and Lizzy walked up to Donald and Annie and they both stared at the cakes. Stella waved them to come over to the table and cut their cakes. Cameras were clicking throughout the crowd as the cakes were cut and the ceremonious first bites were shared. Plates were passed around to the guests. Stella turned the cake serving over to townspeople who offered to help. Annie noticed her mother beaming with joy as she flitted through the gathering of people. Why not, Annie thought to herself. Both of her adult kids were now married with wonderful spouses.

♦ ♦ ♦

As Annie and Donald said goodbye to the last guest, they turned to view their exhausted family sitting in patio chairs near the kitchen door. The newlyweds walked up and sat down on a loveseat. No one spoke for a few moments. It was evening now and all of the excitement of the day had passed.

Annie noticed Lizzy looking at her ring and smiling. Stella had her eyes closed and had her feet up on the patio coffee table. Marie was fluffing her dress, but her eyes were droopy. Rand and Patty were laid back in their chairs staring straight ahead, expressionless.

It was then that Annie noticed Dan watching the house on the hill behind her. She turned and they both noticed someone looking back. The figure quickly moved away from the window. Dan stood and walked to the garage out of view from the house above. Annie continued to watch. She knew that Dan was going to call the police department and have someone check out the house.

"What's going on?" Donald whispered in Annie's ear.

"I noticed a flash of light in the house on the hill," Annie whispered back. "I told Dan just before he and Lizzy walked down the aisle. He suggested I saw a ghost. I guess he is seeing the same ghost now."

Donald chuckled softly, "I heard the house has been vacant for some time now. Laddie and I walked by it several times on our outings. I never saw anything out of the ordinary."

Before Annie could respond to Donald's comment, Dan walked up to the group and suggested they go inside the house. He looked around the yard.

"I'll check the cottage and Stella's apartment to make sure everything is locked up and meet you inside the house," Dan said.

"Do we have ice cream?" Marie asked.

"I believe we have chocolate, vanilla, and strawberry," Stella replied. "Who wants ice cream?"

A chorus of "I do" prompted the group to get up and move to the house. As Annie watched Rand and Patty enter the house last, she held back to speak to Dan. Donald stood with her. They watched Dan check the cottage door and make sure it was securely locked.

"You saw someone in the house?" Annie asked Dan as he approached the couple.

"Yes," he responded. "My guess is someone is staying inside the house uninvited. I asked dispatch to send patrol over to check it out. They will call me after they find out if someone is there."

"But why would someone be watching the wedding?"

"Who knows," Dan said. "They could have been watching the ocean and happen to notice the activity below them."

"Do you know who owns the house?" Donald asked.

"I will do some checking and find out," Dan replied. "Maybe the owner came back to check out the house. It's probably nothing. Let's go inside and get some ice cream."

♦ ♦ ♦

Annie, Donald, and Dan scooped ice cream into dishes and joined the others in the living room. Dan sat down next to Lizzy, who was still admiring her ring and trying to wrap her head around being married.

"Does it seem real yet?" Dan asked Lizzy.

"I am sure it will in a few days, but for now I like being in this dream state."

"We can plan a real honeymoon after I have enough time with the department to take vacation."

"I spoke with Mom earlier and she suggested we go to Italy or somewhere in Europe for a couple of weeks. She said that she and Daddy would pay for it."

"Wow!" Dan said. "I married a rich girl."

"No," Lizzy stated. "I work for a living. My parents are rich."

"I have seen your apartment and the clothes you wear," Dan teased. "You definitely benefit from your parent's wealth."

"Okay. So, my mother spoils me a bit."

Dan and Lizzy turned their attention to the rest of the group when they heard laughter. Stella and Patty were telling stories of how the entire town heard about the wedding and half the town showed up uninvited. Dan rolled his eyes when he heard the Silver Sleuths discovered he had purchased a ring for Lizzy and was planning to ask her to marry him. Stella admitted that it might be her to blame, as she was the one who picked up the marriage license for Dan and Lizzy. The clerk probably told someone who knew someone and it eventually got back to LaVerne, Lorraine, Elsie, and Millie. Once Ione heard the rumor, it was all over town.

Dan's cell phone chirped. He stood and walked to the kitchen to answer in private. Everyone was quiet while listening in on the one-sided conversation with intrepid curiosity. Annie tried to quickly fill them in on what she saw just before she walked down the aisle. The group remained hushed while Dan talked on the cell phone.

Dan walked back to the living room while ending his call. He stood still looking at the silent group, who were all staring at him.

"Well?" asked Annie.

"The house is locked up tight. There doesn't appear to be a break-in. No footprints. Nothing to indicate someone was in the house."

"So, it was a ghost after all," Annie teased.

"A ghost?" asked Marie.

"There is no ghost, Marie," Dan said. "I will go over there tomorrow and take a look around."

"You will do no such thing," Stella said. "You are on your honeymoon, mister. I expect you to spend tomorrow as a newlywed."

Lizzy laughed, "As do I."

"I promise that both of our newlywed couples will have peace and quiet from everyone," Stella advised. "Marie is staying with me tonight and all day tomorrow."

"Patty and I are spending the day sightseeing in Portland," Rand added.

"You mean we have to fend for ourselves?" Donald asked.

"You will manage," said Stella with a smile.

"I can cook, Donald," Annie stated, nudging Donald in the shoulder.

Donald laughed and gave Annie a kiss on the cheek.

"I am going to go get my suitcase and a movie for Mom and I to watch tonight," Marie said, getting up and stretching. She gathered the ice cream dishes and headed to the kitchen. Placing the dishes in the dishwasher, she headed upstairs to gather her belongings.

"A movie?" Patty asked. "Would you mind if we joined you?"

"That would be wonderful," Stella replied. "Annie, do you mind if we take some popcorn with us?"

"Popcorn sounds good," Donald stated.

"I could eat popcorn," Dan joined in.

"You newlyweds have plenty in your honeymoon suites tonight," Stella said, as Patty nodded in agreement.

Marie came back downstairs and joined the family. She had a suitcase in hand and several DVD movies. "I am ready to go watch a movie."

"Before everyone disperses," Donald announced to the group. "Annie and I have been discussing something for about a week now, and we think it might be time to let you in on a little secret."

MYSTERIOUS PAPERCUTS

Die-Cut Cozy Mystery Series

Book 3

Thank you for reading GLUED TO SEE YOU.

Made in the USA
Columbia, SC
29 June 2020